MIND OVER MAGIC

A WITCH IN WOLF WOOD, BOOK 1

LINDSAY BUROKER

FOREWORD

Thank you for picking up my first adventure about witches and werewolves! It's true that werewolves occasionally cavort through my Death Before Dragons books, but they are far from the stars in that series. Everyone knows that if you put a dragon in a novel, *he* instantly takes center stage. In this new series, we're letting the fur people shine.

A Witch in Wolf Wood takes place in the made-up town of Bellrock, Washington, and is not tied in with any of my other series, but I hope you'll enjoy this new adventure. I started it as a fun summer project (I'd been working on a heavier epic fantasy series—Dragon Gate—with much longer books, and I decided I needed some lighter, shorter projects to sprinkle into my schedule).

Originally, I intended to write one book. That turned into three. Will there be more? We'll see, but Book 1 is a complete story, so no need to worry about cliffhangers.

Before you jump in, please let me thank my beta readers (Sarah Engelke, Rue Silver, and Cindy Wilkinson) for following me into another series, as well as my editor, Shelley Holloway.

I hope you have fun with the story!

1

THE RAIN AND THE DOG'S NOSEPRINTS ON THE WINDSHIELD MADE IT hard to see into the twilight gloom ahead. Lucky whined from the passenger seat as Morgen guided the car through mud, over downed branches, and around water-filled potholes large enough to support a small flock of mallards. Possibly a large flock. And their cousins.

Lucky whined again.

"We're almost to the house," Morgen said. "You can hold it."

Lucky snuffled at the cracked window like a hedgehog with nasal polyps and did his best to shove his snout through the gap. His whip of a tail thwacked at the side of Morgen's head, making her regret letting him out of his crate for this last leg of the journey. He stood on the armrest of the door, one paw finding the controls, and the window slid open further.

"Just remember that goes both ways." Morgen concentrated on the road, navigating around another pond-sized pothole. Maybe she should have rented an SUV instead of driving her electric car up here. "If you get your head stuck again, I'm not going to be sympathetic."

As Lucky inhaled deeply, oblivious to the rain spattering his copper-furred head, Morgen checked the GPS again. It had been years—*decades*—since she'd been up to the house. Was it possible she'd turned at the wrong spot? It was hard to believe Grandma had driven up the treacherous mile-long driveway every day on her motorcycle.

A deer shot out of the moss-draped fir trees and darted in front of the car.

An alarm on the screen flashed and beeped. Cursing, Morgen slammed on the brakes as the headlights illuminated antlers and startled deer eyes.

Lucky slid off the seat but was too busy barking out the window to notice. The buck sprang off the road and into the woods.

Morgen smashed the controls to roll up the window before Lucky could leap out, then gripped the wheel with both hands, willing her nerves to settle. That was hard with her dog barking loudly enough to be heard by the crews of freighters sailing through Rosario Strait miles away.

"You're not going after that deer," Morgen said. "You're a vizsla. Vizslas are *bird* dogs."

She was about to nudge the car into motion when a huge gray furry animal ran across the road after the deer. Blue eyes glanced in her direction before the creature—a wolf?—disappeared into the trees.

"Where the hell *are* we? Grandma's estate or Northwest Trek?"

Morgen put the car in park. Her fraying nerves were on the verge of snapping.

Surprisingly, Lucky stopped barking. He sank low in the seat and whined. It was different from the I-need-to-water-a-tree-as-soon-as-possible whine of earlier. This was a concerned maybe-we-should-have-gotten-a-hotel-in-town whine. At least that was how Morgen chose to interpret it.

"We're almost there." She took a deep breath and checked to make sure the keys to the house hadn't gone flying out of the cup holder. "We can—"

The wolf leaped out of the trees and back into the road. Morgen couldn't help herself. As those blue eyes stared through the windshield at her, she screamed.

Lucky sank below the dashboard and whimpered. Morgen clamped her mouth shut, trying to calm herself, but the wolf stood in the mud three feet in front of the car and growled, lips rippling as white fangs flashed in the headlights. It was *not* a calming experience.

If the fir and pine trees to either side of the road hadn't been so close, she would have turned the car around. This was too much to deal with by herself with night encroaching.

She honked the horn, willing the wolf to run away.

Its blue eyes widened, an almost human expression of indignation, and it crouched lower, hackles rising.

As a city girl, Morgen didn't encounter wolves on a regular basis, but she was positive this one was far larger than typical. Its thick gray and black fur did nothing to hide the power of its muscular frame, and she could easily envision it chomping into her tires and stranding her here.

She flashed her headlights at it and tried the horn again, but it didn't budge. Maybe the quiet engine of the electric car didn't alarm it the way a vrooming gas vehicle would have. The silence made it easy to hear the wolf's continuing growls.

"One more try," she muttered, nudging the car forward. She wouldn't hit the wolf, but maybe the bulk of the vehicle would finally scare it into moving. She dreaded the idea of trying to back a half a mile down the obstacle course of a driveway.

Its blue eyes widened again, and it sprang onto the hood, fangs only inches from the windshield. Morgen threw on the brakes, but she wasn't going fast enough for the wolf to fly off. It remained on the hood, snarling at her.

"All right, all right," she said, afraid the thing had rabies and that it might be able to break the windshield to get to her.

Even as she put the car in reverse, something happened to the wolf. It blurred and morphed, as if it were as malleable as clay. Morgen had no idea what was going on, but she didn't want to stick around to find out.

She accelerated in reverse, but the back-up camera was spattered with mud, and rivulets of rain made it hard to see out the rear window. The car had barely gone five feet when a tire sank into a pothole. When she pushed the pedal harder, the tires only slipped in the mud.

As she struggled to maneuver out of the pothole, the wolf's fur disappeared, replaced with bronze skin. Bronze *human* skin.

A naked man crouched on the hood, powerfully muscled arms and legs on display, along with male body parts that Morgen hadn't seen since her divorce.

She was too terrified to think straight. What was *happening*?

The wolf—the *man*—leaped off the hood and landed in the mud beside the driver's door. Now, she had a view of his upper body. Cut abs and pectorals, a head full of shaggy black hair, a mustache and goatee, and those same blue eyes. They were as striking against his dark skin as they had been in the gray-and-black furred face of the wolf. And every bit as angry.

She double-checked to make sure the door was locked.

"No trespassing," he snarled through the window.

She hadn't lowered it, and had no intention of doing so, but she heard his gruff voice clearly.

"Who are you?" she whispered.

"Leave *now*, or I will tear your throat out." His voice was accented, though she couldn't place it, maybe because he was busy threatening her life.

He thrust an arm back down the road, the veins visible under his skin. If she hadn't been terrified that he would punch a fist through the glass and strangle her, she might have admired his physique.

Lucky whined from the passenger seat.

"I know, buddy," she whispered, still trying to navigate the car out of the pothole. Afraid the wolf-man didn't understand that she was attempting to leave, she raised her voice to speak and buy time. "Look, this is 137 Alder Lane, isn't it? I'm not trespassing. This is my grandmother's property."

Technically, it was now *her* property, left to her after Grandma Gwen's passing. Her brothers had been bitter that they hadn't been mentioned in the will, but Morgen wondered now what kind of mess she'd inherited.

"*Get out,*" the man snarled, sounding more like the wolf that he'd just been.

"Communication-link failure," she muttered, quoting an error code she saw a lot at work. Or had before she'd been let go.

Not taking her eyes from him, she grabbed her phone off the console, took a clumsy one-handed picture—though he was standing so close that all she got was his naked torso—then put both hands on the wheel again.

"Maybe the police can use that to identify my murderer when my body is found," she grumbled and wiggled the tires left and right as she tried accelerating again.

This time, the car lumbered out of the pothole. She backed down the road as quickly as she dared. Fortunately, the man didn't follow the car. He merely stood in the mud with his fists on his hips and his legs spread, like some sculptor's statue. Some sculptor's very angry statue.

She spotted a place wide enough to turn the car around, then drove faster toward the road. Lucky grew braver as the wolf-man fell farther behind. He climbed into the back and resumed barking.

"FYI," Morgen told him, her heart still hammering against her rib cage, "that is also not a pheasant."

When she reached the main road, the rain picking up and spattering on the pavement, she turned to head into town. Maybe it was her imagination, but when she glanced back into the woods, she thought she spotted blue eyes watching her from the trees.

2

THE WILD TROUT WAS ONE OF ONLY TWO HOTELS IN BELLROCK, AND
it was the only one that took dogs, though the grumpy clerk had
given Morgen a firm admonition to keep her pet crated and off the
furniture.

As she dialed her phone, Lucky lounged in the middle of the
double bed, his legs stretched out and his head on the pillows.
Earlier, she'd put a quarter in the ancient Magic Fingers machine,
thinking the vibrations might scare him onto the floor, but he'd
only nestled in deeper.

"I can see you were traumatized by our adventure," Morgen
told him, wondering where she was going to squeeze in. Not that
she had sleep on her mind. It was early, and she was too keyed up.
What if she returned to Grandma's property in the morning, and
the wolf was still there?

The *werewolf*.

Unless someone had been playing an elaborate prank on her,
that was all it—*he*—could have been. But werewolves didn't *truly*
exist, did they? They were like vampires and ghosts and witches
and wizards. The stuff of Hollywood movies and fantasy novels.

"Hello?" her cousin Zoe answered. "Morgen?"

"Yeah. Thanks for picking up. I have... a problem."

"You want to list your house? I'd be happy to help. I sell houses all over Seattle and know your neighborhood really well."

"No, Jun got that in the divorce. He's still living in it."

"He got the house? What did *you* get?"

"Lucky, my car, and a lot of questions about my self-worth." Also questions about whether she was as distant, aloof, and cold as Jun had told the lawyer.

All those years together, and she hadn't realized he'd felt that way. He was an engineer, a logical and analytical human being not driven by his passions. She'd thought they were similar types of people and that they understood each other.

"Lucky?" Zoe asked. "That's your dog, isn't it?"

"Yeah."

"He's a nice pup and all, but he's not worth more than a house with ten years of equity in it."

"He's good company," Morgen said.

On the bed, Lucky rolled on his back with his paws crooked in the air.

"You know Grandma passed away, right?" Morgen added.

"I know you were the only one to get anything in her will. *I* don't care, but I bet your brothers are pissed about that. Your sister probably is too. I haven't talked to her in forever."

"She's not pissed. I called her and left a message when I told her about the funeral. She called back and left a message saying she couldn't make it." No need to mention that was what passed for a meaningful interaction with Sian. Jun might have thought Morgen was distant, but he'd called Sian an arctic glacier—based on the two times in ten years that they'd met. Morgen and Jun had been married for three years before the first time. Sian didn't show up for weddings any more often than she came to funerals. "She didn't sound irritated about the will."

"Probably because she's in Botswana chatting up gorillas and can't be bothered with such earthly things as money and houses."

"It's Borneo, and her specialty is orangutans. Let me ask you a question. As a real-estate agent, have you ever driven up to a house with your clients and had something—someone—tell them *no trespassing* and scare them off?" Morgen shivered as she remembered the flashing white fangs less than a foot away from her windshield.

"Uh, sometimes squatters will take up residence on a property that's been vacant for a while. Though I don't know how any squatters would have *found* Grandma's house. From what I remember, it's in the middle of the woods with state land on all sides."

"That's right. I drove up about an hour ago, and a... man leaped out of the woods and tried to scare me away." Morgen winced. "When I say *tried*, I mean he succeeded."

"Was he armed?"

"He looked like one of those guys where his body is a weapon." Morgen didn't mention the werewolf possibility. It was far too kooky to share over the phone. Besides, she was a database programmer, a logical and rational person, not someone who spouted tales of fantastical creatures.

"Oh, yeah? Did you get a picture?" Why did Zoe sound more intrigued than worried for her?

"A blurry one of his chest."

"Send it over. I'll give you my professional opinion."

"Your professional opinion as a real-estate agent? Are you going to appraise him?"

"Absolutely, I will."

Morgen snorted and texted the photo. "I was thinking of calling the police to see if someone would go out there with me in the morning."

At which point, she would feel foolish, because the man

wouldn't show up, and there would be no evidence to suggest he'd ever been there. Wasn't that how these things went?

"If Bellrock has a police station, sure," Zoe said. "Isn't the population there like thirteen?"

"It's not *that* small. And it's not that far to Bellingham."

"My professional appraisal of this chest is that it could indeed be used as a weapon," Zoe said.

"Thanks so much."

"Also that I'd pay fifty bucks to lick his abs."

"That's disgusting."

"No, they're quite nice."

"You didn't see his face," Morgen said.

"Was it horribly maimed and disfigured?" There was that intrigue again.

Morgen should have called her sister. She didn't know what help a primatologist in Borneo could be with this problem, but she was positive Sian wouldn't have offered to lick a stranger's body parts.

"No, just badly in need of attention from a barber. Or maybe a groomer. Does a squatter have any rights to be on a property if they've been there for a while?" It had only been four weeks since Grandma's death, so Morgen couldn't imagine that would have been enough time for anyone to have a legal right to stay on the property.

"Probably not unless he was a renter and has a lease."

"I'm sure Grandma wouldn't rent to a—" Morgen stopped herself before saying werewolf.

"—an Adonis with abs of steel?"

"You're hilarious."

"That's what my clients tell me. Hey, are you going to sell her house? I can't really see you moving to Bellrock."

"If I can get to it and see what kind of state it's in, probably." Morgen had been relieved to have an excuse to leave Seattle and

all the awkward condolences from her colleagues about the disso-
lution of her marriage.

"I can list it for you and get a good deal. I'm licensed to sell
property anywhere in the state, and I'm sure you could use the
money."

Morgen winced at the reminder that she was not only freshly
divorced but freshly unemployed, thanks to her company being
bought out and the new owners deciding to dissolve the IT department. She didn't yet know if this would qualify as the worst year of
her life, but it was in the running. Just last winter, she'd turned
forty and believed she and Jun were on a good path with stable
futures; funny how a few months could change everything.

"I've got my 401(k) and enough in savings to be okay for a
while, but I'll let you know once I get up to see the house."

"Send some more pictures, and I'll give you my professional
opinion."

"Of the house or the, uh, squatter?"

"I'm happy to opine on both."

"Thanks so much." Morgen hung up and searched for a
number for the authorities, her introvert tendencies making her
cringe at the idea of calling strangers. Strangers who would ask
her questions she didn't know how to answer. "It looks like the
county sheriff's department covers Bellrock. At least their office is
close. I'll call in the morning."

Lucky flopped back onto his side and swished his tail against
the comforter.

"Are you going to make room for me in there?" Not yet ready to
tackle pushing a seventy-pound dog over on the bed, Morgen
walked to the window and peered out into the rain.

Across the street, the shops were closed for the night. The
brick buildings with large glass windows and displays inside
looked little different from when Morgen had visited Bellrock with
her siblings when they'd all been kids.

Since their mother's death, none of them had come up here. Grandma had always implied that she preferred to live alone and didn't care much for company, but Morgen wondered if she should have tried harder to establish a rapport with her. Losing her daughter must have been hard on her, and she might have been lonely.

At the least, Morgen should have come up and checked on her. But Grandma hadn't been frail and sickly; the last Morgen had heard, she'd been living on her own without trouble, riding her motorcycle around the state, and reading all the books she hadn't had time for when she'd worked. Even though she'd been ninety, her death had been a surprise.

On the far side of the street, someone in a long dark jacket—or was that a cloak?—stepped out of the shadows between two buildings. A woman? It was hard to tell with the glass reflecting Morgen's own brown eyes and shoulder-length auburn hair back at her. Further, the person wore a hood that hid her face. Not surprising, given the rain, but she turned to look straight at Morgen's window. It was probably only in Morgen's imagination that the woman had a menacing aura.

A braid of damp gray hair had escaped the hood, and something black adorned the ponytail holder at the end. Morgen was too far away to see it clearly, but it reminded her of a spider. It probably wasn't one, but that *would* fit with the menacing aura.

Morgen, figuring she was framed in the window and noticeable with the lights on in her room, didn't want to stare back. She gazed up and down the street, as if she was checking out the scenery of downtown Bellrock. When she looked back, the woman was still staring at her.

Morgen backed from the window and closed the curtains. "Bellrock isn't as friendly as I remember."

She hoped the werewolf would be gone in the morning.

3

The second time Morgen drove up the long muddy driveway, the sun was out and a deputy sheriff's big SUV trailed her car past the water-filled potholes. As she sipped from a cappuccino from Bean Me Up, a drive-through coffee stand on the way out of town, she peered warily into the woods. She didn't see any wolves or anything amiss until they reached the spot where she'd stopped the night before.

And she stopped again. A dead deer lay across the driveway.

Morgen swallowed and closed her eyes, not wanting to look at the mangled body. She loved animals, even wild animals that darted in front of her car. It was one of the reasons she hadn't fought her doctor's recommendation that she become a vegetarian.

Her stomach churned at the thought of having to deal with this. What did one even *do* with a dead deer in the driveway?

A knock at the window startled her.

Lucky barked from inside his crate behind her seat, startling her further. Morgen hadn't wanted him to be tossed about on the bumpy driveway again, so she'd put him in it before they set out.

Fortunately, it was only Deputy Franklin, a big-eared man with a pot belly that slumped over the belt of his olive-green uniform. When she'd mustered enough extroversion to call the sheriff's office and ask for help, she'd envisioned driving up to the property with someone like Wyatt Earp, not Droopy Dog.

Franklin raised his bushy eyebrows and stepped back so she could open the door.

"I saw you stop and got out to see what the problem was," he said as she eased out, mud squishing under her shoes. "You ought to be able to drive around that." He waved to the deer carcass.

Even though Morgen tried not to look at it, she couldn't help but glance and see that it had been eviscerated and partially eaten. Was there a whole *pack* of wolves out here? That was a distressing thought.

And—she blinked and looked again—why was the *head* missing? Did animals usually chew off the heads of their prey? She'd never heard of such a thing.

"Can you check it?" she asked.

"Check it for what, ma'am? It's dead."

"I know, but it's... right in the driveway." Morgen waved at it, wondering if she would sound crazy if she said the wolf might have dragged it there as a message to her.

Stay off the property, or I'll do this to you.

Franklin shrugged. "Someone probably hit it."

"Causing the *head* to pop off?"

"That would have happened later." He stuck his thumbs in his belt and puffed out his chest—and his gut—as if to convey his supreme authority on this matter. "Some scavengers came in to take advantage and had themselves a nice dinner."

"I drove up last night, and *I* didn't hit it. I'm sure nobody else has come up here since then."

Nobody except the werewolf...

Franklin looked up and down the long driveway, trees and

bends hiding most of it from view. Morgen expected to have to argue further, but he shrugged and walked up to examine the area.

Lucky swirled in his crate and barked twice.

Morgen shook her head. "You can run around when we get to the house. Assuming there aren't corpses strewn all over the lawn." She shuddered at the idea.

When Franklin returned, a puzzled furrow creased his brow. He removed his hat and pushed a hand through his short brown hair. "You're right that it doesn't look like it was hit by a car. Some coyotes or maybe a wolf got it."

No kidding.

"Are wolves a big problem here?" *Werewolves?*

"Yeah, there are some wolves in these parts." As Franklin put his hat back on, he peered warily into the trees, losing his earlier nonchalance.

She almost asked him if he'd heard anything about werewolves, but she couldn't bring herself to voice something a normal, *sane* human being would scoff at and say was nonsense.

"This is still a pretty wild area," he continued, "despite our proximity to civilization. Lots of state land around here. Preserves and hiking trails and the like."

"Any hikers ever run into wolves?"

He hesitated. "Sometimes."

"Any hikers ever get *eaten* by wolves?"

"Sometimes."

Morgen blinked. "Are you serious?"

He smiled and thumped her on the shoulder. "Nah. Just joking around with you, ma'am."

She wasn't the best at reading people, but that smile didn't seem authentic, and he glanced into the woods and at the deer again before saying, "We'll drive around. Don't worry. I'll stick with you."

Franklin patted the firearm at his waist before heading back to his SUV.

A part of Morgen wanted to flee back to the safety and normalcy of Seattle, but she already felt guilty about not seeing her grandmother in recent years. The thought of abandoning her property and having it be overrun by squatters and wolves was repugnant.

Morgen took a deep breath and got back in the car. She drove carefully around the deer, wondering again what she was supposed to do with it. If she let her cousin list the house for sale, there would be showings. She couldn't imagine they would go well if the potential buyers had to maneuver past a headless deer carcass on the way up the driveway.

With branches scraping at the windows, Morgen made it around the obstacle. She couldn't keep from peering into the woods as she continued on, afraid she would spot a whole pack of wolves watching her. Or a single pair of icy blue eyes.

But the trees opened up ahead, and she finally glimpsed the clearing where Grandma's old house resided. A large red barn rose up to the side of it, the paint surprisingly fresh and the roof and sides in good condition. The nearby three-story, early 1900s Craftsman was in more need of work, with the green paint and yellow trim peeling and moss growing on the roof. Even so, it was much as Morgen remembered, and she exhaled slowly in relief. Despite triple-checking the sole address sign at the turn-off, she'd started to doubt she was indeed trying to reach the right property.

The fenced garden out front was also in better condition than expected, though weeds had grown up in the weeks since Grandma's passing, mingling with the strawberry plants sprawling across several beds and the green beans and tomato vines growing on trellises. The large lawn surrounding the house and barn had been mowed recently.

Maybe a caretaker had come up regularly to tend the yard for

Grandma? If so, Morgen would have to find out who it was and let them know she'd passed on. Maybe she could employ the same service until she was ready to sell the house.

Reminded of her cousin's request, Morgen got out of the car, intending to take some pictures. The deputy had also stepped out and was looking around with his hand on his firearm. Had he seen something? The naked man? A hulking wolf far too large to be of natural origins?

Morgen felt safer out in the open with the sun shining on the damp grass, but firs, alders, pines, and spruce rose up all around the hilltop property. In the distance, the water of Rosario Strait was visible through the trees. When she'd been a girl, there had been a better view. A real-estate agent would probably want to cut some of the trees down to put *water view* in the description, but Morgen didn't think they belonged to Grandma. The agent would have to list this as a peek-a-boo view.

"I didn't realize how isolated this place is," Franklin said.

"You'd heard of it before? Did you know my grandmother?"

"It's a small town. Everybody knows everybody, but Gwen was a recluse, so I can't say that I knew her. Just heard a few rumors now and then. She rode through town on that Harley of hers even though she had to be creeping up on seventy."

"Ninety, actually."

"Huh, she didn't look all that old. A shame it was the motorcycle that did her in."

"Yeah."

Whines from the car reminded Morgen that she'd promised to let Lucky out. She released him, and he sprang free, beelining straight for the barn. He immediately started sniffing and pawing at the ground next to the wall.

"Might want to keep an eye on him," Franklin said.

"Because of the wolves?"

"That's right. Usually, they'd leave a pup that size alone." He waved to Lucky's seventy-pound frame; the dog was large for his breed. "But people have spotted some big wolves around here."

"Imagine that." For the first time, Morgen thought to check the hood of her car for claw marks. The night before, it had been dark by the time she reached the hotel.

She grimaced at the scratches all over the hood and pointed them out to Franklin.

"That's from your dog?" he asked.

"No. A wolf jumped on my car last night."

He squinted at her. "You only mentioned a man who blocked your way."

"The man was the one who threatened to rip my throat out if I didn't leave." Technically, he may have made the same threat in the wolf language when he'd been growling at her. "That left a larger impression."

Not exactly true. The whole scenario, including the wolf transforming into a naked man right before her eyes, was indelibly imprinted on her mind.

"Are you planning to stay up here?" The car door was still open, and Franklin waved to the luggage visible in the back.

"That was my original plan. I need to figure out what to do with Grandma's belongings and get the house ready to sell."

She dreaded the necessity of sorting through her grandmother's things and deciding what to do with them. Her mother should have been here to spearhead this. Morgen, remembering so little of Grandma, didn't feel qualified. Most of what she remembered was that Grandma had been a librarian and loved books. They'd had that in common. And Morgen knew what it was like to prefer solitude to crowds of people—even family.

Right now, she wouldn't have minded less solitude. Even though she wasn't close to her brothers, she wished some of them had volunteered to come up and help, but they'd all made excuses about how busy they were. She'd sensed their bitterness about not having been left anything and suspected that was the real reason they hadn't come. Grandma had bequeathed all of her liquid wealth to charity, and the house was the only thing Morgen had received, though she wondered why she'd been singled out for that. As far as she knew, she hadn't been any closer than her siblings to Grandma.

"Maybe you should stay in the hotel," Franklin said, returning to the parked cars.

"Oh?"

"I didn't want to scare you, but..." He looked back toward the driveway.

Morgen didn't see anyone, but she had the feeling someone was watching them.

"Is this about the headless deer?" she asked.

"There were prints in the mud around it. Very large wolf prints." Franklin cupped two hands in the air to demonstrate the size.

Morgen nodded. After all, she'd seen the wolf that made them.

"Also, it looked like it was dragged into the road after it was killed."

"Like... to make a point?"

"I wouldn't necessarily attribute that much intelligence to an animal, but..." Franklin paused, then shook his head. "Never mind. I don't want to worry you. It might not mean anything."

Uh huh.

"I'll look around the property a little more," he offered. "See if I see anything peculiar or dangerous."

"Thank you."

As Franklin headed off to do an investigation of the property, Morgen grabbed the keys out of the cupholder in her car. Her fingers trembled a little, and she couldn't shake the feeling that someone was watching her.

After making sure Lucky hadn't gone far—he was still sniffing around the barn—she headed for the covered front porch. The wood had recently been sanded and sealed. Courtesy of the caretaker who'd mowed the lawn? Most of the house appeared old and in need of repairs, but parts here and there looked good, with the barn almost gleaming, though it had to be a hundred years old, if not older.

She halted at the top of the porch steps. A large firewood box rested on the doormat and blocked the door. Odd.

Morgen bent, intending to push it to the side, but a twinge of foreboding came over her, and something made her reach for the wooden lid. She lifted it and screamed for the second time in a day. The decapitated deer head was inside, dead eyes staring up at her.

4

MORGEN'S HANDS WOULDN'T STOP SHAKING AS SHE WALKED AROUND the exterior of the house, taking pictures from different angles. Deputy Franklin was toting the firewood box with the buck's head inside to the back of his SUV. She had no idea if he intended to run fingerprints on the hinges of the box or do any kind of investigation or if he was simply calming the terrified newcomer to his town by taking it away.

Morgen had only screamed once, but it had been enough to bring him running up to her side. He'd admitted it was disturbing and apologized for not offering to go inside the house first.

After he put the box away, he took the keys from her and went in to look around. Normally, Morgen prided herself on being the independent type and not needing a man's help for anything, but the last twelve hours had worn down her bravery. She poked around outside while Franklin went through the rooms inside, making sure there weren't any more body parts in boxes lying in wait.

She came to an old root cellar, the grass grown up to either side of the yellow double doors. A path around the house to them suggested Grandma had visited often. Since she had the garden, that probably made sense.

Morgen tried to remember if she'd ever been under the house as a kid, but she didn't think so. Curious, she reached down to tug one of the doors open, though a part of her wondered if she was making a mistake. Maybe she should ask the deputy to check out the root cellar first.

She was almost relieved when the doors didn't budge, though it was puzzling, because she didn't see a lock. Maybe Grandma had done some remodeling, and the cellar was now accessible from inside the house.

A star-shaped indention in one of the doors made her take a closer look. Cut into the wood and painted in dark blue that stood out from the surrounding yellow, it was a little larger than an old silver-dollar coin. She touched it, and a buzz of electricity ran up her arm.

Startled, she jerked back and looked at her finger. It was already turning red, as if she'd been burned.

"Because this day wasn't weird enough," she muttered, frowning at the indention.

She'd touched wood, not metal, so she didn't see how current could have been conducted through it. She glanced up, as if she might spot high-voltage electrical wires running over the house that she hadn't noticed before, but the only notable thing was a crow perched on the peak of the roof. Or was that a raven? It was large to be a crow.

"None of the wildlife is normal-sized around here."

She touched the indention again, to see if it had been a fluke. It buzzed her once more. Almost as if it were an alarm or a warning not to touch the doors.

"Huh."

"Ma'am?" Franklin had come around the corner of the house

and frowned at the doors. "Do you want me to check down there too?"

"They're locked."

"Good."

She raised her eyebrows. "Did you find something in the house?"

Something that would make him reluctant to explore further?

"Oh, no. I'm just..." Franklin gazed out into the woods again. Ready to get the hell out of here, his eyes said, though he didn't voice the words. "No, there's nothing in the house that you need to worry about. Your grandmother was a little quirky, but that's all. You should be fine looking around. But uhm, I'm still going to recommend the hotel. I don't think a woman should be out here alone in the woods at night."

Never mind that Grandma had lived alone here for years after Grandpa passed.

"I have Lucky." Morgen pointed to the dog, who'd taken a break from sniffing to roll on his back in the grass.

"He looks ferocious."

She decided not to mention how he'd spent the night on the bed at the hotel with his head on both pillows.

Franklin handed her the keys to the house. "I can wait while you look around if you want."

Though she was tempted to say yes, she didn't want to keep him out here all day. "That's all right. Maybe you could just take that head away and, uh, who should I call to have the rest of the body removed from the driveway?"

"I'll take care of it."

"Thank you."

He smiled and tipped his hat. "Call if you need anything."

Morgen flipped through the keys on the ring she'd inherited, looking for something to match the star-shaped indention, but nothing was similar.

Lucky bounded up to the deputy, demanding to be petted before he left. Franklin might not have been the badass law enforcer Morgen had hoped for, but at least he indulged the dog.

She headed into the house to look around and take more pictures. As she stepped into the living room, scents of sandalwood and sage enveloped her, and she remembered the pungent smells from visits in her youth. She vaguely recalled Grandma burning candles and pouring oils into diffusers.

Floorboards creaked as she walked through the house and into the kitchen. A surprisingly modern gas range was wedged between chipped yellow countertops, with numerous copper pans hanging from a rack over it. Maybe preparing meals here wouldn't be that bad. Though the word *icebox* came to mind when she looked at the pale blue refrigerator with rounded corners. It probably ran on electricity, but she wouldn't be surprised to find a compartment for a block of ice.

As she wandered through the second floor, the house large for only one person, more memories returned, mostly of her in her room reading while her brothers ran through the hallways and played outside in the yard. Her sister had always claimed the library full of books and locked herself inside, not even letting Morgen in to share the solitude. She'd done her reading from a ledge atop a closet, filling the nook with blankets and pillows. Their father had admonished them for spending their summer vacation with their noses in books and told them to go out and play in the woods. If giant wolves had been lurking in the trees back then, Morgen was glad she hadn't heeded that request.

She'd never been in her grandmother's room before, and when she ventured in, the scents were even stronger, as if incense had been burned in there recently. Wrinkling her nose, she opened a window wide to air the place out.

The artwork on the walls was an eclectic collection of pressed leaves, dried berries, and words in foreign languages. A number of ropes were coiled decoratively on the ceiling above the bed, made from braided horsehair or something of that nature. A desk held a mortar and pestle and numerous candles. Maybe this had been the room that had led Franklin to label Grandma as quirky.

A number of belts and necklaces dangled from a bedpost. Not that big on jewelry, Morgen started to ignore them, but a hunch drew her over, and she sorted through the collection. A silver chain with an emerald-green star-shaped medallion made her think of the root-cellar doors. She couldn't see how it could be a key, but she removed it to see if the medallion would fit in the indention.

A caw came from the window, and she dropped it. The raven that she'd seen outside now perched on the sill. To her shock, the big black bird flew into the room, cawing loudly.

Morgen sprang back, bumped the bed, and almost pitched to the floor. Black wings flapped, feathers flying, and the raven dove toward the medallion.

"What the—" Though alarmed, Morgen lunged for it.

No way was she going to let some bird *steal* her grandmother's jewelry.

Wingtips brushed her face, almost beating her about the head, but she snatched up the medallion. Talons flashed, and pain stabbed the back of her hand. She almost dropped the medallion again, but she tightened her grip and ran into the hallway. She slammed the door shut and plastered her back to the opposite wall.

Several caws of protest came from the bedroom before the house fell silent again. Morgen stared at bloody gouges in the back of her hand and the heavy medallion she gripped.

She was tempted to leave the door closed and walk away, but if the raven was left inside, it could tear up the room and make a mess.

"I'm starting to think that preparing this house to sell won't be easy." Morgen ran to the kitchen, grabbed a broom, and returned, bracing herself in case she had to battle the raven to drive it out of the house.

But when she opened the door, the bird was gone. After double-checking, she hurried to the window to close it. The raven cawed at her from the roof of the barn.

Lucky ran back and forth below, barking up at it.

"I guess that's closer to a pheasant than the other things you've been trying to get," Morgen muttered.

As she headed downstairs, she sent the photos she'd taken to her cousin. She resisted the urge to text: *if you don't hear from me again by tomorrow, send the police.* Though maybe it wouldn't have been a bad idea.

The raven was probably a fluke—weren't they known for stealing shiny objects and squirreling them away in nests?—but the werewolf squatter was another story.

She left the broom in the kitchen and grabbed a butcher knife. Just in case.

Outside, Lucky continued to race back and forth while barking at the raven on the roof of the barn. From thirty feet above, it looked down, indifferent to the dog.

Morgen kept the medallion close, in case the bird was still contemplating theft. Deputy Franklin had driven off, so she would be on her own if she had to retrieve it from some forest nest.

"You barking at it isn't going to make it fall off the roof and into your mouth," Morgen told Lucky as she passed him. This common sense did not leave an impression on him. She finally called, "Treat!" to get him to stop.

It didn't always work, but this time, it did. He raced over and sat in front of her, his floppy ears cocked.

"Good boy." She dipped into the treat bag she kept in her jacket pocket and gave him a piece. "How about giving your vocal cords a rest for a while?"

He licked her hand, dropped to his back, and rolled in the grass.

"That works."

A call came in from Zoe as Morgen knelt in front of the root-cellar doors.

"What do you think?" Morgen answered, assuming her cousin had looked through the photos.

"It's got good bones. You should remodel it before listing it. You'll get a lot more. People with money want granite countertops, walk-in closets, and heated floor tiles in the bathrooms. Even better if there's a steam shower, a jetted bathtub, and towel warmers."

"Towel warmers?" Morgen placed the star-shaped medallion into the indention.

It was a perfect fit. Coincidence?

"After you spend a few million on a house, you don't want to have to endure chilled towels when you step out of the shower."

Morgen scoffed. "This place isn't worth millions."

"It's only five minutes outside of town, and it's on a bunch of land, right? And Bellrock is close to Bellingham and not all that far from Seattle. Trust me, that much land by the water is going to go for a fortune."

"I think it's mostly state land. There's only an acre or so around the house."

Morgen tried turning the medallion, though the indention was cut into the wood, so she didn't see how it could turn. And it didn't. It lay there, the emerald glass gleaming in the sunlight but nothing else happening.

"Are you sure about that?" Zoe asked. "It's not unheard of, but it would be uncommon to find a private parcel surrounded by state land."

"Pretty sure. If it was truly worth a lot, Grandma never would have been able to afford the property taxes. She was a retired librarian, and I don't think Grandpa left her much when he passed."

"Seniors can get discounts on property taxes. Let me check on it. Text me the address."

"All right."

Wingbeats sounded as the raven flew off. Lucky growled, but he wasn't looking toward the bird but into the woods. Morgen didn't see anything among the trees, but she again had the feeling that she was being watched.

"Let me know what you find," she told her cousin, the urge to finish searching around and get out of there as soon as possible filling her. Another night at the Wild Trout sounded more and more appealing. "Bye."

She was about to give up on the medallion doing anything but decided to try pressing it. It didn't depress far, but a click sounded. When nothing else happened, Morgen pulled out the medallion. She tried opening the doors again. This time, they creaked open, revealing wide earthen stairs that descended under the house.

A hodgepodge of strong scents that she couldn't identify wafted out, making her wrinkle her nose again. It was even worse than in the house. How did discerning buyers who liked jetted tubs and towel warmers feel about homes reeking of incense, dried herbs, and who knew what else?

"Stand watch, Lucky."

He'd returned to sniffing around the barn, making Morgen wonder if another dog—or a wolf?—had been marking the area.

As she descended, she hunted for a light switch, but the walls were made of dirt. It truly was a root cellar.

Except that it didn't contain jars of pickles and cans of tomatoes.

Enough daylight filtered down for Morgen to make out unfamiliar tools on pegboards and shelves filled with quirky potion bottles, ceramic crocks, and jars holding everything from powders to agates to organs and eyeballs in formaldehyde. Some of the powders were *glowing*. Would the real-estate listing have to mention that parts of the house were radioactive?

Boxes and crates were stacked against the back wall, along with bookcases that overflowed with weathered tomes that might have been older than the house. With some books stacked horizontally and others perched vertically or leaning diagonally, they didn't seem to be categorized in any way, and the urge to spring into the morass and arrange them in a logical organizational paradigm made her fingers twitch.

But the sheer strangeness of everything collected within kept her feet rooted to the floor as she gaped around. The rest of the walls were lined with counters and workbenches, the tops cluttered with daggers, vials, bottles, cauldrons of various sizes, and more mortars and pestles. A staff with antlers attached to the top leaned next to the stairs. In the center of the sprawling cellar, the packed dirt floor held a pentagram in a circle painted in red. *Blood* red.

If one of Grandma's motorcycle helmets hadn't dangled from a hook next to the staff, Morgen would have thought she'd wandered into an alternate dimension. Or that Grandma had unknowingly rented out her root cellar to a witch.

But the key to this place had been in *her* bedroom.

Morgen shook her head and set the butcher knife down next to a wavy-bladed kris. The kitchen tool looked like a toy in comparison to it.

Her grandmother had kept to herself and been aloof, but that ran in the family. It wasn't *that* weird. This... What was Morgen supposed to do about all this? Put it in the description for the listing for the house under *bonus room*?

Lucky barked, and the rumble of a car engine floated down.

Now what?

5

A WHITE LAND ROVER ROLLED UP THE DRIVEWAY AND PARKED IN front of the house. Lucky had stopped barking, but Morgen grabbed his collar as soon as she came out of the root cellar—the *witch* cellar. He was more likely to jump on a stranger and knock him over with an energetic greeting than to bite anyone, but not everybody appreciated that.

The windows were tinted, so Morgen couldn't see inside, but the owner soon stepped out. He had short white hair, a bushy handlebar mustache, and wore a denim shirt under a brown suede jacket with fringes. A ten-gallon cowboy hat topped off the ensemble. In Texas, he might not have looked out of place, but jeans and flannel were more typical along the misty coast of western Washington.

"Morning, ma'am." He tipped his hat toward her.

Lucky woofed.

"Morning, hound."

Lucky wagged agreeably.

"Hi," Morgen said.

"I'm Magnus Christian, best real-estate agent in these parts."

"Ah." Morgen could already guess what this visit was about. Maybe she shouldn't have shut the doors to the root cellar on her way out. Seeing all of the bizarre paraphernalia might have deterred an agent from wanting to list the place. "Morgen Keller," she said, still getting used to using her maiden name again. "I inherited this place from Gwen Griffiths."

"Wonderful to meet you." Christian smiled and reached for her hand.

Morgen hid a grimace as she let go of Lucky's collar so she could accept the clasp. She'd never been one for hugs—or hand-shakes—from strangers, but people tended to raise their eyebrows when she jerked her arm away.

Fortunately, all he did was clasp it and nod to her before letting go. "You're the daughter of the deceased?"

"Granddaughter. I guess that's what I get for not bothering with makeup."

Christian blinked and looked her up and down. "I didn't mean to insult you, ma'am. You don't look a day over thirty, and if I were to walk through the shopping district with you, I'd feel quite smug at having attracted such a young lady." He winked at her. "I just hadn't realized that Mrs. Griffiths was old enough to have grown grandchildren."

"She was ninety."

"Really?" Christian patted Lucky. "Did you hear she died in a motorcycle accident?"

"Yes, how did *you* hear about it?" Morgen forced a smile, though she was already inclined to be suspicious of this man.

How had he known she was up here? It hadn't even been a full day since she arrived in town. Had Deputy Franklin said something? And if so, to whom? And why?

For some reason, Morgen thought of the woman who'd peered into her hotel room window the night before.

"It was in the local news a few weeks back," he said, "and I'd met Mrs. Griffiths a few times. She contacted me this past spring about selling her property. She was thinking of moving into a condo up north. One of those assisted-living facilities."

Given what Morgen had seen in the root cellar, she highly doubted Grandma had been contemplating anything of the sort. Assisted-living facilities had to have rules about how many cauldrons and jars of organs one could store in one's room. And surely, drawing pentagrams on the floor was discouraged.

"Interesting," Morgen made herself say, though she was already contemplating how to get rid of this guy. Lucky had lost interest in him and returned to investigating the barn—or whatever creatures might be living under it. "My cousin is a real-estate agent, so I'm sure Grandma would have used her if she'd been serious about selling."

His eyes narrowed. "An agent where?"

"In Seattle."

Christian scoffed and waved dismissively. "You can't use an agent who doesn't know the local area. That would be ludicrous. I'm sure I can get you much more. I understand you *are* the sole heir to the estate?" He lifted his brows.

"Not to be rude, but how do you know that?"

He shrugged easily. "As I said, it's a small town. I regularly have lunch with Abraham, the estate attorney who handles most of the cases in these parts."

So he could find out which aggrieved descendants might be willing to list properties with him and beat his competition to their doors? This time, Morgen didn't bother hiding her grimace. She eyed his SUV, decided it had cost him a fortune, and felt pleased about the fresh mud spattering the sides. If nothing else, he would have to pay to have it scrubbed after coming out here. Somehow, she doubted he was the type to wash a car himself.

"I can help you get a great offer," Christian said. "I already know lots of developers who are interested in Bellrock and are buying up land all over the area for their projects. Do you realize how rare it is to find an estate this size left this close to town? I'm surprised the county hasn't already rezoned it. A developer could put hundreds of houses and condos in there. And is that a view of the water over there?" He peered off toward the Strait. "If you cut down those trees, you'd be able to see the sunset and all the ships passing below. *Magnificent*."

"Cut down all the trees?" Morgen wasn't as anti-progress as some, but the idea of bulldozers coming in and clearcutting the woods—even if they *were* infested with werewolves—horrified her. The local deer were having a hard enough time staying alive as it was.

"Oh, they'd leave some, I'm sure. For aesthetics." He waved his hand. "People like trees."

"Yeah, I hear they're good for the planet."

"I'm more interested in getting you what's good for your pocketbook." He glanced at her hand. "I don't see a ring on that finger. Are you single? Divorced? It's not easy for a single lady to make it in the world, is it?" His pitying smile made her wonder if he'd researched her and knew she was out of work.

Morgen gritted her teeth. "Look, Mr. Christian. I just got up here, and I need to sort through Grandma's things. I'm not thinking about selling right now."

"Of course, of course. Take your time." He pulled out a gold card holder encrusted with emeralds and diamonds—were those *real*?—and withdrew an embossed business card. "Call me when you're ready."

He pressed it into her hand, tipped his hat, climbed back into the hulking SUV, and drove off. She hoped the wolf leaped onto his hood and threatened to tear his throat out for trespassing.

"I'll call you the first of never," she muttered and tore up the card.

"Do you object to him personally or to developing the proper-ty?" a man with a growly voice asked from behind her.

Morgen swore and spun, realizing that she'd left the butcher knife in the cellar. What had she been thinking?

She recognized the owner of the voice right away, though he'd been naked the last time she'd seen him. Now, he wore jeans and a brown leather vest that revealed almost as much of his muscled chest and arms as his *last* outfit had. A single tooth—some animal's fang—hung on a thong around his neck, and wide stud-ded-leather bracers circled his wrists, as if he were an archer who needed them to protect his forearms. He towered six and a half feet tall, making her feel much shorter than she usually did at five-eight, and was close enough that he could have reached out and grabbed her.

Morgen skittered back, wishing she had the knife, especially since his cool blue eyes hadn't changed. They lacked warmth, and they reminded her of the wolf he'd been the night before. The wolf he still seemed like with that wild black hair and powerful build. This was a predator, whether he was in fur or flesh.

"Do you object to him or to developing the property?" he repeated slowly, as if she were an idiot who needed help compre-hending simple words, though he was the one for whom English had to be a second language. Was that a Mexican accent? What would a Mexican werewolf be doing in Washington?

"Both." Though Morgen was afraid to look away from him, she glanced around for Lucky, worried the man might have done something to him. Otherwise, he should have barked to alert her to a stranger—to a threat.

Lucky stood off to the side. He didn't appear injured, but his tail was clenched between his legs and his head was low, as if he'd been scolded.

"You will not sell the property?" the man asked.

"I don't know yet, but not to someone who wants to bulldoze

the woods and put in a thousand houses and condos."

He watched her with those cool eyes, and she wasn't sure if she'd given him the answer he wanted. Maybe she should have said a plain and definitive *no*. But that wasn't the truth, and what business was it of his anyway? *He* was the trespasser here.

"Gwen was your grandmother." He didn't ask it like it was a question. He already knew.

The people in Bellrock knew far too much about her.

"Yes. I'm Morgen. And you are?"

Besides the freak who'd threatened to rip out her throat after leaping naked onto her car...

"He who protects this place," he said.

"That doesn't roll off the tongue as easily as you might think."

"Follow me. I will show you something." He strode toward the front of the barn.

"Uh." She glanced at Lucky, who'd lowered to his belly in the grass, as if commanded to stay. His tail was still clenched. If the werewolf tried anything, she couldn't count on her dog to help. "Be right there," she called, then ran back to the root cellar.

She grabbed the butcher knife off the workbench, then wondered if she would be better off grabbing the kris or antler staff, but shook her head and stuck with her first choice.

The werewolf was waiting at the large rolling door, the wood scorched with a symmetrical pattern that reminded her of snowflakes. Without explaining it, he shoved it aside, but he pointed at her knife before walking in.

"You intend to prepare a meal?"

"No. A wolf jumped on my car last night and threatened to kill me. It seemed like a good idea to be armed."

He grunted. "You should have grabbed the boline knife."

While Morgen wondered if that had been one of the tools in the root cellar, he strode into the barn.

Though still hesitant, and not at all certain he wouldn't kill her, she followed him inside.

Wood chips scattered the cement floor of the cavernous interior. When Morgen had been a kid, there had been horse stalls on the left side of the barn, but those had been taken out, replaced by a huge workshop. Tables, benches, and even a totem pole in progress rose up amid power tools and sawhorses. Some of the furnishings had fine wood carvings in the flat surfaces, and a few had been decoratively charred, as if by a blowtorch.

To the right of the work area, stairs led up to what she remembered as a loft but now looked like more of an apartment. Near the base of the stairs, a tarp lay over something lumpy. The werewolf tugged it off, revealing a wrecked motorcycle.

Morgen grimaced. "Is this... was this... Grandma's?"

"Yes. By the time I learned of the crash, the paramedics had pulled her body out of the ravine. I found this at the bottom, mangled among the trees." He nudged a couple of parts that must have fallen off in the crash. "At the time, I didn't yet know that she was dead. I brought it back in case she wanted it."

"Wait, do you live here?" Morgen glanced at the steps leading to the apartment.

"Yes."

"Do you pay rent?" She thought of her cousin's words that if the werewolf had paid rent, it might be more difficult to evict him from the property.

"Why?" His eyes narrowed, and his words turned into more of a growl again. "Do you wish to charge me to stay here?"

"No. I..." Maybe saying she wanted to evict him wasn't a good idea either, not when he crouched there, radiating menace toward her. She didn't know what this guy had against her, but she definitely got the feeling he didn't like her. "I was just asking. Grandma didn't mention you."

"*You* never came here. How could she *mention* me?"

"Well, there are these things called phones." Morgen almost

brought up email too, but she hadn't seen a computer in the house and couldn't remember Grandma ever communicating with the family that way.

"Which you did not use to call her."

Was that what he had against her? Morgen had always thought that was what Grandma wanted, to be left alone in peace. But what if she'd resented that her grandchildren hadn't come up to visit? It boggled her mind that this werewolf might have known her grandmother better than she did.

"This was on the bike when I found it." He pointed to a bone-colored clip fastened to a fluid line. Or maybe the clip was *made* from bone.

Was that the brake line? Morgen had put together her own computers when she'd been in her teens and twenties, but she knew little about cars and even less about motorcycles.

"Touch it," he told her, the words a command, not a request.

She bristled, not wanting to obey him—or crouch shoulder to shoulder beside him. But curiosity kept her from voicing a protest. She bent over, touched a finger to the clip, and jerked her hand back when it buzzed her the same way the indention in the root-cellar door had.

His eyes glittered with triumph. "It is magic, yes? I *knew* it."

"Uhm." Nothing more articulate came to mind.

"And you have the witch blood of your line."

That deserved another *uhm* or maybe something more profound, but Morgen couldn't do anything but alternate between staring at him and at the clip. It had felt like an electrical current had buzzed her—not *magic,* whatever the hell magic felt like—but as with the door, the clip didn't appear to be made from a material that could conduct electricity.

"I don't know what any of that means," she said.

He pointed at the clip. "*That* means that someone murdered your grandmother."

6

"YOU THINK SOMEONE TAMPERED WITH THE MOTORCYCLE?" MORGEN asked.

"Yes. That was under a housing before." The werewolf pointed at the bone clip. "It would not have been visible to Gwen. I am surprised she did not sense it, but I do not know how witch magic works." He squinted at her. "Do *you* sense it?"

"Sense it? No, but I'm not a witch." Nor did she believe in witches, magic, hexes, potions, wands, or werewolves, for that matter. "I'm a database programmer. I also enjoy reading, organizing, cooking, hiking with my dog, and music with lyrics that mean something. As you can see from my list, I have no witchy hobbies."

"You felt its magic."

"I felt... something." Morgen rubbed the finger that had been zapped. "Like electricity."

"Magic can feel like many things. Often, it is painful." He grimaced, as if remembering some specific incident. "You will research this device." He removed it from the motorcycle with a faint snap. If it buzzed him, he gave no indication of it. "You will learn who made it and tell me their name."

"You like to give orders, don't you?"

"Gwen allowed me to take the fallen trees from Wolf Wood for my work and to live on this land. I owe her. You will find out who murdered her." He held out the clip.

Morgen hadn't the foggiest idea how to research a magical item, nor did she want to get zapped again by taking hold of the thing. "The sheriff's report said my grandmother died in an accident, that it was late, the roads were wet, and she went around a curve too quickly."

"She was murdered." He stepped closer to her. His height and prominently displayed muscles would have made him intimidating even if she *hadn't* seen him transform from a wolf into a man. "You will find out who did it so I can kill them."

"How about if you want my help, you offer me something or at least ask politely instead of being a big bully?" The words came out braver than she felt. After the day—and night—she'd had so far, she wanted to run and hide somewhere, not deal with this guy.

"I am *not* a bully."

"You haven't given me your name, you're ordering me around, and you're about to knock my face in with your prodigious pecs. What would you call that?"

He squinted down at her for several long seconds, and she didn't know if he was debating whether his actions—and his pecs —were or weren't bullying, or if he was contemplating throwing her over his shoulder and locking her and the clip in the root cellar until she solved his mystery.

Finally, he stepped back. She realized she was gripping the handle of the knife so hard that her knuckles ached.

"My name is Amar Guerrero. *If* you research this item, find out who put it on the motorcycle, and tell me, I will..." He looked around the barn for inspiration. "Make you a table."

"A table?" She appreciated that he was taking her advice and offering her something, but what was she supposed to do with a table? Especially a giant table made out of slabs of wood hauled in from the wilds? She didn't even have a house these days, unless one counted the small apartment she'd rented in Shoreline. If the chunky furnishings in the barn were indicative of his typical work, she wouldn't be able to get anything he made through the door.

"Or a bench," he said.

"You could just buy me dinner." Morgen meant it as a practical suggestion, especially since she hadn't yet had time to grocery shop, but belatedly realized it sounded like she was fishing for a date.

No, she was not looking for that, not from any guy, and especially not from the werewolf who'd threatened to rip her throat out. Besides, what did he eat that a vegetarian could have? Deer was not on her menu, especially not freshly eviscerated deer. She shuddered.

Fortunately, he seemed more puzzled by than interested in this suggestion. Apparently, she wasn't his type. That was fine with her. She shuddered again.

"A bench would be fine," she said. "I'll fend for myself for food. I've got a bag of cauliflower puffs in the car."

Maybe she could put his bench on the front porch here. Then she wouldn't have to worry about transporting it, and the people who came to look at the house could sit aghast on it after seeing the pale blue icebox and the lack of towel warmers.

Though it occurred to her that selling the house, the original and only plan she'd had when driving up to Bellrock, might not be a good idea. What if everyone wanted to develop the property instead of living on it? No, she wouldn't let that happen. As long as there were multiple offers, she could be selective. Maybe she could find a nice family that wanted a fixer house with room for the kids to run. Though small children might not be appropriate for a property with a werewolf living in the barn.

She rubbed her face, wondering if she would wake up to find out this bizarre day had been a dream.

"Cauliflower what?" he—Amar—asked.

"Puffs. They're a snack food. A mix of cauliflower and sorghum."

"Sore gum?"

"Sorghum, yeah. It's an ancient grain. And an environmentally responsible sustainable crop. No need to feel guilty about your snacking pleasure." Morgen stopped short of telling him about the fiber content. As her husband—*ex-husband*—had been quick to point out, nobody wanted the details of her *hippy health kick*, as he'd called it.

She couldn't help it that her doctor had traumatized her with ominous threats and stern lectures about her questionable health and how her body would only decline further in her forties if she didn't change something. At first, she'd been reluctant to give up her diet of fast food to learn to cook vegetable-based meals at home, but she'd gradually gotten used to it. These days, cauliflower puffs didn't even seem that odd. They were handy for car trips—and prompting strange conversations with werewolves.

A werewolf whose brow remained furrowed and unenlightened.

"I'm a vegetarian," she explained. That tended to clear things up—or at least helped people to categorize her crazy. "I like animals," she added, wondering if he'd been the one to put the deer head on the doorstep. Who else could it have been?

Maybe she was crazier for standing here and talking to him than for her food choices.

"Huh," was all he said.

"A bench would be great."

"Yes. Good." Amar held out the clip again, looking more exasperated than pleased by her acceptance. Or maybe he was just exasperated with her. She probably should have told him she liked deer puffs.

She tugged her sleeve down, hoping a fabric barrier would keep the clip from zapping her again, and accepted it. He folded his arms over his chest and stood like a statue, as if he meant to wait there until she finished her research and brought him the answers he wanted.

How likely it was that she could, she didn't know, but if Grandma *had* been murdered, Morgen wanted answers too.

She walked back outside, and Lucky bounded over. He jumped up on his hind legs, planted his paws on her shoulders, and licked her face.

"Yeah, yeah," she said, nudging him back down. They'd gone to obedience classes for months to work on the jumping thing, and she'd thought he'd grown out of it, but maybe this was an extenuating circumstance. She had, after all, just walked out of a werewolf's lair.

As Morgen headed toward the root cellar, figuring a witch's laboratory—or whatever it was called—was the appropriate place to research a magical bone clip, she pulled out her phone to take a picture of it. Maybe an image search on the internet would be enlightening.

She didn't find anything exactly like the clip, just a lot of sites ensuring her that working with skulls, bones, and animal remains was typical in modern witchcraft, shamanic practices, and folk magic.

"That's a relief. I was hoping my day would turn *typical.*"

Lucky bounded along at her side and sniffed at the clip.

"No buzzy bones for you," she said, even though that sounded like the name of a product for her treat pocket. "And if you're coming into the root cellar with me, you have to keep your nose out of things."

Lucky ran off to sniff at the side of the barn again. Maybe he couldn't be constrained by such rules.

Morgen descended the stairs, the strong scents making her dread the idea of spending hours down there, and headed straight for the bookcase. She ducked her head to avoid hitting twists of strange dried things dangling from the ceiling beams.

The collection of paraphernalia gathered down here wasn't any less daunting the second time. If she needed to find any specific item, she wouldn't know where to start. If this had been her workshop, she would have tagged everything with RFID and entered the items into a database before sorting and storing everything in a logical manner. Her fingers groped at the air with longing as she imagined instilling such order on the place.

When she reached the bookcase, she was relieved that most of the titles were in English, though the fancy calligraphic script on the bindings made the texts seem just as old as she'd guessed. Some were even handwritten.

"*Grimoire of Sacred Knowledge*," she read on one as she scanned the titles, hoping something would pop out at her as possibly relevant.

The part of her that had read numerous detective stories believed it might be a better use of her time to wander around town and speak to people who'd known her grandmother—such as that smarmy real-estate agent who'd apparently been talking to her about selling the property—but the introvert in her cringed at the idea of starting conversations with strangers. She would rather spend days in a library—or a cellar full of grimoires—than wander around asking people questions.

But she wouldn't be able to find anything in this disorganized mess. After again eyeing the books, the jars, the bottles, the crocks, and bags of what had to be ingredients for potions or creams or who knew what, Morgen ran to her car to grab her laptop. Sadly, she didn't have RFID tags along, but she could improvise some labels and at least get a thorough inventory of everything. Maybe in the process, she would come across something identical or similar to the bone clip—and instructions telling her all about it and who made them.

She'd been working for two hours, thankfully finding a chain to turn on a naked light bulb mounted in a socket between ceiling beams, when the phone rang. Zoe's name popped up.

"Hey," Morgen answered. "Thanks for calling back."

"No problem, coz. And have I mentioned that you're my *favorite* cousin? And that I'm a brilliant real-estate agent who will gladly lower my commission if you let me sell that house for you?"

"Since I've already inventoried the root cellar and know there isn't a stash of gold bars down here, I'm going to assume it's on more land than we all thought." Morgen could have guessed that based on Christian's comment about hundreds of houses fitting on the property. She knew developers crammed a lot of houses into small areas these days, but nobody would put a hundred on an acre.

"Good guess," Zoe said. "The house itself is on a two-acre tax lot, but here's what Grandma never mentioned. She owned it and the six tax lots surrounding it. The easternmost one *does* back up to state land that stretches over to the interstate, but everything you can see from the house all the way down to the water was hers. Is *yours* now, I guess. There's over five hundred acres."

Morgen swore, far more daunted than excited. "How did the lawyer not mention that? There's going to be a huge estate tax due at the end of the year, right?"

Morgen would have to sell the land to pay that. Even though it was what she'd planned to do after hearing she'd been left the property, the idea of being *forced* to do it was distressing.

"Uhm, not necessarily. Grandma—actually, I think this was *her* grandmother—had it designated as forest land a long time ago. Looks like that comes with an agreement to sustainably manage the forest. More importantly, it means the maximum assessed value of the land is a lot lower than it would be if you put it on the market and sold it to someone who was going to try to get it rezoned for residential development."

Exactly what Amar didn't want to happen. Even if she didn't like him, Morgen couldn't blame him for not wanting to see the forest destroyed. What had he called it? Wolf Wood.

"She also had a veteran's exemption on her taxes—that must be because Grandpa served—and a senior citizen exemption too. It looks like she wasn't paying for anything more than the property the house is on. Are you sure the lawyer didn't tell you all about this? That's odd."

Morgen sighed. "I don't know. I never talked with her over the phone. These last couple of weeks have been tough." The last couple of *months* had been tough. "And I don't like talking with strangers under any circumstances."

"Even strangers who are giving you things?"

"Yeah. She ended up sending a big packet along with the keys to the house. It's all in the car. I was going to look everything over this week."

"Well, she probably would have warned you about the estate tax if the property value meant it crossed the threshold and you had to pay it, but you will *definitely* have to pay it if you sell the land and make millions. It's not that big a deal, since you'd make F-U money out of the deal, even after paying the taxes. Like I said, I'm happy to take care of it for you."

Yes, everybody would be happy to sell the property for her. Morgen could think of worse problems to have, but she was starting to wish Grandma had left the place to her sister.

"And if I don't want to sell it, what then? I just have to worry about the property taxes?"

"Essentially, but they're going to go up a ton because you don't have any exemptions."

"Can you define a ton?"

"Uh, not really. There aren't any comps around for me to look at it, but it might be a lot. And you said you're not working, right? Morgen, you have to sell it. You can't afford to move up there. There aren't any programming jobs in Bellrock. There's a fudge store, three tchotchke shops, the woo woo place that sells crystals and weird powders, and two hotels that probably don't even have computer systems. Just sell the place. We barely went up there as kids. It can't mean that much to you. And don't you want to be a millionaire?"

"I don't know what I want yet."

No, that wasn't true. Morgen eyed the bone clip lying on a counter next to a mortar and pestle. She wanted to find out if the werewolf was right, if someone had killed Grandma.

7

IT WAS ALMOST FULL DARK BY THE TIME GRITTY EYES AND AN ACHING back made Morgen give up on her cataloging-and-organizing project. She'd barely made a dent in the mess.

Admittedly, the project might not need to be done—maybe she'd given herself the only kind of task she was perfectly suited for because everything else was too daunting to deal with. But she couldn't help but think the answer to what the bone clip was, what it did, and maybe even who had made it, could be in the cellar somewhere.

At the least, she ought to familiarize herself with what had been her grandmother's secret life—at least secret to her family— especially if Amar had spoken the truth and Morgen had inherited some predilection for... witchiness. Witch ways. Witch blood.

Was that possible? If she hadn't been inexplicably zapped twice today, she would have scoffed and dismissed it all, filing away everything in the cellar as a sign of an odd hobby and possible senility. But as she rubbed her fingertips together, the memory of the electrical buzzes fresh in her mind, she feared there might be something to it.

A blast of worry struck her as Morgen stepped outside, looked around, and didn't see Lucky. She'd had the doors to the root cellar open while she'd been down there, and she'd heard him snuffling around from time to time, and he didn't usually go far from her, but what if he'd chased something into the woods and gotten lost? Or what if he'd irked a werewolf who'd decided to eat him?

She glanced toward the two windows in the apartment above the barn, but no lights were on. Either werewolves saw in the dark, or Amar had gone out for a hunt. Or he was skulking around in the dark somewhere.

Morgen shivered. By the fading light, she grabbed Lucky's dog dish and bag of kibble, along with the big envelope of papers she'd told Zoe about and hadn't yet read. As soon as she found Lucky, she would go inside and peruse them.

She jogged to the porch to turn on whatever outside lights the house had so she could see more of the yard.

A *thwap, thwap, thwap* greeted her, and she could just make out Lucky lying on his side on the floorboards. The wood probably held lingering warmth from the sunset.

"I was worried about you, and you were up here napping?"

Thwap, thwap.

"Did you wear yourself out pretending to hunt all day? And had to collapse exhausted on the porch?"

Thwap.

Being a good dog, Lucky didn't point out that she'd been pretending to research all day and had also exhausted herself.

"Do you want dinner?"

Lucky sprang to his feet and whined at the door.

"I thought so."

As with *treat, dinner* was one of the handful of words he knew. And even though he'd never been in this house, his doggie instincts told him that food would be found inside.

In truth, most of what little food she'd brought up was in the car. Since she hadn't grocery shopped yet, she hoped she would find canned soup or something in the pantry that she could open for herself. She wondered what it said about her that she thought more about provisions for her dog than herself.

To her surprise, a new scent filled the house when she walked in. Tomato sauce?

Had the werewolf—Amar, she reminded herself—*cooked* something?

Something about imagining the shaggy-haired man standing in the kitchen and stirring sauce over the stove was bizarre. Even when he was in human form, he seemed like someone who should be out in the wilds, springing over logs and crouching in the ferns as he hunted some animal.

Morgen headed warily to the kitchen, not wanting to run into Amar inside. Even if he'd had a rental agreement with Grandma for the barn, it didn't seem right that he should feel free to wander through her house.

But it was dark in the kitchen before she turned on the lights, and she didn't hear him clomping around in the house anywhere. Lucky ran around the kitchen table, claws clacking on the beige-and-brown vinyl floor, and didn't give any indication that he found anything amiss—like a predator crouching behind the couch in the living room.

A window was open, and a distant howl floated in from the woods.

"Guess he's out getting his own dinner," Morgen said.

Radishes and carrots freshly pulled from the garden, with dirt still sticking to the roots, lay in a clump on the red-and-white checkered cloth covering the kitchen table. On the stove, she found pasta floating in a ridiculously large stock pot next to a saucepan with spaghetti sauce simmering over low heat. The jar it had come out of rested on the counter and was labeled *pepper and sausage* medley, but a bowl next to it held a bunch of tomato-sauce covered lumps. The... sausages? There was a dirty strainer in the sink.

"I think I have to give him points for trying, right?" Morgen assumed he'd found the sauce and noodles in the pantry and had made the best of what was there.

Lucky's tail thwacked against the kitchen table as he pointed his nose toward the bowl of sausage bits.

"Last night, he was threatening to kill me. This is substantial progress."

Thwack, thwack.

"Of course, he's expecting me to solve a murder case for him. What happens if I can't? Or if he was wrong, and Grandma's death was truly an accident?"

Morgen snorted. Even that story was different from what the authorities had originally reported to her family. They'd said Grandma had died of natural causes. Such as the natural cause that occurred when one's motorcycle tumbled through a guard railing and crashed into a ravine a hundred feet below.

When she'd found out about the accident, she'd assumed someone had made a mistake on the report. But now, she wondered...

Lucky whined.

"Sorry, you're right. We should eat it while it's warm."

Another howl floated through the window.

"And not think about what he's eating." Morgen wondered if Amar was the only wolf around or if there was a pack out there. Wolves traveled in packs, didn't they? Though there was the expression *lone wolf*. "Maybe I need to Google wolves and learn more about them." She poured kibble into Lucky's bowl. "Or I could call my sister and ask her opinion on all of this. Such as whether I should trust this guy or take the deputy's suggestion and go back to the hotel for the night." She dumped the sausages onto the top of the kibble. "Maybe Sian has encountered werewolves before. She spends all that time in tents in the wilds. Do you think Borneo has werewolves?"

Lucky leaned against her leg and gazed avidly at the bowl.

"You're a lot of help with wrestling with these issues."

Morgen set his bowl down. His tail wagged vigorously at the extra toppings.

After filling a water dish for him, she cleaned the strainer so she could remove the noodles from the water. She had little doubt that they would be mushy after floating so long, but given that she'd thought she would be eating cauliflower puffs out of a bag for dinner, she wouldn't complain.

As she ate, she read through the papers in the envelope and found information on the various tax parcels Zoe had mentioned. She was surprised to find a letter from Grandma. Since she couldn't have anticipated her death, Morgen hadn't expected anything like that, though at her age, maybe she'd assumed it was coming sooner or later. A date in the top corner was from the previous year.

Dear Morgen, it read. *You and your sister are the only of my kin who always shared my love of books—your mother never read much nor cared to learn about her heritage. I trust that when you look around the house, you'll discover yours, and I hope your curiosity will drive you to learn about it.*

Her heritage? The witch stuff?

Morgen rubbed her fingertips again as she read on. *I do not believe your sister feels your sense of connection to this place, so it is unlikely she would ever fall in love with Wolf Wood.*

Wolf Wood? Grandma had called it that? Not only Amar? Maybe werewolves had always been lurking here.

I remember you reading in the tree branches one summer.

That had been because her brothers had figured out how to lock her out of her room, not because sitting in a tree had been comfortable. She did like nature though, and she'd gone on walks with their dog Angus out here as a kid.

I believe that once you learn the secrets of Wolf Wood, you'll agree that it must continue to be protected by our family.

"Uh."

Lucky issued a questioning whine. He'd polished his bowl and was sitting on his haunches, gazing hopefully at the table.

"I'm getting the feeling Grandma didn't want this place sold."

And what *secrets* did the woods have? It didn't sound like she was referring to the unexpectedly witchy root cellar.

Would Amar know? He had to have traveled all through the trees, but he wasn't a witch, so would he know what one found interesting? Maybe some special trees grew in the area. Something with medicinal flowers or leaves that could be used in potions or tinctures or whatever witches made and shared with friends—or enemies?

"I think I'm in over my head, buddy," Morgen said before reading the last few lines.

Lucky put his paws on the table and nudged her bowl with his nose. She admonished him and pushed him back down, though he must have worked up a larger appetite than usual running all over the property. She was out of sausages, so she gave him a carrot to nosh on.

Some dogs liked vegetables, or so she'd heard. Thus far, she hadn't seen much evidence of it. Still, Lucky chewed heartily.

There are many who desire Wolf Wood for various reasons, the letter went on. *Please protect it and maintain it as it is. Amar will help you if you let him. He can come across as gruff and occasionally ferocious, but he also cares for the land. He came from the south, but he's come to love it as a native. Just don't irk him, or I can't speak to what might happen. His kind have tempers.*

Best wishes,

Gwen.

Irk him, such as by failing to figure out who'd arranged for Grandma's motorcycle to crash?

No, she *would* find that out. And when she did... she could point the irked Amar at the guilty party.

Snuffling came from the floor. Lucky had chewed the carrot into dozens of tiny orange bits and was nosing them.

"I should have known you would make a mess of that. I remember what you did to the blueberries you insisted you wanted last summer." She probably shouldn't feel smug that the stain beside the coffee table had never fully come out and that her ex-husband was the one who had to live with it now.

The phone rang. She almost hoped for her sister, that Sian would have somehow sensed that Morgen wanted to talk and called, but it was a local number.

She let it ring several times as she stared at it, her natural proclivity to let unfamiliar calls go to voice mail before deciding if she wanted to return them, but she had a hunch who it might be, and an idea percolated into her mind.

"Hello?" she answered.

"Hello, ma'am," Magnus Christian drawled. "I just wanted to see how you're settling in."

"Fine, thanks." Morgen knew exactly what he wanted and that it had nothing to do with her settling anything. But it occurred to her that if she listed the house with him, that would be one way to find out exactly who wanted it. Maybe someone had wanted it so badly that they'd been willing to kill for it. Whoever put in an offer right away might be the responsible party.

"Have you had any more time to think about listing the property?" he asked. "I'd be happy to buy you dinner tomorrow to discuss it."

"Oh? How do you feel about cauliflower puffs?"

"Pardon?"

"Never mind. You don't have to buy me anything, but I guess

I'd be open to hearing about your plans and what we might be able to get for the place." And *who* would be willing to pay it...

"Fabulous, fabulous. Let's meet for dinner at six tomorrow—I insist on treating you—at the Timber Wolf. The locals love that place. You'll get a great hearty meal, and I'll give you all the details."

"Okay, thanks."

"Looking forward to chatting with you, darling. Good night."

After Morgen hung up, she Googled the restaurant, having a feeling from the name that the vegetarian offerings would be scant. She was right.

"Ten kinds of steak, venison, elk, bison, and bear. Appetizer of prairie oysters. I wonder if the *locals* are all werewolves."

Resolving to eat before she went and to bring back something in a doggie bag for Lucky, she debated if she should tell her plan to Amar. She had better warn him before he saw the listing in the paper. They seemed to have a truce, at least for the moment, but that might change if she started letting real-estate agents wine and dine her.

"I'll figure out a way to let Amar know without irking him." She thought of Grandma's warning in the letter. "That should be possible, right? Just because Jun said I'm as warm and charismatic as a frozen pond in a remote wilderness doesn't mean I can't charm a werewolf, right?"

Lucky, disappointed with the carrot, returned to his empty bowl to lick it for a fourth time.

8

MORGEN WOKE TO A LOUD BUZZING NOISE AND LURCHED UPRIGHT IN bed. She forgot where she was and clunked her head against the frame of the bunk above her.

Swearing, she rubbed the sore spot. It hadn't seemed right to sleep in her grandmother's room, so she'd claimed the room she and her sister had stayed in as kids. As the older sister, Sian had taken the double bed on the bottom while Morgen had been stuck in the twin above. With no competition this time, Morgen had opted for the larger bunk, believing it would be spacious enough for an adult, but that had been before Lucky burrowed under the covers and expanded throughout the night. Now, his legs were straight, paws sticking out from under the sheets, as he took up most of the bed. Morgen's own legs had been mashed against the wall.

"Remember when I was married, and we had a no-dogs-in-the-bed rule?" She couldn't remember when she'd decided to relax that rule, but Lucky was softer and cuddlier than Jun had been, so it wasn't that awful. *Most* of the time.

He was snoring too loudly to hear her. Whatever that obnoxious buzz was hadn't disturbed *his* sleep.

Morgen maneuvered around him, clambered out of bed, and padded to the window to peer toward the barn. Fog blanketed the hilltop, making it hard to tell how late—or early—it was. Amar stood in front of the barn, facing a log perched atop a stump and wielding a chainsaw like a sculptor using a chisel and hammer. The beginnings of what might have been a bear were forming under the noisy blade.

Morgen closed the window and glanced at her phone. It was only a few minutes after six. "If Grandma didn't have a no-chain-saws-before-nine rule, she should have."

While Lucky snored on, Morgen went downstairs and made coffee, relieved she'd found an unopened can of ground beans in the pantry—alongside another five jars of the *pepper and sausage medley*.

With the warm beverage in hand, she returned to the window and debated how to tell Amar about her plan to have dinner with Christian. Her natural inclination to avoid starting conversations with strangers—and near-strangers—made her muse that maybe she didn't *have* to tell him.

But it would be better to let him know her plan rather than risking him jumping to assumptions. She just worried he would think it was idiotic. He thought the answer was with that bone clip and seemed to believe her blood would make it easy for her to discover it.

Morgen checked the time in Borneo and called her sister. It was after nine at night there, but Sian ought to still be up. Assuming she answered. Sian was as apt to let calls drop to voice mail as Morgen, maybe even more so.

"Is everything all right?" Sian answered.

"Yes. Hi."

"Hi."

A long pause followed.

"Normal social conventions suggest I ask you about your work and how things are going in Borneo," Morgen said, "and I would be happy to hear about such things, but you usually show such disdain for small talk that I'm guessing I should just ask my question."

"Yes. If you wish an update on my work, you can read my upcoming paper in *Nature* on homosexual behavior between orangutans in the context of both affiliative and aggressive interactions."

"I'll do so. The copulating habits of primates never fail to be of interest."

"This is true. What is your question?"

"I'm up in Bellrock dealing with Grandma's estate, and there's this... Well, I wouldn't believe it if I hadn't seen him transform in front of my eyes—on the hood of my car, precisely—but there's a werewolf here."

An even longer pause followed.

"I don't expect you to believe me," Morgen said, "but since you're an expert on animals, I thought you might give me some insight. I don't want to, uh, *irk* him. Grandma's letter specifically suggested avoiding that. But he's kind of a renter or a squatter here or something. They had an agreement, I guess. And I'm going to have to work with him."

"I'm a primatologist who specializes in great apes."

"Yes, I know. I was at your graduation and suffered through countless watchings of *People of the Forest* with you when we were kids. But you studied other types of animals in school, right? I distinctly remember you doing a paper on wolves and talking Mom and Dad into taking us to Wolf Haven in Tenino one weekend."

"That was when I was in fourth grade."

"You practically have an eidetic memory. I'm sure you remember a lot." Morgen was starting to regret calling.

"I remember a great deal, such as errors in pack behavior that were propagated at the time and falsely linger into this century. They were based on studying wolves in captivity rather than wild wolves. To this day, I cringe every time I hear the term *alpha male* or *alpha female*. Most wolf packs are simply the pair-bonded parents and their four or five offspring that have not yet reached maturity and headed out on their own. In the wild, dominance fights between other wolves are rare. Captivity forces unrelated wolves into close quarters, so it's a strange and unnatural relationship."

"That's interesting," Morgen said, though it wasn't what she wanted to know about. Thus far, she wasn't dealing with a pack.

She was about to ask about lone wolves, assuming that was what Amar was, but Sian went on. "There are some exceptions where larger packs form and hunt together, such as with the wolves in Yellowstone National Park, which were reintroduced to the area approximately twenty-five years ago. There, the higher prey densities created different conditions, and they ended up with a lot of packs in very small territories. The packs get larger as more wolves are forced to work together. It is less common then for pups to forge off on their own at a young age, and they may stay with their parents and other wolves for up to four years."

"I knew you knew a few things about wolves. Though I note you're not commenting on *werewolves*."

"I'm pretending you're an intelligent, educated human being and wouldn't bring up something so farcical unless you were teasing me because you know I struggle with sarcasm and practical jokes. If you truly believe in werewolves, I am concerned. It's possible that the unexpected termination from your satisfying and mentally stimulating employment has resulted in the development of a psychological condition that you should be assessed for."

"You think I should blame any issues I've developed on losing my job rather than my divorce?"

"Certainly. Your work has been a crucial part of your identity for nearly twenty years. Your husband was... obnoxious."

"You find all men obnoxious."

"Yes. Most women as well. Non-human primates are more intriguing to me."

"It's good that you do work that calls to you. What about lone wolves? I'm dealing with one at the property. Are they outcasts or dangerous?"

"Is it a wolf or a *werewolf*?" Sian asked.

"He can be whatever you need him to be in order to answer my question. Though right now, he's making chainsaw art on a stump in front of the barn."

Maybe she shouldn't have said that. The third pause was the longest yet.

"Lone wolves are typically those who have yet to find an unclaimed territory and a mate, or they have lost their mate. Their goal is presumed to be to find a new mate, settle down, produce pups, and start their own pack. Occasionally, lone wolves will linger on the outskirts of an existing pack until such a time as they can join to replace an existing breeder. There are some false beliefs that packs are required for wolves to kill large animals and survive, but a study of wolves in Minnesota showed that lone wolves killed more prey per wolf than a pack of five. Lone wolves and pairs are very capable hunters on their own."

"If one is choosing to live alone, is it because he can't find a mate? Are all wolves driven to mate?"

"It is a biological imperative for most, though exceptions do arise." Sian's tone had turned dry.

Was she thinking of herself?

Morgen was fairly certain her sister hadn't ever gone on a date, but since she had never enjoyed courtship herself, and had married Jun less out of passion-fueled love and more because they'd seemed like a logical match with common interests, she couldn't fault anyone for that.

"My dessert is waiting for me," Sian said. "Do you have further questions?"

"Just one." The only one Morgen had truly wanted to know. "Do you have any suggestions on how not to irk a lone wolf?"

"Lone wolves are typically circumspect and wish to avoid straying into another pack's territory, lest there be repercussions. I'd worry more about irking any packs that might be in the area, though as a human, you shouldn't have to worry about any of this. Avoid scent-marking the trees around Grandma's house, and you'll be fine."

"Thanks so much for the tip. Can I send you anything? Fudge from Bellrock?"

"Would it be *vegan* fudge?" Sian was about as disdainful of Morgen's diet as a werewolf might be.

"Probably not. And I'm vegetarian, not vegan. I will eat butter and milk, though my doctor suggested olive oil or rice bran oil as an alternative."

"Do not send me fudge with rice bran oil in it."

"I don't think that's a thing."

"Good. You know my preferences for gifts. Practical with touches of whimsy."

"Yes. I remember the bamboo underwear request."

"Bamboo underwear is practical. It's soft, dries quickly, resists odors, and is hypoallergenic."

"I thought you just liked the last set because it was purple with pink flowers."

"That satisfied my need for whimsy. Goodnight."

As Morgen hung up, Lucky stirred, oozed out from under the covers, and stretched.

"I'm not sure if I'm any more enlightened about my chainsaw-wielding tenant than I was twenty minutes ago," Morgen said, heading downstairs to let him out. "But if Amar is the *circumspect* wolf in the neighborhood, I really don't want to run into the local pack."

9

It was late morning and Amar was still working outside when Morgen walked toward the barn with a coffee mug and a bag of vegan granola. It was one of her road trip snacks, and not likely something that would excite a werewolf, but she felt she should offer Amar something in case he was hungry after his morning of chainsaw aggression toward stumps.

She'd spent several hours continuing to look for clues and organizing the cellar, but she still hadn't found anything related to bone clips. Amar had ignored her trips in and out of the house, as if he preferred to pretend she didn't exist. Maybe he did.

The fact that he was still wielding the big power tool made her hesitant to approach, but she wanted to explain her plan to Amar before the news in the gossip-loving town found its way to him.

Morgen circled widely around him, not wanting to startle him or take a flying wood chip to the eye, and stood where he could see her. Talking over the roar of the chainsaw would have been difficult, so she waited for him to stop and ask what she wanted. Except that he didn't. Frowning, he kept working, his blue eyes almost scary with intensity as he focused on his art.

It must have been a workout, for sweat dampened his wild hair. A bead ran down his biceps, leaving a trail in the fine wood dust that coated his bare arms. If Morgen were the type to ogle a man's physique, Amar would have been ogle-worthy. Fortunately, she was a mature and rational woman, not one driven by her hormones.

He finally turned off the chainsaw and looked at her, exasperation furrowing his brow. "What?"

"I wanted to thank you for dinner."

He grunted. Was that the wolf equivalent of *you're welcome*?

"Is that all?" he asked. "A client is waiting for this piece. I need to finish it today."

"Yes, but I brought you coffee. And food if you're hungry." She held up the granola bag, wondering if she should have put it in a bowl, but since she didn't have any almond milk—or any other kind of milk—that had seemed unnecessary. When she was in a hurry, she usually ate it dry.

"That's food?" he asked in his gruff voice. He always sounded like he was on the verge of breaking out into growls.

"Espresso-flavored granola. It's high-protein and low-sugar. And has caffeine in it, though since you were up making chainsaw art at dawn, I guess you don't need caffeine in the morning."

He looked at the bag the way a bear might eye a trap in the woods with leaves scattered atop the iron teeth. Make that a *wolf* in the woods. "What *kind* of protein?"

"Uhm." She read the label on the back. "Watermelon-seed protein."

"What is *that*?"

Morgen dug out her phone and Googled it. "A highly digestible plant-based protein rich in B-vitamins and magnesium. How is your magnesium, Amar?"

His expression turned from suspicious to disgusted. He strode up to her, and she pulled the bag to her chest, worried he was going to knock it aside. The last thing she needed was Lucky running over to Hoover up caffeinated granola. He was looking for gophers in the holes proliferating the lawn near the garden, but he had a knack for hearing the drop of food from miles away.

Amar halted in front of her, took the cup of coffee, and guzzled it down in a long drink that gave her a prolonged view of his bobbing Adam's apple—and his chest when a few droplets dripped down to slither between his pecs. Like his arms, they were covered in a fine wood dust. That vest didn't offer a lot of protection from dirt, dust, or coffee droplets.

Amar handed the empty cup back to her and returned to his stump.

"Happy to be of service," she said.

That earned her another grunt. She decided it was not only his equivalent of *you're welcome* but also *thank you.* Maybe even *good morning, have a nice day at work,* and *your hair looks good today.*

As he hefted the chainsaw, she lifted a hand. "Wait, there's something I wanted to tell you."

He looked at her over his shoulder, his scruffy hair hanging in his eyes. "Is it about Gwen's murderer?"

"Related to that, yes. You were here yesterday when the local real-estate agent, Magnus Christian, was talking to me right? Do you know him?"

Fury flared in his eyes, making Morgen take an involuntary step back.

"I know him," Amar growled. "He tried *many* times to talk Gwen into selling her property. He has talked *many* older people in the area into selling their homes that are on acreage, because developers from up north are moving into this area and wish to turn it into housing communities and *golf courses.*"

"I imagine you prefer trees to golf courses."

"Unnatural grasses that are not native to the area and are full of chemicals that make your fur itch when you roll on your back are despicable."

"Your fur?" Since he'd transformed from wolf to human on the hood of Morgen's car, she supposed he wasn't trying to hide his secret. Maybe it wasn't a secret at all. Maybe all the townsfolk knew about the lone werewolf who haunted the area.

"My fur and my skin. Christian is an enemy to the pack."

"Oh, there is a pack? I'd wondered. You seem... solo."

"I am solo." His eyes narrowed. "But there is a pack. There are *two* packs that compete for this territory. It is one of the few areas along the western coast that has not been completely destroyed by the encroachment of civilization. *So far.*" His eyes remained narrowed as he watched Morgen like the predator he was, making her uneasy about the survival of more than her granola. "Why do you ask about this man?"

"You heard that he wants me to list the property through him, right?"

"You said that you would not." His eyes narrowed further.

Why did she get the feeling that he would spring over and throttle her if she said the wrong thing?

Though she wanted to scurry farther back, she made herself hold her ground and look him in the eye.

"I did, but I'm thinking of letting him list it—that wouldn't obligate me to sell it—so I can find out who wants to buy it. I thought that whoever made an offer might be the person who... arranged for Grandma's motorcycle to have an accident."

"Who arranged for her to *die*," he said.

"Yes."

"You did not find answers about the magical clip?"

"Not yet. I'm trying to find information related to it, but until yesterday, I had no idea about any of that." Morgen waved toward the root cellar. "Or that my grandmother had a quirky hobby."

"She was a witch," he stated, as if that was a completely normal thing. To a werewolf, maybe it was.

"Right. She neglected to mention it to the family."

"Perhaps because her family never came to visit." His still-narrowed eyes radiated icy disapproval, making Morgen wince and once again wonder if she'd misread Grandma, if she'd only said she preferred her privacy but had secretly felt alone these past years after her daughters died.

Morgen still missed her mother terribly, the only person who'd ever accepted her and Sian as they were and hadn't tried to force them to be more extroverted or social or *normal*, like their brothers. The loss had been horrible for Morgen, but she imagined it had been as bad if not worse for Grandma, who'd lost not one daughter but two. Aunt Alys and Mom had both died of cancer, as if they'd been marked by the same faulty genes.

Faulty genes that Morgen often feared lurked in her own blood. That had more than a little to do with her decision to adopt a healthier diet.

"She always told us she preferred her privacy," Morgen said quietly. "And Sian and I—that's my sister—are both like that, so we assumed she was telling the truth."

"She was a private woman. That doesn't mean she always wished to be alone."

"Maybe she should have told us that then. We're not mind readers." Morgen clenched her teeth. Even though she was too wary to do anything but step lightly around Amar, she didn't appreciate the lecture.

He only glared stonily back at her.

"Forget it," Morgen said. "I just wanted to let you know about my plan and that I'm not really going to sell the property." Unless the taxes made it impossible for her to keep it... But she would worry about that later. "But like I said, I want to see if I can lure out the person or persons who want it. Who maybe want it badly enough that they killed to remove the primary obstacle to getting it. I'm telling you so you won't freak out if you see it listed. Maybe I won't have to go that far. I'm having dinner with Christian at a place called the Timber Wolf, and if I can learn who the prospective buyer is, we might not have to—"

"The Timber Wolf?"

"Yes. It looked like your kind of place. There's a dearth of watermelon-seed protein on the menu."

"It is not *my* kind of place. The Loups Laflamme claim that pub."

"Flame wolves?" Morgen asked.

"Yes. They are the rival pack to the Lobos Sanguientos."

"Uh, blood wolves?"

"Yes." For the first time, his eyes lost their irritated squint. "*¿Hablas español?*"

She shook her head. High-school Spanish had been a long time ago. "*Un poco*, sorry."

"That's more than most here."

"We're a ways from the Mexican border. French wolves seem like more of a fit."

"They are *not* a fit." There went his eyes narrowing again. "The Lobos were here first, when this territory was not claimed by any."

"That's your pack?"

He hesitated. "I have no pack."

"Because you're waiting for the, uh, breeder to die so you can take his place?" Morgen didn't know if the werewolves actually *used* the terminology her sister had shared, but Amar seemed to understand what she meant.

His nostrils flared, and his back stiffened. "My *brother* leads the Lobos. I do *not* wish him to die."

Maybe she shouldn't have trotted out her newly gained wolf knowledge and assumed it applied to him. "Ah. Sorry. I was doing some research on wolves earlier and trying to figure you out."

"Why do you care?"

Good question. Mostly, she didn't want to annoy him.

"Grandma said you helped her." Morgen shrugged. "Just because I wasn't here doesn't mean I don't—didn't—care about her."

"This place is special. It needed a protector. *She* needed a protector."

And how the heck had he come to be in that role? Morgen flashed back to him leaping on her car with his fangs on display. He was about as protective as stinging nettle.

"She should not have left the property so much," Amar grumbled, turning his back on her. He dusted wood chips off his project. "She was independent and refused to be told what to do. Or to take suggestions regarding her safety. She believed, as a witch, that she could take care of herself."

For the first time, his voice was soft and touched with an emotion other than gruff surliness.

Morgen bit her lip, not sure how to react to the change. She wasn't much better than her sister at knowing what to do to comfort people, and it wasn't as if he was a typical or predictable *people.*

A soft, "Yeah," of agreement was all she could manage.

Amar looked to the foggy gray sky, as if wrestling with some decision, then turned back to her. "I will take you to the Timber Wolf and make sure the Loups do not bother you."

"That's not necessary. I can't think of any reason why French werewolves would care about me."

"It *is* necessary. Because now, you control this." He extended his arms toward the trees in both directions.

"Why does that matter to werewolves? This can't be the only forest land around here." Though she admitted it was likely difficult to find hundreds of acres of unbroken wilderness nestled between the towns along the coast. The Cascade Mountains were full of national forest and had to be appealing for wolves, but perhaps other packs lived out there and claimed that territory. Or perhaps werewolves, unlike regular wolves, had to live near civilization so they could have jobs and homes. After all, they were human half of the time. Or most of the time? She didn't even know. A day ago, she hadn't believed they existed.

"It is special land. Magical." Amar lowered his arms. "Come. I will show you."

"Uh." She glanced at the clock on her phone, but the conversation hadn't been that extensive, and she still had a long time until her date with Christian. "All right. Lucky." She called the dog away from his gopher hunt. "Do you want to go for a walk?"

Walk was one of the words Lucky knew, and he bounded up, ears flapping and tail wagging, though he slowed down when he drew close to Amar. He dropped to his belly and whined uncertainly.

"Amar is going with us. He's recently guzzled coffee, and he's probably feeling perky."

One of Amar's eyebrows twitched, but he didn't reply, simply heading off toward a trail behind the barn.

Morgen followed, wondering what he would show her and what she'd gotten herself into by agreeing to dinner at a restaurant claimed by one of the local packs. Hopefully, any werewolves that lurked at that restaurant didn't hang out there before sunset.

10

As Morgen trailed Amar deeper into the woods behind the barn, the fog thick among the trees and a creek burbling off to their left, she worried that coming out here alone with him hadn't been wise. He had such a short temper, and that warning in Grandma's letter not to irk him kept coming to mind.

Lucky didn't seem concerned. He trotted through ferns alongside the well-worn trail, sniffing at whatever critters scurried about under the dew-damp fronds.

The woods themselves weren't eerie, though the evergreens, with curtains of moss hanging from their branches, might have felt more welcoming in sunlight. It was her guide who set her on edge, and she didn't get too close as they walked, letting him lead and simply watching his broad shoulders and the thatch of black hair that hung partway down his back. A few wood chips were tangled among the strands—even under the best of circumstances, he didn't look like someone who used a hairbrush—but there was no way she would presume to pluck them out.

"Do you think Christian is working for or associated with the

Loups?" she asked, finding the silence uncomfortable, even if it probably didn't bother Amar.

"Werewolves do not *work* with humans. Christian knows what they are and nuzzles their jowls."

"Is that a wolf expression? Like kissing up? Or kissing ass?"

He gave her a long look over his shoulder, as if the expressions were beneath him. Or maybe he wasn't familiar with them? His English was as precise as anyone's, but who knew how long he had lived here?

"It is wise to treat the packs with respect," he said.

"Does that mean I should be nuzzling something of yours?"

His brows rose in surprise. "Witches and wolves do not *nuzzle*."

"Right. You'd want to avoid interspecies cooties, I imagine."

He shook his head slowly, as if she were a very remedial student toddling after him on a field trip, and looked forward again.

Well, at least she didn't have to worry about him hitting on her. Not that she truly imagined there was much chance of that. She knew she wasn't hideous, but she'd grown older and didn't put much effort into fashion and makeup. Even before she'd gotten married, that had been true. She'd rebelled against the idea of going out of her way to dress to attract a man, feeling that anyone who might become her soulmate ought to be able to see through such superficiality.

But she hadn't found a soulmate, had she? She'd found someone to be comfortable with, or so she'd thought. But she'd been wrong, and now, she had nobody.

Not for the first time, she wondered if it had been a mistake not to have children. Since she and Jun had been dedicated to their careers, and since she didn't fit many definitions of *maternal*, they'd always put it off, saying *maybe later*, though she wasn't sure either of them had truly dreamed about it. But sometimes she wondered if she'd made a mistake, if deep down, she might have enjoyed taking care of more than a dog.

But if they'd had kids, the divorce would have been more complicated. Maybe it was for the best that they hadn't.

The trickle of water grew louder as the trail veered down a slope. The creek came into view, as well as a deep pool with mossy green rocks all around it. Old-growth trees grew close, many of their gnarled roots visible above ground. A weathered cement bench rested in the shadows, the legs almost as coated in moss as the rocks. Here and there, patches of mushrooms sprouted from soil dusted with fir and pine needles. The moss and mushrooms were so vibrant they almost seemed to glow.

There was a serenity to the place that made Morgen forget about her ex-husband and lose her concerns about Amar. After all, he'd cooked her dinner. He couldn't be that bad of a guy.

"Gwen called this the Mystic Pool." Amar stepped aside so she could walk closer. "It's fed by a spring as well as the creek. She proclaimed it was magical and drank regularly from it."

"Without a filter?" Morgen wrinkled her nose but, when Amar frowned at her, refrained from pointing out that it could be rich with arsenic and other toxic chemicals. Grandma had lived to ninety—and who knew how long she might have gone on if not for that accident—so there probably wasn't anything terrible in it. If it truly was magical... too bad Mom and Aunt Alys hadn't visited more often for sips.

Amar knelt by the edge, scooped water into his cupped palm, and drank from his hand.

"Well, you have that beard," Morgen said. "That probably filters things."

"Are you always so irreverent?"

"Yes. Are you always so surly?"

"Yes."

"I bet there's nobody nuzzling at his jowls," she muttered to Lucky, though he was busy snuffling under a log.

Amar sniffed at the air and gazed off into the fog.

"Do other wolves come into these woods? Wolf Wood, you and Grandma both called it." Morgen knelt to wash her hands in the water. She wasn't ready to commit to drinking from the pool, but she rubbed some over her face. Even though it was midsummer, the morning was cool, and the water was icy.

"Many animals come here. There are signs that inform human hunters that it is private land and not to trespass. I help enforce the rules."

"But it's okay for you to hunt here? And leave deer carcasses on the driveway?" Morgen grimaced, reminded that the carcass might still be there. The deputy had said something about having it removed, but if he hadn't, or if the service that handled that took days to come, she might have to do something about it.

"I had her permission. And nature is not a vacuum. Scavengers of all sorts feed on carcasses and they are soon gone, only a few bones and blood remaining to nourish the earth."

"Nothing like blood nourishment." She hoped Bellrock didn't have any vampires lurking around. She could only deal with one fairytale coming to life at a time.

"A tradition long favored by gardeners in the area is to bury fish heads in the soil. As they decompose, the nutrients feed the crops."

Morgen made a face as she remembered the carrots and radishes she'd eaten the night before.

"I'm not always able to stop all trespassers," Amar admitted. "There is a woman who comes—I've caught her scent—but for some reason, she is difficult to track. I believe she's a witch."

"There are other witches in the area?" Morgen didn't know why she was surprised. If there were packs of werewolves, why not packs of witches?

"There is a coven," he said in a clipped tone, as if he didn't want to speak further about them.

"And wolves don't like witches?"

"No." His tone was even more clipped.

Though she ached for information, she let it go.

As she knelt back from the water, Morgen noticed a patch of mushrooms with blue caps hunkering in the shade of the bench. They didn't look like any she was familiar with from the stores, and they truly did seem to glow, especially there in the shade. They were so striking that she couldn't resist reaching out to touch one. She would have to poke around in Grandma's library to see if there were any books for identifying mushrooms.

A buzz of electricity zapped her finger, and she jerked back. "What the—"

"Many of the plants—and fungi—that grow around the spring are magical," Amar said, as if there was nothing strange about being electrocuted by mushrooms.

"Does that mean I better not touch any trees or ferns as I'm getting up?" Morgen planted her hand carefully in dirt devoid of vegetation as she pushed herself to her feet.

"Likely. Or you could start wearing a witch amulet."

"Which is what exactly?" Morgen thought of the star-shaped medallion she'd used to open the root-cellar doors.

"I am not certain I could identify one, as werewolves do not sense magic the way those with witch blood do, but I've been told they nullify the effect of positive magical charges meeting negative."

"Magic is like a battery?"

"Those with magical blood emanate a different kind of energy field than magical things found in nature and items crafted by witches. Perhaps if you study further about that clip, you will understand more."

"Yeah, yeah." Morgen had time enough before dinner to do

more research, but after spending hours down there, she was starting to question if the answers were in the root cellar. "Are the other witches from this coven in town?"

Maybe the real-estate agent wasn't the only one who might have useful information.

"Some are. Gwen interacted with a couple of witches on occasion, but she tended to be solitary by nature. A lone wolf." Amar lifted his chin, as if he approved.

Maybe they'd connected over that.

"If you see any when we go to town, will you point them out to me?" Morgen thought again of the woman who'd peered through the hotel window at her.

Was it possible *that* had been a witch? And she'd somehow sensed that Morgen was related to Gwen? That they'd shared blood?

If so, the menacing aura that person had given off didn't bode well for future relations. Morgen didn't know why witches would care one way or another about her, but she was beginning to get the feeling that everyone in town resented that Grandma had owned this land—and hadn't been willing to sell it.

11

EARLIER THAN MORGEN EXPECTED, AMAR PULLED UP TO THE HOUSE in a pale blue Ford pickup truck that had to be from the sixties. She'd seen it in the back of the barn the day before but had assumed it was something that Grandma had inherited along with the property, not something anyone still drove.

A modern interpretation of a totem pole and two live-edge garden benches filled the bed. They were wrapped in blankets and tied down, but so much of the pole stuck out from the back that it looked like it might tip the truck onto its rear wheels.

Morgen grabbed her cauliflower puffs out of the front seat of her car before joining Amar. She highly doubted this restaurant would have anything vegetarian-friendly. Maybe she could talk Amar into stopping at the grocery store afterward. She would offer to buy him a few slabs of meat.

A whine of protest came from one of the front windows of the house. She'd left Lucky inside with a rawhide snack and water, but he'd probably already scarfed down the treat.

Normally, if the weather wasn't warm, she would take him along on errands, but the thought of this Timber Wolf being rife with werewolves made her hesitant. Besides, if the late-afternoon sun burned through the clouds, it might be too hot for him to wait in the car. Somehow, she doubted the Timber Wolf was the kind of place with outdoor dining that invited well-mannered dogs onto the patio with their owners.

Amar got out of the truck and jogged back into the barn, as if he'd forgotten something. He returned with a toolbox and a blow-torch and tucked them into the bed. Maybe he anticipated the new owner wanting more of the burnt-wood look on the benches.

The door stuck as he returned to the driver's seat. He grunted, muscles flexing, and yanked it open with a noisy creak.

"Are you sure you don't want to take my car?" Morgen asked.

As the truck idled, the engine chugging loudly, it reverberated like an off-kilter paint mixer.

"I need to drop off furniture on the way." Amar looked at her car. "That's flimsy. One of my wooden bench legs would crush it."

"A wolf almost crushed it the other night."

"Yes. The wan metal dented and nearly crumpled under my weight."

"I'm sorry the hood of my car wasn't sufficient to hold your massive bulk. That's clearly a deficiency the manufacturer should address in future models."

He eyed her. "You had better practice ass-kissing before you talk to any of the Loups."

"They're not invited to my dinner."

"They are if you're having it in their restaurant. Don't expect that runt-of-the-litter Christian to protect you from them."

"I won't, though I thought you were coming along to loom protectively and keep me out of trouble."

"As a favor to Gwen, I will attempt to do so, but I am one wolf without a pack. They would be wise to acknowledge my strength, but I've never known the Loups to be wise."

As Morgen climbed into the passenger seat—technically, the passenger side of a bench seat—she thought about texting Christian to see if he would be amenable to changing locations. Unless these Loups were tied in with Grandma's death somehow, she had no reason to seek them out. She would prefer to avoid *both* wolf packs.

"Do you ever get in fights with the Loups?" she asked.

"Once." Amar lifted the side of his vest to show old scars—claw marks—in his side.

"Did the other guy get hurt just as badly?"

"The other *guys* did." He gave her an aloof sidelong look, as if she'd offended him by not assuming he was the supreme warrior in the land who'd handed out multiple ass-kickings.

"I should have known." Morgen patted around for a seat belt but didn't see one. It wasn't missing. It just wasn't there. Maybe they hadn't existed in the sixties. "Do you ever get in fights with the sheriff over not having seat belts?"

"A deputy pulled me over once. I showed my fangs and growled at him, and he wet himself."

"You think you're pretty badass, don't you?" Morgen gripped the handle bolted to the door as the truck rumbled off down the driveway, the furniture clunking and shifting in the bed behind them.

With her other hand, she gripped the star-shaped medallion she'd donned earlier and hoped it was lucky. At first, she'd scoffed at the idea of a witch amulet that could protect her from being zapped by magical items, but as an experiment, while she'd worn it, she'd touched the bone clip and the indention in the cellar door. Neither had shocked her. She'd then removed the amulet, touched the clip again, and it had left a painful red mark on her finger. That was enough to convince her to wear it, at least as long as she was in Bellrock. When she returned to Seattle, she trusted she wouldn't have to worry about such things again. Witches hadn't cavorted through her previous life any more frequently than werewolves.

"I am a capable warrior," Amar said. "You should be honored that I will accompany you today."

"Oh, I am. I'm giddy."

He gave her another sidelong look as he navigated the potholes. This one was harder to read.

"Many females in town are attracted to me," he stated.

"I'm sure. The sleeveless vest is like a display case for your arms."

"When you asked me for dinner yesterday, I assumed you wanted to have sex with me."

"No, I was just hungry."

"Because of the insufficiently filling vegetable puffs."

"Yup." Morgen rattled the bag. "I'm also recently divorced. I'm not looking for a hookup with a werewolf or otherwise."

"Good."

She decided not to be offended that he sounded relieved, though it was a little insulting.

The deer carcass was gone, and she breathed a sigh of relief as they passed the spot. Amar didn't comment on it.

"Did you leave the head in the box?" she asked, fairly certain he had, but if he hadn't, and someone else was trying to send her a message, she had better figure out who.

"Yes."

"To scare me?"

"Yes." They reached the paved two-lane road, and he turned onto it and headed toward town.

"Why? You knew by then that I wasn't trespassing."

"If you were scared away, you might leave forever and never do anything with this land. If you came here to sell it..." His voice lowered into familiar throaty-growl territory as he said, "You know I do not wish this."

"Yeah, you haven't been shy about expressing your feelings on the matter."

They reached a stop sign, turned, and the main street of Bellrock came into view, the Wild Trout and a gas station on the left and shops on the right. She eyed the alley where the cloaked woman had spied on her, but nobody was loitering there this evening.

They passed the Wild Trout's sole competition, the cedar-shingled Roaming Elk Inn, with a few tourist amenities across from it, including miniature golf and a Go-Kart track, both looking like they'd been installed around the same time Amar's truck had come off the factory line. The Go-Karts probably didn't have seat belts either.

Before reaching the handful of restaurants that presumably included the Timber Wolf, Amar turned the truck onto a side street that led up a hill with a view of the Strait. It curved past houses and driveways half-hidden by trees. There were more residences up there than Morgen would have guessed.

After another turn, Amar pulled up in front of a house with a big grassy yard and numerous trucks parked out front. Sawing and hammering noises emanated from the open front door, and a landscaper in denim overalls with no shirt underneath was putting in a brick-paver driveway. The various construction workers were all brawny bronze-skinned men with dark hair, many shirtless or in tight T-shirts that showed off more than they hid. Other than the unappealing yellow pit stains on some of those shirts, the fit group looked like they could star in a Chippendales calendar.

Amar sighed and curled his top lip, a hint of a sharp canine tooth showing.

"Problem?" Morgen asked.

"No. Stay in the truck." He climbed out and started unwrapping the blankets from his furnishings.

At first, none of the workers seemed to notice him, but one who was carrying lumber into the house paused, nostrils lifting in the air to sniff like a hound.

With a start, Morgen realized these might also be werewolves. In fact, they looked a lot like Amar. Was this the pack he'd spoken of? The Lobos?

The one doing the sniffing spun, spotted the truck, and nudged the one who'd been laying pavers. They muttered to each other, set down their materials, and sauntered down to the truck.

As they drew closer, they appeared even larger and brawnier, with jagged veins running down their thick forearms. Staying in the truck seemed like good advice.

The two men glanced curiously at her but walked past to address Amar in Spanish. Hostile and surly Spanish.

Morgen listened through the window, but with her meager experience with the language, all she caught was that Maria wasn't there, and Pedro would beat Amar if he found him sniffing around. Amar said something about his furniture, maybe that he was there to deliver it and nothing else.

One of the men propped an elbow on the side mirror near Morgen. He was in his early twenties, much younger than Amar, and might have been considered handsome, but all she could focus on was that he wore a tank top that left his matted armpit hair on display for her.

She reached up and tried to lock the door, but it didn't work. Hardly surprising in an ancient truck with no seat belts.

The man noticed her through the window, cocked his head, and sniffed. He looked toward her chest, though she wasn't wearing anything revealing or designed to accent curves. Still, his gaze lingered. Was it possible he somehow sensed the amulet? She was wearing it under her thin hoodie, so nothing but the chain should have been visible.

Amar said something gruff, walking past with a bench over his shoulder. As chunky as the log it had been hewn from, it looked like it weighed hundreds of pounds.

"*Déjala*," he growled over his shoulder.

The man eyeing Morgen chuckled and lifted his hands innocently. "*Sí, sí, primo.*"

The other man followed Amar up the walkway, not offering to help carry the bench. If these people were his relatives—his former pack?—Morgen felt sorry for him and wondered what had happened to drive a wedge between them.

Amar glanced around as he carried the bench, a wistful expression on his face as he looked at someone on the roof with a hammer. Because he missed the work? Had he once been a part of their construction crew?

The truck door opened, and Morgen swore. She should have remained focused on the man lurking outside her window instead of trying to decipher the moody Amar's looks.

"Witch lady," Tank-top Man said. "You sleeping with my cousin?"

"No. He's giving me a ride to town."

He looked her up and down, checking out her chest again. "You're a new witch. Haven't heard nothing about you."

"I like my privacy and for the door to remain shut. Not good to catch a chill, you know." Morgen tried to tug the door closed, but he'd leaned his arm against it, and it didn't budge.

She hoped Amar returned shortly. If these were the Lobos, they seemed just as much a danger to her as the Loups he'd said he would protect her from.

"You one of those witches who keeps a pet wolf?" His lips rippled back, revealing pointed canines far more prominent than typical for a human.

"Nope. I've got a dog. He's very un-wolf like."

"You control him with your magic? Make him a *slave*?"

"No, I give him treats. That does the trick. Why don't you go back to work? I believe there's a homeowner in need of a burly man with unkempt armpit hair."

The sneer turned into a smug smirk. "Yeah, she was. I took care of her. Me and Juan Martín did last night."

"How lovely that your construction company provides extra services. That's how you get those five-star reviews."

"It is, but we don't serve witches. Even Amar isn't desperate enough to let some witch control him. If we find out you're using a wand on him, we'll come find you."

"I'm wand-free currently." Morgen wanted to scoot across the bench seat and get away from him, but she realized he might be a source of information. "Are witches known to do that? Try to control werewolves? That seems dangerous."

"It *is* dangerous. But magic evens the odds, and some witches like danger." His eyelids drooped partway. "Maybe you're one of those witches. You know Amar has a temper, *sí*? Better not let your magic wear off, or he'll tear your throat out."

"He's just giving me a ride."

"That's what the crystal witch's sister used to say about Miguel. Turned out, she had him on his knees like a slave, forcing him to *serve* her."

"Bautista," Amar snapped, jogging back down the walkway. "I said to leave her alone."

"Just watching out for you, *primo*."

"You don't care for me. You just hate the idea that someone who used to run with the pack could end up like Miguel."

Bautista's lips rippled again. "That was an *embarrassment*. The Loups don't let us forget it." Bautista pointed at Amar. "You let a witch control *you*, and we'll put a stop to it."

"Help me with this pole. You're on the clock."

"Sure, *primo*. Sure." Bautista flashed his fangs at Morgen, then slammed the door shut.

She rubbed her face, relieved when he left, carrying the totem pole by himself. Amar walked past with the other bench, and he glanced in at her.

Morgen schooled her face into a neutral expression, not wanting him to know she was rattled. It wasn't so much by the leering or the hostility as the fact that people she'd never met believed she was a witch. And hated her for it. If werewolves had bad blood with witches, how ever had Amar ended up friends with Grandma?

Morgen envisioned people in this town—werewolves—trying to kill her because they believed she was a threat. As if she knew anything about witchcraft or how to enslave a wolf or anyone. Maybe wearing the amulet had been a mistake. That might be what had made this guy think she was a witch.

She removed it, intending to stuff it in the glove compartment instead of wearing it to dinner, but pens and a huge stack of folded papers occupied the space. She pulled them out, hoping to shift everything around to make room, but a couple fell off the pile and to the floor.

Worried Amar would catch her snooping, she glanced up to make sure he wasn't returning yet, then bent to retrieve the papers. She meant to simply put them away, but curiosity got the best of her, and she unfolded them.

One was a drawing of a fancy table with drawers and hidden compartments. Some project he planned? Relieved that the sketches weren't something more personal, she glanced at the second one and started to refold it and put it away before she fully saw it. But it was of a person, not a piece of furniture. A beautiful woman with thick hair that tumbled to her shoulders. Her eyes gleamed with warmth, and her full lips parted in a smile, a cute nose crinkled slightly with laughter. A loving hand had drawn the portrait. Or... the hand of a lover?

A bang at the window made Morgen jump and crack her head on the roof of the cab.

"Put those *away*," Amar snarled, fire in his eyes.

"Sorry," she blurted, hurrying to fold them and return them to the glove compartment as he strode to the driver's side, his back even stiffer than it had been that morning.

All the warnings about his temper leaped to mind, and she gripped the door handle, tempted to spring out and take her chances with the pack. Or simply leave all of them. She was close enough to the restaurant that she could walk there herself.

Indecision made her hesitate, and Amar opened his door and climbed in, the bench shuddering as his weight settled onto it. Jaw clenched, he started the truck without looking at her.

"Sorry," she repeated. "That man—your, uhm, cousin?— thought I was a witch casting a spell on you or something. I thought it was my grandmother's amulet that made him think that." Since it was still in her hand, she held it up, as if it might work as proof of her innocent intentions. "I was afraid I would be a target if I wore it into the restaurant, so I was going to put it in the glove box for now. I shouldn't have touched the papers."

"No," he said curtly, turning the truck back toward Main Street.

She wanted to ask who the woman in the drawing was—could it be the Maria that one of the men had mentioned?—but a cloud of disapproval and displeasure hung about Amar, so she didn't dare. She had no ability to control werewolves or anyone else, so if he got physical when he lost his temper, she wouldn't have a way to defend herself. Maybe she should have brought the butcher knife along.

"Is there somewhere else I can leave it where it won't be stolen?" she asked as they turned toward the collection of restaurants, a sign out front of a log building proclaiming it was the Timber Wolf.

He glanced over for the first time. "Wear it. It'll offer some protection."

"Against werewolves?"

"Against other witches who might cast spells on you."

"Does that... happen often at the restaurants in Bellrock?"

"The coven here is active, and nobody likes them. Some specu-late that half the town is under their control. But *not* the were-wolves." He glared over at her, as if he expected her to argue.

Morgen lifted her hands. She didn't know what she'd gotten herself into, but arguing was far from her mind.

Still glaring, Amar returned his focus to the road, swinging the truck into a parking lot behind the log building.

She thought about making a joke about jowl nuzzling but decided to let him cool off instead. As irked as he looked now, she doubted she could count on him to defend her inside. All she could hope was that Christian came alone and neither witches nor werewolves showed up to make the meal more interesting than she already feared it would be.

MORGEN HEADED ACROSS THE PARKING LOT TO THE ENTRANCE OF THE Timber Wolf alone, Amar saying that they shouldn't be seen together but that he would be _around_. She had no idea if that meant he would skulk into the restaurant and hide in the shadows under a table or if he planned to wait in his truck and that she should flee outside to him if she got in trouble. Or maybe he intended to take off as soon as she was out of sight and leave her to find her own way back to the house.

"Should have insisted on bringing my own car," she muttered.

The amulet lay heavy against her chest, and her doubts about it returned, along with the temptation to remove it and stuff it in her purse. But she doubted that would make a difference. If were-wolves could sense it on her, they would sense it in there too.

A squawk came from the edge of the roof as she reached for the door. A raven perched there, its head cocked as a single beady eye stared down at her.

Morgen doubted it was the same one that had flown into Grandma's room at the house, but she flattened her hand against her chest, just in case it was thinking of swooping down and trying to steal the amulet.

The door opened, and an elderly couple walked out wearing matching T-shirts that read *King of the RV* and *Queen of the RV* respectively. They glanced at her chest, maybe wondering why she was touching herself on the threshold of a restaurant.

Morgen lowered her hand, eyed the raven one last time—it hadn't moved—and stepped into the restaurant. The back entrance that led into the parking lot was more popular than the front, and she had to weave through a crowd of people grabbing raincoats and umbrellas before venturing out.

The coat hooks mounted to the log walls were bronze wolf heads, and the theme continued into the restaurant where howling wolves adorned ceiling lamps, wall sconces, and iron wall art. Next to the cash register, a fountain featuring a wolf standing atop a waterfall burbled while a teenager with pigtails rang up tabs on a system that had been state of the art in the eighties.

The tables were full, with more people milling in a waiting area, but Morgen spotted Christian alone at a large booth, his hat taking up half the bench beside him. One of his arms was draped over the back of the seat while he sipped an amber liquid on the rocks. As Morgen made her way toward him, marveling that a town with such a small population could have so many people at this restaurant, she looked warily around for burly men who might be belligerent French-Canadian werewolves with a thing against witches.

Fortunately, retired couples taking a break from their summer travels were more typical. Given the scents of charring meat and sizzling bacon wafting from the kitchen, Morgen would have expected a clientele with younger, haler arteries.

Christian spotted her, lifted his glass, and waved her to the seat opposite him. "Glad you could make it, ma'am."

"Yes." Morgen slid into the booth, glancing around one last time for werewolves, but she didn't see anyone similar to the brawny construction werewolves—or Amar—nor was anyone paying attention to her. That was a relief. "Thanks for meeting me. I'm eager to hear your plans for the property."

If they got straight to business, maybe they could finish in a few minutes. She could skip the dining portion of the meal entirely and head back out to join Amar.

"Certainly, certainly. But let me order you a drink first." Christian waved for the waitress.

Morgen sighed, having a feeling that straight-to-business wouldn't happen.

"The Timber Wolf isn't our finest dining experience, but the locals and tourists enjoy it, and it gives you a taste of what Bellrock is about. You get to pick your steak off the beef trolley, and they prepare it to your specifications." Christian pointed to a server in an apron pushing a wheeled cart of slabs of raw meat out of the kitchen.

Even though Morgen didn't consider herself the kind of vegetarian who vociferously proclaimed the cruelty of the meat industry and condemned others for their tastes, she couldn't help but curl a lip at the glistening slabs of beef lined up on the cart.

"How much would I have to pay to see an offering from the tofu trolley?" she asked.

Christian blinked slowly. "You might check at the froufrou coffee shop down the street for that. They have some baked goods that are gluten-free, soy-free, sugar-free..." He sipped from his glass as he muttered, "Flavor-free," to finish.

"I will. Thanks."

Christian started detailing plans for the property, including sending a photographer to capture the estate at its best. Morgen decided she would lock the root cellar for that. Even though she'd been organizing the shelves, pegboards, crates, chests, and everything else down there, she doubted the pentagram on the floor and the ceremonial daggers would entice buyers.

A server brought menus as Christian spoke, and Morgen perused the selections under the wolf-head logo, hoping for trolley-free offerings. There wasn't anything strictly vegetable-based, but she occasionally ate fish, and could have opted for the salmon, but it came with a steak on the side. All of the seafood offerings were some version of surf and turf. Maybe she would get a plate, eat the side salad, and take the rest out to Amar. He had to be hungry after a day of chainsawing logs into artwork.

"Can I send the photographer over tomorrow?" Christian asked. "Have you had time to tidy up the place?"

"Uh." Morgen thought of the shelves full of embalmed organs that she'd alphabetized and the rooms in the main house that she hadn't touched. "I'll finish working on it tonight. Sure."

The sooner the house was listed, the sooner she would find out who wanted to buy it.

The pigtailed teenager from the cash register came up to the table and handed an envelope to Morgen. "This is from the Crystal Parlor. The old lady who works there said to give it specifically to you, that you look like you could use a two-for-one voucher." She glanced at Christian and shrugged.

"I'm the only one who gets one?" Morgen asked.

"Yup." The teenager stuck her hand in her jeans pocket, tamping down the tip of a five-dollar-bill that had been hanging out. Had someone paid her to deliver the envelope? "Most of the randos who hang out here aren't the crystal types."

"I'll be sure to check it out."

"Said no one ever." With another shrug, the teenager wandered off.

Apparently, the five-dollar tip hadn't been sufficient to convince her to talk up the place.

"It's a tchotchke shop for people who will believe anything." Christian eyed the storefronts across the street, including one labeled the Crystal Parlor.

The words *crystal witch's sister* floated into Morgen's mind. The werewolf had said them in a scathing way, making it clear she was an enemy, but maybe one of the witches in town could tell Morgen something about that clip.

A server came to take their order, and as Christian was relaying a long list of instructions on how he wanted his wagyu prepared, Morgen opened the envelope. She was disappointed when the first thing she pulled out was indeed a two-for-one voucher, good on all crystals, geodes, and tumbled stones, with a special deal on selections from the Chakra Collection. But the next handwritten page was more interesting.

Without preamble, it read, *The Timber Wolf isn't safe for our kind. If you have trouble escaping, you can use Gwen's amulet for assistance. Simply incant, "Under the moon's magic, allow me to sleuth and reveal thy silvery truth," to learn the weaknesses of your enemies and exploit them.*

Morgen hoped *incanting* was the same as *saying* and that she wouldn't need to do either. How had whoever sent this known that she wore the amulet? It wasn't as if she'd taken it out from under her zipped hoodie, and the silver chain itself was unassuming.

For some reason, the raven popped to mind. What if it was a witch's familiar, and it was spying on her?

As much as she cringed at the idea of strolling into shops and chatting up the employees, she might have to step out of her comfort zone to speak with whoever had sent this. Clearly, it had been someone at the crystal shop. The owner? The *crystal witch*?

The server cleared his throat. "And your order, ma'am? Do you want to make a selection from the beef trolley?"

"No, that's not necessary. Just... the salmon and steak is fine. With a large salad."

"We only have one size of salad, ma'am." He used his hands to shape a small plate in the air. If his portrayal was accurate, it could hold a maximum of four lettuce leaves.

"That's fine. Thanks."

"Anything interesting?" Christian pointed at the envelope.

Morgen read the incantation again to memorize it, then slid the paper back into the envelope, showing him the coupon so he would believe it was nothing of importance. "Only if I need my chakras realigned."

"Bunch of woo-woo crap." He took out his phone. "I'll need to send over some documents for you to sign, permitting me to represent you and ensuring you won't let anyone else list the property. What's your email address?"

Morgen hesitated, the idea of signing something and committing to this line of action bothering her, though she knew she wouldn't have to accept any of the offers. Christian would be disappointed if she didn't—especially if they were for substantial amounts of money—but he could get over it. If he'd truly been harassing Grandma for months and trying to get her to move into an old-folks home, he deserved it.

She gave him her email address, not expecting him to rush her to sign anything, but he kept glancing at her phone as they ate their appetizer salads, and she got the impression he wanted her to sign everything before he let her out the door. Since there wasn't wifi at Grandma's house, and the cell reception was a little spotty, maybe it wasn't a bad idea. The sooner she did this, the sooner she could find Grandma's killer.

The server raised his eyebrows when Morgen asked for a doggie bag as soon as he set their entrees down. She restrained her humor by *not* asking for a wolfie bag, though, given the decor, he probably wouldn't have thought anything of that.

After signing Christian's documents electronically on her phone, she ate the handful of vegetables that had come with the meal while stealing glances out the window at the Crystal Parlor. Unfortunately, the wares were the only things visible through the shop's large display window. She couldn't see anyone peering out at her.

"I'll take care of the bill." Christian picked up his hat and plopped it on. "Thank you for your time, ma'am. I'll send up the photographer tomorrow."

"Thanks."

With the business concluded, he didn't dally. Morgen was glad. As she swooped up her take-out box, she thought about heading straight across the street to investigate the crystal shop, but she felt obligated to check in with Amar. Also, it wouldn't hurt to ask if he knew anything about the crystal witch and if she was likely the one who sent the note, or if that person had nothing to do with the parlor at all.

The crowd had thinned by the time Morgen opened the back door, so she was the only one exiting the building, but she almost crashed into Amar's broad back. He crouched with his fists up, facing three pale-skinned men with neatly trimmed brown hair. They were as big and muscular as Amar, but their gold watches and North Face and Ralph Lauren clothes were a lot different from his style.

"Let us in, Lobo," one growled in a raspy voice similar in tone to Amar's, though the accent wasn't the same.

Morgen had a feeling these were the Loups.

"That's *our* restaurant. We own it, and we run it," the man continued.

He hadn't yet seen Morgen through Amar, but one of his buddies had. He squinted at her as he sniffed the air in her direction.

"We have the right to go inside whenever we want," the speaker added.

"That's her." The other man pointed at Morgen. "The new

witch."

"Get her," the third one said. "We'll make *sure* she doesn't sell Wolf Wood."

13

ONE OF THE LOUPS SPRANG AT MORGEN, AND SHE JUMPED BACK BUT couldn't go far. She bumped into the door.

Fortunately, Amar blocked her attacker with his body as he threw a punch. It slammed into the man's chin, deterring him, but one of the other Loups charged toward her from his other side.

Morgen spun and grabbed the door handle, hoping they wouldn't follow her inside. Even as Amar traded punches with the first werewolf, he kicked out at the second one, keeping him from reaching Morgen.

That was a good thing because someone had locked the door behind her. What the hell?

She dropped her take-out box and tugged with both hands, thinking it was jammed or someone else was pulling from the other side, but no. It was locked.

Movement at a nearby window drew her eye. Someone pulled the curtains. What, because a fight in the parking lot would disturb the diners?

Morgen spun back, amazed that Amar was holding off three men but afraid he wouldn't be able to do so indefinitely unless she could do something to help. Thinking of the note, she pulled out her amulet. Seeing their *weaknesses* didn't seem that helpful, but she hurried to whisper, "Under the moon's magic, allow me to sleuth and reveal thy silvery truth."

The amulet warmed in her hand, but nothing happened to the werewolves. Two punched and kicked at Amar as one growled and whipped out a knife.

Morgen glanced at the sky, afraid the incantation only worked at night, under the moon, or that it didn't work at all. It wasn't as if she were truly a witch and knew how to cast spells. She didn't even know what *incanting* meant.

The sky had grown dimmer as the sun descended in the west, but if the moon had come out, it was behind the clouds.

As Amar blocked a stab from the knife-wielder, one that would have driven the blade into his eye, Morgen said the words again, speaking more firmly this time, hoping that would help. She didn't have any weapons, and even if she had, it wasn't as if she knew how to wield anything more powerful than a keyboard.

Only when Amar dodged another attack did she get a good look at one of the men and realize that something *had* changed. He was glowing now. All three of the Loups were, a silvery nimbus outlining their forms. They didn't seem to notice it as they kept attacking Amar. The glow shifted around two of the men, showing flames outlining their bodies, as if a wizard from a fantasy novel had hurled fireballs at them.

For an instant, Morgen saw two versions of the men. The fearless snarling attackers trying to take down Amar to get to her and terrified men glancing in horror at the flames around them. A different shadow fell over the third man, and she saw him both fighting and also having advanced to an extreme age and being killed by a powerful young adversary.

Confused, and distracted by the men continuing to try to lunge past Amar to get to her, Morgen didn't at first understand what she was seeing. Then she realized these had to be the men's weaknesses. Two of them were afraid of fire and one of getting old and being taken down by a younger, stronger werewolf.

If she had some fire, maybe she could do something, but all she could think of was the blowtorch that Amar had stuck in the truck bed. Would such a small tool scare the men, or would it take a forest fire roaring down on them? The blowtorch was all she had access to, so she would have to hope for the best.

Morgen scooted along the wall, hoping she could get to Amar's truck while the men were all busy fighting.

"Stay behind me," Amar barked.

But she didn't. As soon as all three of their foes were focused on him, Morgen charged for the truck. She pulled herself into the bed, but one of the men spotted her and broke away from the melee.

Fortunately, with the furnishings gone, it was easy to get to Amar's tools. She grabbed the blowtorch but fumbled it as she tried to figure out how to turn it on. She'd never used such a tool before in her life.

The Loup sprang up to the bed of the truck without using his hands. He landed on the edge, snarling at her.

A chilling growl came from the pavement, and a gray-and-black wolf charged toward the truck. Amar. He sprang, leaping far higher than a typical wolf should have been able to do, and crashed into the man's back.

Morgen threw herself to the side, shoulder hitting the bottom of the truck bed as the men—man and wolf—clawed and thrashed in the other half.

That gave her the time she needed to turn on the gas and find the ignition button. The tool clicked and flared to life. Morgen scrambled to her feet, the blowtorch shooting out a blue stream that didn't look much like the crackling orange flames she'd seen in that vision.

As Amar's attacker kept fighting him as a man, his face and hands bloodied, the other two Loups turned into wolves. They were the ones who'd been afraid of fire.

Morgen made herself face them as they ran across the parking lot, powerful legs carrying them fast. With one foot on the edge of the truck bed, she held up the blowtorch.

One faltered and didn't jump, but the second one's amber eyes were so focused on her that he didn't seem to notice the tool. He sprang, jaws snapping for her throat.

It took all her courage not to shriek and jump away—she'd thought they wanted to capture her, not *kill* her.

Morgen held her ground and thrust the flame into his lupine face. The wolf shook his head, growls turning into a yip of alarm, and the stream of flame struck him in the eye. He closed his jaws shy of biting her, but his momentum carried him into her.

Two hundred pounds of werewolf slammed into Morgen, and she crashed back into the truck bed, cracking her head on the side. She barely managed to keep hold of the blowtorch and thrust it above her, turning the flame on her attacker's chest. With another yip of pain, the wolf sprang out of the truck on the far side.

Next to her, Amar came out on top of his opponent and sank his fangs into the man's shoulder. The human cry of agony assaulted Morgen's ears, but she made herself stand up again, afraid the third wolf would attack. As soon as she brandished the blowtorch again, he and the one she'd scorched took off, fleeing the parking lot and disappearing behind another building.

Amar snarled, sounding almost like a lion roaring, and the still-human Loup scrambled out of the truck. He gripped his torn shoulder, blood seeping through his fingers, and shouted, "You'll regret tangling with the Loups, *solitaire* Lobo. You don't get in the way of the pack and live."

Amar snarled again, blood dripping from his fangs. Even though he faced their enemy, Morgen took an involuntary step back. When he was in that form, his head came up to her shoulder, and he was even more intimidating than he was as a human.

Their enemy limped off after the others. Despite his bravado, he glanced back often, as if worried Amar would spring after him.

But Amar turned to face Morgen, his blue eyes unblinking.

She still gripped the blowtorch, and she reached down to flick it off. A dark shadow lurked over his heart—something lingering from the visions the amulet had given her? She didn't know what it meant, but it didn't convey that fire was his weakness. Not that she expected to have to exploit whatever his weakness was anyway.

At least, she didn't think she would. As he gazed unblinking at her, she shifted uneasily.

When he was in that wolf form, was it possible he didn't think as his normal human self did? What if he thought like a wolf? Like a predator eyeing someone who could make a tasty dinner?

"If you're hungry, I brought a doggie bag." Morgen pointed to the box she'd dropped by the door, though someone had stepped on it and mangled it.

Hopefully, the food inside was still edible. How picky would a wolf be? If Lucky could get away with it, he ate week-old hotdogs found under picnic tables.

"Thanks for the help, by the way," she said, hoping that speaking would remind Amar of who she was—and that he didn't need to stare at her like that. "I don't understand why everyone in this town has it out for me because they think I'm a witch, which I'm really not, but it's clear I need a bodyguard. And you do a good job. Maybe I could pay you for your time. I'm not flush with cash at the moment, but I do have a semi-substantial 401(k) that I've been contributing to faithfully for eighteen years. I've even got some stock in the company that just let my team go. Come to think of it, I should probably sell it, because their business is going to tank now that they let go of the IT department."

Morgen heard herself babbling and struggled to stop. Having him standing there, his cool eyes staring at her and blood droplets and saliva spattering the truck bed under his jaws, made her uncomfortable.

Though she got the sense that he was trying to convey something to her. She hadn't the foggiest idea what. Apparently, werewolves weren't telepathic.

"I'd like to go to the Crystal Parlor before it closes to talk to the owner and see if she knows anything about that bone clip." Morgen tilted her thumb over her shoulder. "Do you want to come along? Or wait here?"

Amar emitted what sounded like the wolf equivalent of a sigh, then slowly morphed into human form, the process surprisingly quiet. It seemed that such a dramatic change should involve the painful snapping and cracking of bones.

When the transformation completed, Amar stood before her, utterly naked.

Twilight was approaching, so the shadows somewhat dulled the starkness, but she had no trouble making out his form. She looked away, lest he think she was ogling him and dreaming of having sex with him, though this wasn't the first time she'd seen him naked. It hadn't occurred to her that his clothes would disappear when he shifted forms.

As she looked away, she noticed something on the pavement. His vest. And were those his jeans by the door? And boots. The jeans appeared to be torn. Maybe that happened when he shifted in the middle of a fight and didn't have time to remove his clothing first.

"I was trying to convey to you that you might want to get out of the truck if you didn't want to see me naked." Amar hopped down to the pavement and grabbed the vest.

"Oh, I thought you were riveted by talk of 401(k)s and unemployed database programmers."

"No."

"Well, nudity isn't a big deal. I mean, I've already seen you naked more than my husband in the last year of our marriage, but that's perhaps not surprising. We weren't that, uh, conjugal at the end." Admittedly, they hadn't been that conjugal for a long time, which was perhaps what had led to him labeling her as cold and aloof.

Amar glanced at her as he put on his vest, and she grimaced, not sure why she'd brought such a topic up with him. She set down the blowtorch and climbed out of the truck bed.

He picked up his jeans, but they had indeed been ripped.

"I guess I'll have to include a clothing stipend, if you're going to be my bodyguard," she said.

"You will not pay me." Amar tossed the ripped jeans in a garbage can, picked up his boots, and—despite the refusal of payment—grabbed the semi-mutilated takeout box before heading to the driver's seat. "I will protect you because Gwen would have wished it."

"Are you sure? I don't want to get in the way of your work or anything."

Amar didn't answer, only pulling out a set of jeans from under the seat. They were still folded with a tag sticking out. He pulled it off and put them on, sans underwear. Morgen winced, fearing for his nether regions and things being caught when he zipped them up. Maybe underwear wasn't practical when one had to remove—or lose—one's clothing every time one changed.

But how often was that? In the movies she remembered from her youth—a dubious gift that her father had shared with her and her siblings, along with his passion for all the country-western music of the time—werewolves had only been able to change if there was a full moon. And there'd been a lot of biting of innocent people to turn *them* into werewolves. Did that actually happen? Or was it a hereditary affliction? If the former, would she be in danger if Amar got cranky and decided to chew on her?

"Get in," he said once he was dressed again.

"I need to make a stop first."

"The grocery store?"

"That too. And a coffee shop that sounds like a must-visit for me, but I specifically had the Crystal Parlor in mind. I think I could learn something there." She summed up her encounter with the teenage cashier and showed him the note she'd received. "If magic was used to kill my grandmother, it makes sense to talk to a witch, don't you think?"

Amar regarded her, his blue eyes the same as they'd been as a wolf, though she trusted he wasn't trying to convey impending nudity this time. "The witches here are unpleasant. And one or more of them may have been responsible for Gwen's death."

"From what your pack—uhm, your acquaintances at the construction site—said, it sounds like werewolves think all witches are unpleasant."

"They use their magic to control animals, including those of us with moon blood."

"Moon blood? Is that like witch blood?" She remembered him using that term.

His eyes narrowed. "It is very *different* from witch blood." He kept glowering at her, as if offended that she'd implied they were anything alike. "But both convey to the owner a certain ability to use magic," he admitted, almost reluctantly.

"If you hate witches, and my grandmother was a witch, how come you didn't hate her?"

"I did not like her at first. I only wanted her wood."

"Uh, what?"

"The trees that fall in Wolf Wood. They are not exactly enchanted, but some that come from the center of the forest have magical properties."

"Like those mushrooms?"

"Not usually that strongly imbued, but yes."

"Does that mean the bench you said you would make me won't zap me in the butt when I sit on it?"

"It should not."

"That's good. That would be a jarring gift."

"A *jolting* gift."

She blinked. "Is that a joke?"

"Yes."

"I wouldn't have guessed you made those. Your humor seems..." She kept herself from saying *nonexistent,* since that might offend him. "Subtle."

"Yes." He pointed toward the street and the buildings on the other side. "I will wait outside while you speak with the shop owner."

"Do you think I'll learn anything useful? Is she a witch?"

"She is, and it is more likely you will get yourself into trouble."

"*More* trouble? It's a good thing I now have a werewolf protecting me, one who doesn't mind ripping his jeans and getting furry for me." She smiled, tempted to pat him on the shoulder, but that also might offend him. He was a bristly werewolf.

He regarded her without humor. "Perhaps it's unfortunate that my bench won't zap you."

"I'm not sure that's another joke, but I'll pretend it is."

He grunted and led her out of the parking lot.

14

MORGEN HEADED INTO THE CRYSTAL PARLOR WITH HER COUPON IN hand. Amar remained outside, leaning against the brick wall and noshing out of the takeout box. Morgen imagined he'd worked up a good appetite during the fight and couldn't blame him for snacking, but she found the idea of eating a meal directly after biting people unsanitary. Who knew where those Loups had been before staging their ambush? What would Amar think if she got him a toothbrush and toothpaste kit to keep in his truck along with his spare jeans?

She stepped into a shop so stuffed with shelves, racks, bins, and rotating display cases that she worried she would break something. Was there a rule somewhere that witches had to be hoarders?

A strong mishmash of scents permeated the air, something like a Christmas tree fencing with lavender stalks while adorned in charred citrus peels. Morgen hoped burning incense and candles and who knew what else wasn't a witch requirement, though she imagined a bored bureaucrat at the supernatural permitting counter refusing to give her a license to practice until she recited all the kinds of incense and promised to burn them religiously.

She weaved through the shop carefully, hoping to glimpse items made from bone, ideally labeled with the purpose and the maker identified. Finding the information she sought without actually *speaking* to the owner would be preferable. Though she did feel obligated to thank the person for the incantation. Given her dearth of experience with the occult, and previous lack of belief that magic even existed, Morgen was surprised it had worked.

Throughout the cluttered display room, only crystals and gems and various types of rocks were on display. Unless they were supposed to have magical power, she didn't see a clear link to witchdom.

An open door in the back showed a room full of bags, jars, and tubs of what appeared to be powders and seeds—they reminded her of bulk-food bins at grocery stores—but from the colors— more blues, purples, and grays than anything else—she doubted they were edible. A chain across the doorway with a sign hanging from it said the area was off-limits and to ask for help.

"I thought you might show up here," a woman said from a corner, half-hidden by a carousel of keychains featuring agates and crystals.

Olive-skinned with curly graying brown hair, she wore a colorful ankle-length garment that reminded Morgen more of a dashiki than what Hollywood assured her was traditional witches' garb. Maybe the black dresses and pointed hats were reserved for Halloween.

"Hi." Morgen picked her way toward the corner.

The woman sat in a comfortable chair, reading from an old book. Nobody else was in the shop.

"I'm Morgen," she offered.

"Yes. I am Phoebe Aetos."

Not the Tabitha or Glinda that Morgen had half-expected, but if Phoebe didn't have a black dress and a nearby broomstick, maybe she couldn't be expected to have a traditional witch name. The lack of a black cat skulking through the aisles was a little disappointing.

"Are you the one who sent me the note?" Morgen asked.

"Yes. I was informed that you were about to enter a werewolf haven."

"Informed? By the raven perched above the door?"

Phoebe smiled cryptically.

"I noticed him—or her—because another raven, or maybe the same one, tried to take my grandmother's amulet from the house." Morgen had tucked it back under her hoodie and didn't pull it out. "I was surprised you knew about that when we haven't even met before."

"Are you making accusations? After I gave you a coupon?"

"Oh, no. Just polite conversation. I'll take some rocks from the Chakra Collection to show that there are no hard feelings." Morgen smiled, though she had no desire for rocks, crystals, or anything else. But it would be a small price to pay for the information she wanted.

"The fate of Wolf Wood is of concern to many," Phoebe said. "Zeke was keeping an eye on the place for me."

"Zeke... the raven?"

"Zeke, my familiar. He didn't wish any of Gwen's belongings to fall into the hands of an unschooled mundane."

"What about an unschooled relative who apparently has witch blood?" Morgen raised her eyebrows, wondering if Phoebe could confirm that for her. Despite the numerous zappings she'd received now, it was still hard to believe that she was the heir to magical blood that allowed her to cast spells.

"That is almost as bad. We did not know who would arrive or what blood you would have."

"If I wanted to learn about magic, would there be a good place for that?" That wasn't what Morgen had come here to ask about, but she admitted to being the tiniest bit curious about her heritage and wished Grandma had said something about it while she'd been alive. These days, Morgen didn't feel particularly special, and there was something appealing about the idea of having some uncommon... ability. Her sister was right that it had been a blow to her self-worth to be let go from a job that she *thought* had been crucial. She'd thought *she'd* been crucial. "Is there a school?" she added. "Or do you, ah, tutor?"

"This isn't Hogwarts, and I'm not Dumbledore," Phoebe said dryly.

"So, I'm stuck relying on websites and YouTube videos?"

"Grimoires are more useful, but you can really only learn witchcraft from a master. And that requires that the master wishes to take you on as an apprentice." The dismissive look that Phoebe gave Morgen suggested she had no interest in doing so. "But you're too old to learn. I suggest you return to your regular life, leave witchcraft to those who've been versed in it from their earliest days, and put your grandmother's property into some kind of trust. You should leave it to someone who will care for it and ensure it remains as it is."

"I'm too old to learn? Retired people go back to college to get degrees. And I'm not retired. I'm just... on sabbatical."

"Witchcraft isn't a *college degree*. You can't learn from lectures. A master must take you on personally and instruct you in the ways."

"Then why did you send me a note with a spell?"

"Even rubes can chant incantations if they have a proper foci." Phoebe waved toward Morgen's amulet. "That isn't witchcraft. A real witch customizes and makes up her own spells and creates potions tailored to specific maladies and desires. It's an art, and a secret and guarded art at that."

Phoebe could say what she wanted, but Morgen was *positive* the internet was full of videos on her secret art.

"But you are welcome for that smidgen that I gave you. I trust you found it useful."

Did that mean Phoebe knew about the werewolf battle? She'd probably heard the snarls and yips from here.

"I did. Thank you. I was a good student back in school. If you'd be willing to teach me a few things, I'd put my heart into it." Especially if it gave her an opportunity to snoop around the shop and try to learn more. "I would pay you for your time, of course."

"Are you earning a lot while on your sabbatical?"

"Probably as much as you're earning from your booming customer base." Morgen waved at the empty shop, though as soon as the words came out, it occurred to her that being insulting to the tutor she wanted to hire wasn't a good idea.

Phoebe's eyes turned as cool as the crystals lined up on the ledge behind her chair. "I'm not interested in your money."

"Is there some other way I could help you? In trade for your time? I'm not planning to move here forever. It wouldn't be a long-term commitment."

"Of course, because witchcraft is something you can learn in two weeks."

"I could come up for occasional weekends too."

"This isn't the National Guard."

Morgen drummed her fingers on her thigh, searching around for inspiration, though she only ended up sneezing as some draft stirred up dust—or one of the strange powders in the back room. Maybe this was pointless.

"The only thing I can truly use right now is help in the store," Phoebe said.

"Really? Does it get busier at other times of day?"

Phoebe hesitated. "Not so much lately, but the economy can't stay good forever."

"The economy?"

"Yes. During booming times, people are less likely to turn to our ways for answers to their many problems. When your home and your stock portfolio are appreciating twenty percent a year, who needs advice from the spirits within the crystals?"

Who ever needed advice from spirits within crystals? Morgen kept that thought to herself.

"My sister used to help out around the shop, but she's been gone for months, and I can't afford to hire outsiders."

Was that the crystal witch's sister that the Lobo had mentioned? Who had enslaved one of the pack? It sounded like she had passed away, so she couldn't be a problem now.

"Besides," Phoebe continued, "teenagers looking for summer jobs aren't qualified to work here. They know nothing of potions and powders."

"I hear that's not covered in high school these days."

"No." Phoebe frowned at the front window. "Is that werewolf loitering outside with you?"

"Yes. He didn't think he would be welcome in here."

"He wouldn't be. He's also not welcome to rub his scent all over my storefront."

"He's just standing there eating salmon."

"You should be careful around him. I trust he's not under your control, since you don't know how to *do* anything yet."

"He's not under my control, no. He's just..." Morgen almost said he'd only given her a ride into town, but it didn't feel right to dismiss Amar's help in the parking lot so blithely. Without him, she would be chained up in some werewolf den by now, if not dead. One of those wolves had been snapping for her throat. "He's helping me out."

"Why? What's in it for him?"

"My irreverent charm. He finds it endearing."

"You're a dreadful liar."

"Is a knack for mendacity required to become a good witch?"

"It is not. It's useful, however, for customer service. If someone picks out a gem or earrings that don't look good on them, but you can smile, nod, and make the sale, you'll do fine in my shop." Phoebe gestured to the display cases.

Why did Phoebe want Morgen to work here? She likely knew even less about potions and powders than the local teenagers. Admittedly, Morgen could help organize the place. Maybe even enter everything into an inventory-management system for ease of tracking and re-ordering.

"Have you thought about selling some of this stuff online?" Morgen asked. "The number of people who come through Bell-rock each year must be somewhat limited."

"It is, but I don't know enough about computers to do that."

"I could help you set something up. Even if you didn't want to sell online, it would help you immensely to have inventory-management software to let you know how much of everything you have and what's selling and what's not. Given your current organizational paradigm, I bet you run out of some items regularly and have far more of others than you need."

"That's not... untrue. I also have a tendency to order more of some gems and crystals because they're high quality and genuinely useful, and people *should* want to buy them, even though they always go for the pretty, decorative things that have little to no power. It's madness, really."

"Right. Will you take my help setting up software and getting you online in exchange for teaching me?" Morgen might end up here all summer if she got involved in this project for Phoebe, but... did that matter anymore? There wasn't anything calling her back to that drab apartment in Shoreline.

"Very well. I'll agree to that. Come back when you are prepared to start. I'm here all hours that the shop is open and then some. In the evenings, I make my potions." Phoebe pointed toward the back room.

"Good. Uhm, one more question before I go. I have reason to believe that Grandma's death might not have been an accident. There was a bone clip attached to her motorcycle before it crashed. Can witches make magical tools that could cause such a thing?"

"Bones aren't the most ideal medium, but they can be infused with magic, yes. Bring it to me when you return, and I'll look at it."

"Thank you. I will." Morgen turned toward the door, but Phoebe spoke again.

"A werewolf is not a friend of a witch."

"I've heard that." Morgen paused and glanced toward the window, though Amar was staying out of sight. How Phoebe had known he was loitering, Morgen didn't know. "But he seems all right. He rented an apartment from my grandmother, and I guess they were friends."

"Friends." Phoebe scoffed. "It's more likely that Gwen controlled him with a spell or even an idol or brand. If the werewolf hasn't realized it yet, he will one day, and then he'll feel vengeful toward her and her kin. Werewolves are not *friends* with our kind."

"Why not?"

"They are shaped and easily affected by magic but are not able to cast it themselves. That makes them bitter and resentful."

"From what I heard," Morgen said, choosing her words carefully so she wouldn't offend her potential new tutor, "some witches have treated werewolves badly. You just said my grandmother might have used magic on Amar." Morgen hoped that wasn't true, but she *had* been wondering how those two could have ended up as friends.

"If they weren't such surly bullies, witches wouldn't feel compelled to use their magic on them. Those two warring packs were a threat to this town before the coven stepped in. Further, as women, we often have need to defend ourselves, especially against savage bullies, and we can't be blamed for using our powers to protect ourselves and our kin."

"By ensorcelling others?" Morgen had almost said *enslaving* others.

"To avoid being preyed upon? If necessary, yes. If they would leave us alone, and leave the innocent townspeople alone, we would leave them alone, but *they* started it. And you had better be careful. If that werewolf is pretending to *help* you, as you said, it's because he wants something. Likely what everyone else wants. Access to Wolf Wood and for it and its magic to remain unchanged."

"That's not what everyone wants." Morgen thought of Christian's insincerely smiling face.

"The old world and the new have always battled over progress. Don't cross the wolf until you've learned to control him. Even then, it wouldn't be wise."

"I wasn't planning to cross him."

Or try to control him.

"Let's hope Gwen didn't. A scorned werewolf is a dangerous enemy, an enemy who might arrange one's death."

"They weren't enemies," Morgen said certainly, though she did catch herself thinking again of the warning in Grandma's letter about not irking Amar. Had she done that at some point? How else would she have known of the danger?

"Don't be so certain. I promise you they weren't friends."

Morgen shook her head and walked out, not willing to believe her grandmother had been controlling Amar somehow. If she had, he wouldn't be protecting Morgen now.

15

IT WAS FULL DARK BY THE TIME THE TRUCK TURNED ONTO THE LONG pothole-filled driveway, Morgen's grocery bags tipping over and dumping everything from cantaloupes to cans of cream-of-mushroom soup all over the bed. The bag of dog food she'd picked up for Lucky, who would be starving by the time she fed him tonight, skidded back and forth with each turn. She resolved to take her car, with its modern amenity of a trunk, into town for her next grocery run.

A clunk sounded as something hit the side of the bed. Hopefully, not the label maker she'd purchased right before the small stationery-slash-office-supply-slash-printing-slash-mailbox store closed for the night. She'd been delighted by the find and planned to put it to use in the root cellar, at least on the things she could identify. A lot of the jars weren't labeled, and a check of her phone's app store had shown her programs for identifying plants and trees, but nothing aimed at recognizing strange powders used by witches.

As he drove, Amar sat silently, no lights on the antiquated dashboard to illuminate his face. He'd barely spoken since

Morgen walked out of the Crystal Parlor, admitting that Phoebe was willing to show her a few things, but she sensed that he didn't approve. Maybe she shouldn't have said anything. All he wanted— and all she'd said she wanted when she'd walked into that shop— was to find Grandma's killer.

But after being targeted by so many dangerous people, Morgen wanted to learn something about her heritage. *Especially,* she wanted to learn to defend herself.

Back in the suburbs of Seattle, she hadn't felt the need, but Bellrock was different. *Very* different.

"I'm going to have to clean the house tonight and in the morning," she said, the seat making her voice vibrate as the truck bumped and swayed up the muddy road. "There's a photographer coming to take pictures of the property tomorrow."

Long seconds passed before Amar replied. "You are certain this is only a ruse?"

"Absolutely certain. Grandma left me a letter that I read last night and asked me to keep the woods intact. Even if I'd been thinking of selling the property before—" which, she admittedly *had* been doing, "—I wouldn't do it now that I know it would be against her wishes."

"It would also be against *my* wishes."

Morgen hadn't known him two days ago, so that wouldn't have swayed her nearly as much, but she said, "I know. And I'd prefer not to annoy you."

"Good."

"But because I want the ruse to work, it might be a good idea if you would refrain from wandering around in front of the barn with your chainsaw while the photographer is here."

"You do not think a picture of me would help interest a buyer?"

"One of you holding a chainsaw would be alarming and not make anyone want to put in an offer."

"Then I should prowl about in every room as the photographer takes pictures."

"Ha ha. Also don't turn into a wolf, please. You, with blood dripping from your fangs, would also put off a buyer." Morgen said it lightly, but the disturbing memory of that image had imprinted itself in her mind.

"I cannot become a wolf when the sun is out."

"That's the rule? I'd wondered if it only worked at night. Are full moons required?"

"No. Only that the sun be down or hidden behind deep cloud cover. It is painful, however, if the light level rises and forces a change back, so night is the ideal time to become the wolf."

"Is it... painful the rest of the time? Transforming?" Morgen imagined that having one's bones and body magically contorted into another shape had to hurt.

"It is not pleasant," he said tersely.

"Then why do it?"

Now, she felt guilty that he'd had to change into his wolf form to help her at the restaurant.

"The moon calls."

"Meaning you can't resist it?"

"You can resist, but it grows more difficult with time. For one or two nights, perhaps it is only an itch that longs to be scratched, but the urge grows as more time passes without turning. Also, at night, there's a great urge to hunt, to consume the hot fresh flesh of the prey that travels the forest." Amar looked over at her.

Hopefully, not thinking about how humans were prey that one might feast upon.

"Carrots and cabbage don't satisfy that urge, huh?" she said after a long uncomfortable moment.

"No." Amar looked back to the driveway as they ran into a pothole with a jolt. "The hunt is even more exhilarating than the feast afterward. I am also stronger and more deadly in my wolf form."

Thinking of his muscular arms, she wondered if that was true. He seemed like he would be deadly as a human too.

"There are times when it's an advantage to turn," he added.

"Like at the Timber Wolf."

"Yes. But you have to be careful once you turn. It's easy to get lost in the blood lust, to forget the difference between friend and foe, to simply wish to strike." His voice lowered to a husky whisper. "To kill."

"Such a pain when that happens." Maybe she shouldn't have made jokes, but the conversation was making her uneasy, and she longed for the house to come into view so she could escape inside. It was her fault for asking questions.

"It is *a pain* when you are also a man and judged by the laws of men," Amar said. "Even if you are judged as a wolf, men will come after you if you've killed their kind."

Their kind. As if he weren't truly one of them.

"They are weak, but their guns can kill even one of us," he said.

"Have you always been a werewolf? Is one born into it?"

"No."

She waited, expecting him to tell her the story, but he didn't. Maybe it was something painful that he didn't want to share, like the picture of the woman in his glove compartment.

Amar sniffed the air, then rolled down the window, and sniffed some more.

"Are you... smelling prey now?" Morgen sniffed tentatively, but her nostrils didn't give her anything except the smell of the forest, damp after an earlier rain.

"No. I smell smoke."

"Like a campfire?"

"No."

Though the driveway hadn't grown any less bumpy, Amar gripped the wheel with both hands and accelerated. If the bench had been making her teeth vibrate before, now it threatened to knock them out of her jaw and onto the floor of the truck. She grabbed the door bar and, there sadly being no oh-shit handle, pressed her other hand against the ceiling.

Before the house came into sight, the smoke Amar had smelled reached her weaker nose. The first inkling of fear entered her gut. She'd left Lucky in the house. If it was burning, he wouldn't be able to get out.

Orange light flickered over the trees. She leaned forward on the bench. Not only was there a fire, but there was a *big* fire.

As Amar rounded the last bend in the driveway, the clearing came into view. The clearing and the barn. Flames burned all along its roof and leaped through the broken windows of the loft apartment as plumes of smoke rose up into the dark night.

How had those windows broken? Had someone—some arsonist?—thrown Molotov cocktails through?

Amar swore, accelerating toward the barn. For now, the house wasn't on fire, but the barn wasn't so far away from it that it was guaranteed to be safe.

He halted the truck and leaped out. Morgen grabbed her phone to call 9-1-1 as he ran toward a hose reel on the side of the house. She shook her head bleakly. That little hose wouldn't do anything to stop those flames.

As she called, wondering how long it would take for a fire engine to navigate those potholes and reach the place, she ran toward the front of the house. Surprisingly, Lucky wasn't barking. She couldn't believe he would be inside sleeping when the barn was on fire.

The smoke hung thick under the roof of the porch, and she coughed as she opened the front door. Again, she was surprised, because her dog didn't sprint out, as she would have expected. Maybe he sensed the danger and was hiding?

"Lucky!" she called as soon as she gave the address to the dispatcher and hung up. "Come on, Lucky! Let's get you outside."

She ran through the house, checking all the rooms. Since most of the windows were closed, it wasn't that smoky inside, so she didn't have trouble seeing or breathing, but she didn't spot him.

"Lucky, I brought food for you. Dinner. Treats!" She threw out all of the words that usually made him come, but he wasn't anywhere on the first floor.

What if the arsonist had let him outside, and he'd been afraid and run off into the forest? He could be lost or hiding under a log somewhere.

Morgen was about to run upstairs to look for him, but a masculine scream came from the yard. Amar?

He hadn't screamed or so much as yelped in pain when he'd been battling those three werewolves. What could have made him cry out? He wouldn't have been foolish enough to run *inside* the burning barn, would he?

Though she was worried for Lucky and wanted to keep searching, Morgen ran back outside. She halted on the porch steps as she spotted Amar on his knees, his back arched and the hose in the grass beside him. Outlined by the light of the fire, three women in dark dresses had come out of nowhere and faced him, each carrying a stick—no, a *wand*—and an amulet. They gripped the jewelry in their hands rather than wearing it around their necks and pointed their wands at Amar as they muttered arcane words.

And those words, or those items, were hurting Amar.

Morgen almost shouted for them to stop, but if they'd taken him to his knees, they would have no problem knocking her on her ass. She gripped her amulet and whispered the only magical words she knew, the incantation from the restaurant.

"Under the moon's magic, allow me to sleuth and reveal thy silvery truth."

Once again, it took a moment for anything to happen, and Amar continued to gasp and writhe on his knees. Morgen gripped the porch post, wanting to help him, not hide uselessly in the smoke and shadows. Had she been able to think of anything in her grandmother's house that could be used as a weapon, she would have run back in to get it. The fireplace poker? That was the only object that came to mind.

There were all those knives and even that antler staff in the root cellar, but she would have to run around the house, and likely into sight, in order to get down there.

The double-vision returned, showing her the witches and what they feared. An illusionary man appeared, grabbing one woman and forcing her against something. Did that signify a mugging? A rape? Either way, Morgen didn't know how she could use that fear to get her to leave Amar alone. Another woman was afraid of growing old and dying. The last feared... werewolves. In her vision, a man turned into a black wolf and sprang at her.

Morgen cursed, unable to think of how to exploit any of their fears, and ran into the house for the fireplace poker. It was all she had.

As the barn continued to burn, another scream ripped from Amar's lips.

Morgen ran back outside with the poker and followed the shadows of the porch, hoping to get close enough to whack at least one witch before they saw her. She didn't know how they were holding Amar prisoner or what pain they were inflicting on him, but their lips kept moving. If Morgen could make them stop the incantation, maybe their spell would falter.

She reached the closest witch and slammed the iron poker down onto her wrist. The woman shrieked and dropped her wand. Morgen spun, intending to do the same to the other two, but they'd seen her. One sprang back, her mumbling stopping, but the other frowned at Morgen and focused even more intently on Amar. He'd gotten one foot under him, but she renewed her chanting and thrust her wand toward him. His back arched, and he screamed again.

"Stop it, you bitches!" Morgen lunged past Amar, wanting nothing more than to crack the woman on the head.

But the first witch recovered and snatched up her wand. She pointed it at Morgen, and something that felt like a lightning bolt struck her. Her entire body spasmed, and her legs gave out. She pitched into the damp grass, flopping like a fish at Amar's side, unable to keep her legs and arms from twitching wildly.

A snarl came from a few feet away.

"He's changing," one of the women cried. "Stop him!"

The electrical current flowing into Morgen stopped, though her limbs continued to shake. Her whole body was shaking, but she made herself pat around, trying to find the poker. She found a piece of leather clothing—was that Amar's vest?—but not the poker.

"Stop right there." Something cool pressed against the side of Morgen's neck.

A gun? No, it was the metal of one of the pendants, touching her skin as the witch bent over her. It was hot, like a branding iron, and Morgen winced, trying to pull away.

"This is my property," she said. "You all better get off right now. The sheriff's department is on the way."

"The sheriff knows better than to interfere with our justice," one of the witches said.

"*Justice*? Burning down my barn and attacking the renter?"

More snarls came from her side, followed by a yip of pain. One witch still had a wand pointed at Amar. He'd started shifting into his wolf form, but they'd stopped him somehow, and he was stuck in the middle of changing, now neither man nor wolf.

Morgen slowly got to her feet, not daring to ignore the tip of the amulet pressed to her neck but refusing to sit in the grass and do nothing.

The wail of a siren reached them. It was probably a fire engine coming and not law enforcement, but the witch with the amulet pulled it back and glanced uncertainly toward the driveway. One of the others did too. Only the witch with the wand, the one focused on Amar, kept her focus, her eyes full of anger—or was that hatred?—as she glared at him. That was the woman whose fear was werewolves.

Morgen spotted the poker and snatched it up.

"Don't fight us," the youngest of the women said, a girl who barely appeared old enough to legally drink. "We came to save you."

"By burning my *barn*?" Morgen demanded.

She feared she would regret it, that she would be zapped again with electricity or worse, but she stepped in front of Amar—in front of whatever magic the witch was firing at him from that wand.

Surprisingly, nothing hurt her. She didn't feel anything at all. Behind her, Amar gasped and pitched backward, reverting to his human form.

"By burning *his home*. You'll never be safe as long as a werewolf claims this property as his own."

"He's not claiming anything. He's my..." Her what? Morgen didn't know. She barely knew Amar. She hadn't even figured out yet if he'd been paying rent for the barn. "Protector."

"He's a werewolf, not a *protector*," the woman with the wand said. She hadn't lowered it, but she was scowling at it now, as if betrayed that it wasn't zapping Morgen. "He hates our kind, and if he's pretending to help you, it's only because he wants something."

"Yeah, to protect me. Because he was my grandmother's friend." Even as she said the words, Morgen wondered if they were true. Phoebe's warning came to mind, that Grandma might only have gained Amar's allegiance by casting a spell on him.

"He was her *servant*, not her friend. That is the only way for our kind to have a relationship with their kind, the cruel bullying bastards." This time, the woman who spoke was the one who'd feared rape, at least according to Morgen's incantation. She shook her head vehemently, loathing in her eyes as she stared at Amar.

The sirens were growing closer, vehicles maneuvering up the driveway. The glances the witches sent in that direction promised that they didn't want to be caught here, even if they'd claimed the law didn't interfere with them.

"Amar isn't like that," Morgen said. "Whoever hurt you, it wasn't him."

She couldn't truly know that, but she believed she was right. Maybe Amar was fierce and aggressive and had threatened her life, but he hadn't so much as glanced at her chest. Not like the smarmy Christian.

"They're all the same," the woman said. "*All* of them."

"That's not true," Morgen said. "Now, get off my property so I can put out that fire. Put out your *arson*. How the hell did you think burning down the barn would help *me*?"

"He was supposed to be *in* it, not riding around with you. You're a fool to trust him at your side. The minute you try to sell the woods, he'll tear your throat out."

The headlights of the approaching fire engine flashed through the trees.

One of the witches swore and grabbed the arms of the other two. "We have to go."

They ran between the house and the burning barn and into the woods.

Two fire engines *and* a sheriff's department SUV pulled into the clearing. By now, the barn roof was collapsing, and the sides of the loft apartment were charred black. The witches might not have succeeded in burning Amar to death, but they'd destroyed his home. And possibly all of the furniture and projects he'd been working on in the barn below.

Distressed on his behalf, Morgen turned to help him as the firemen leaped from their trucks.

He was naked and on his knees, a fist pressed into the grass, his jaw clenched as he glared at the earth. Thinking of his admission that shifting form hurt, she could only imagine what being knocked back mid-change did. And the witches had clearly been hurting him further with their magic.

Morgen didn't know if she could believe them, but if they'd come here to *help* her, this was her fault. She dropped to her knees beside Amar and risked putting a hand on his bare shoulder.

"I'm sorry. Is there anything I can get you? Tylenol?" She had some in her purse. "Bandages?" She eyed a cut at his temple that dribbled blood down the side of his face. "Cauliflower puffs? I know you're a fan."

Amar snorted, shook his head, and rose, indifferent to her hand—maybe to her. He gripped the back of his neck, as if some of their magic had struck him there, but he dropped his hand and looked with determination at the barn. "I have to put the fire out."

The firemen were already on that, but he grabbed the garden hose, the grass sodden since it had kept spewing out water while the witches worked him over, and strode toward the barn. She didn't think the firemen needed him, but she couldn't blame him for wanting to help. After all, that was his home. She didn't know how long he'd lived there, but it must have been a while to accumulate all that wood and start so many projects. Projects that might be little more than ash now.

Morgen shook her head, again feeling for him, but he only glared at the flames and shot hose water onto the barn, standing naked in the orange light of the fire.

A deputy headed toward her, nobody commenting on the

naked man on the lawn, and Morgen braced herself to answer questions. But a distant bark came from the house, and she spun toward it.

"Lucky?"

She waved to the deputy and shouted that she would be right back, then ran into the house. She charged straight up to the second floor where she'd left off her search. The library door was shut, and she didn't think she'd left it that way. Had the witches come into the house to snoop around and locked Lucky in there when he'd barked at them?

She raced and opened it.

Lucky jumped up, putting his paws on her shoulders, and knocking her into the wall. He licked her face before dropping to all fours and running toward the stairs.

"Wait, boy," she blurted, afraid he would charge outside and be hurt or get in the way.

She chased him out of the house, prepared to lunge after him if he ran toward the fire. But he veered abruptly from the steps to the closest bush, where he lifted his leg. She slumped against the railing.

"I guess I was gone for a while," she admitted as he continued. And *continued*. "My apologies. I did bring back dinner."

Though she didn't know when she would get a chance to make it. The deputy had spotted her and was heading her way again. What she would tell him, she didn't know. The witches had disappeared into the woods. She hoped she never saw them again, but she doubted she would be that lucky.

16

AFTER FEEDING LUCKY AND SPENDING TIME ON HER LAPTOP researching software inventory solutions for Phoebe, Morgen grabbed a camp lantern and walked out to the barn. What *remained* of the barn. Most of the roof and the top halves of the walls on two sides had burned before the firefighters had been able to douse the flames. If the three witches hadn't interfered, maybe Amar could have done more to get the fire out earlier but probably not. The garden hose hadn't been sufficient for the task.

Morgen looked for him as she padded across the damp grass, charred pieces of wood littering the lawn. The photographer would have to be selective in what he or she took pictures of in the morning. Even though the witches had spoken of driving out—or killing—Amar, Morgen suspected they'd heard about the upcoming real-estate listing somehow and wanted to make sure her attempt to sell the property went badly. She couldn't imagine what reason they would have for targeting Amar now, when he'd presumably lived here for years.

Though she supposed she didn't know that. She still didn't know much about him. He could have moved in three months earlier and might only have remained to, as Phoebe suggested, keep an eye on Wolf Wood and make sure the new owner didn't sell it.

Maybe Morgen was naive to call him her protector. Even if he was helping her, it would only last as long as she agreed not to sell the property. What would he do if she changed her mind about that?

She didn't plan to. And remembering him the way he'd been the first night they'd met was enough to make her wish to stay on his good side. If she couldn't do that, she had better get out of the area as quickly as possible.

Morgen found Amar inside the barn, his clothing back on but sodden from the water dripping from the charred remains of the rafters. The stars were visible between them, moonlight shining onto puddles on the ashy cement floor. The farther she walked in, the stronger the scent of wet burned wood grew.

The stairs that had once led up to the loft apartment were gone, most of the wood flooring up there burned away. Since she'd never been in Amar's home, she didn't know what furnishings and personal belongings he'd lost, but it might have been everything he owned, save for the extra clothing and whatever else he kept in his truck.

It was his woodworking projects that held his focus now. Even with her lantern driving back the shadows, he barely seemed to notice her enter. He was too absorbed in wandering between the tables, chairs, benches, and other furnishings, many now charred beyond saving, all of them sodden. Some of the ones that had been finished and sealed, and had missed the brunt of the flames, might be salvageable, but Morgen wasn't sure about the rest.

"I'm sorry you got caught up in this." She stopped several feet away, afraid to get too close.

He might lash out, blaming her for what had happened. Even though she'd never seen those witches before, never known anything about witches at all even two days ago, she couldn't help but feel that her problems were trampling over him.

"Now you know," he said so softly that she barely heard him, "why werewolves hate witches."

He rubbed the back of his neck.

"Yeah, those three seemed kind of bitchy." It was an understatement—they'd been *torturing* him—but Morgen didn't feel she knew him well enough to slather him with sympathy. She'd never been good at that anyway. Her family had always opted for making jokes over expressing feelings. Clever word play was admired. Admissions of emotions less so.

Amar slanted her a sidelong look that was hard to read. *"Kind of."*

"Do you want to stay in the house tonight?" Morgen glanced up at the destroyed apartment. Even though the idea of him wandering around in the same house she slept in was uncomfortably intimate, she had to offer. She didn't want him to have to sleep in his truck or curled up as a wolf in the woods.

"No."

"There are plenty of rooms. And Lucky doesn't mind sharing."

There was that sidelong look again.

"I'll even make you breakfast. I bought cantaloupe and granola and... sausages." She realized he might not like her admittedly faux sausages, but how fussy could one be after having one's home burned down?

"What are long-pause sausages?"

"Technically, they're plant-based breakfast patties."

"The rest of the Lobos would beat me up if I ate something as girlie as that."

Rest of the. As if he still considered himself a part of the pack. Morgen wondered what had happened, but given how frosty he'd gotten when she'd glanced at a mere picture in his glove compartment, she wouldn't pry.

"First off, *boys* become vegetarians too. And second, if you can't ooze sufficient manly menace after eating plant-based sausages, that's more of a personal problem than anything wrong with the food."

He grunted and pulled a few shop towels out of an ash-covered locker in the back and started drying off his projects.

"Do you want help?" Morgen asked.

He didn't answer at first, merely focusing on wiping water off a table, and she thought about leaving. She'd made her offer. He could accept it or not.

But he surprised her by tossing a couple of folded towels toward her. She set down the lantern where it would provide light for both of them, though werewolves could probably see in the dark, and started drying a table with a pedestal support made from braided branches of gnarled wood.

"Tonight, I will hunt," Amar said, "and tomorrow, I will start rebuilding the barn."

"You don't have to do that."

Even with the woodworking tools that appeared to have survived the fire largely unscathed, she couldn't imagine one man taking on such a large project.

"It has been my home. Gwen let me live here without paying rent. All she asked was that I helped out with repairs to the property and kept an eye on things. I will rebuild the barn." His firm tone made it a promise, if not a vow.

Morgen didn't fight him on it. In truth, she found that she didn't want him to leave, not with so many threats lurking. The local witches and werewolves all seemed to have it out for her. Maybe she was being a fool for chumming up to Phoebe.

"Thank you," she said. "How long have you—did you—live here?"

"Three years. Ever since..." Amar shifted to another piece of furniture. "Never mind."

"Ever since you left your pack?" she guessed.

"It is not my pack. It is Pedro's."

"Who's he?"

Not the schlub who'd pestered her in the truck, she hoped. No, the werewolves who'd come to the truck had spoken about Pedro. Pedro and Maria.

For a moment, Amar's eyes seemed haunted, more pained than they'd been when the witches had been tormenting him.

"My brother," he said quietly.

"Did he kick you out?"

"I would prefer not to discuss this."

"Sure. Sorry. I shouldn't have pried."

"Not about me, no. You should pry to find Gwen's killer." Did that look imply he was irritated with her lack of progress?

Morgen bristled. It wasn't as if she could snap her fingers and figure everything out. Usually, she liked puzzles, but she was overwhelmed by this strange new world she'd landed in. To hope to solve a mystery after two days wasn't reasonable.

Still, she made herself say, "I know. I'm working on it." After the night he'd had, she could refrain from sarcastic retorts. "I'm doing a favor for Phoebe, and I'm hoping she'll give me more information. I doubt she knows who may have arranged Grandma's death, but she must know a lot about town and the witches here. I'm going to show her the bone clip the next time I see her. I'll also ask her who the heck those three arsonists were."

Amar grew still, his towel pausing mid-wipe. "What kind of *favor* will you do for her?"

"I'm bringing her shop into the modern age so she can take orders over the internet. It'll be a big project. Hopefully, she'll be suitably appreciative."

"You shouldn't get into bed with her."

"I'm helping her with inventory, not becoming her business

partner. Or her sex partner. Whatever the hell you're implying." It was getting harder for her not to retort with sarcasm.

"Her sister used to prey on the young werewolves in the area. The Loups *and* the Lobos. She ensorcelled them and took them to her bed."

"I got the impression her sister is dead."

"She has not been seen in town for a time. That doesn't mean she's dead."

"Well, has Phoebe done those things? She can't be blamed for her sister."

"She has done *plenty* to our kind. With her magic, she can take control of a bird or an animal. Or a *werewolf*." Amar growled low in his throat, sounding more like a wolf than a man, and touched the back of his neck again. "You should not become her ally. Or learn her ways."

"I'm just trying to find out more about my heritage. I'm not going to learn how to ensorcel any werewolves or anyone at all." Morgen shifted uneasily, thinking of Phoebe's certainty about Grandma, that she'd cast a spell over Amar to make him her protector. Was there any truth to that?

"All you need to learn is who killed Gwen. You don't have to become a witch."

"Trust me, it was never a life goal for me." Even if she was somewhat intrigued by it, Morgen wouldn't admit it to him, not when he was bristling like a dog. Like a *wolf*. "I just want to be able to protect myself while I'm here. And help out my werewolf friend when he's attacked by a gaggle of witches or three other werewolves."

"I did not ask for your help," Amar said. "I can take care of myself."

"Fine," she said curtly, annoyed that he wouldn't acknowledge that she'd been useful. "Next time, you can fight a pack by yourself. And you know what? You can clean up this mess by yourself too." Morgen left the towels, grabbed her lantern, and stalked for the door.

He was impossible. She shouldn't have tried talking to him.

"Stop," Amar said and strode after her.

Morgen paused in the doorway and looked back, still wary around him, still not certain what he would do if he lost his temper.

He slowed down as he approached, lifted a hand toward her, then dropped it. Surprisingly, he seemed as hesitant to get close to her as she was to him. Because she had witch blood? She shook her head bleakly.

"I misspoke," Amar said. "Your help was not unappreciated."

"That's vague. Who appreciated it? The wolf I torched?" As soon as she spoke, she regretted it. He was trying to apologize. She shouldn't make it difficult.

"*I* appreciated your help," he said before she could apologize for her sarcasm. "And I appreciated seeing Pierre's belly fur lit on fire."

"Good. I also thought he looked better in flames."

Amar smiled faintly. "Yes. I... do not blame you for wishing to learn to defend yourself. There are many dangers here. But perhaps you would enjoy a firearm or a crossbow more than witch magic. I could show you how to use such weapons."

"A crossbow? You don't think that's a little antiquated?"

"Casting hexes, poxes, and turning men into goats are also antiquated, but that doesn't stop the local witches from such practices."

"Oh? Are there a lot of goat men in town?"

"Rumors abound about a herd of goats up on Seaview Point." He pointed toward a distant mountaintop.

"Given how poorly I did at sports as a kid, I think an academic way of protecting myself might be more up my alley. I was more of a mathlete than an athlete."

"*Math*lete?"

"Yeah. There was a team at my high school. In the mornings before classes, we practiced solving problems and memorizing trivia and theorems, and in the afternoons, we competed against other schools in math bowls."

He mouthed, "Math bowls," then shook his head.

"Memorizing incantations would be my cup of tea. But look: I promise I'm not going to hex or pox you. Or turn you into a goat. I'm sure you'd find that a huge demotion from being a wolf."

"Yes."

"Though goats aren't picky eaters, so I bet I could interest one in my plant-based breakfast patties."

"Also your rose bushes, draperies, and bootlaces."

"*Exactly*. Not picky. Goats are amenable creatures. Not at all surly and gruff like werewolves."

Amar opened his mouth, as if he would object to these adjectives, but he closed it again. "Just be careful around the local witches. They are... our enemies. I appreciate that you defended my honor tonight, even though you do not know me well." He stepped forward and rested a hand on her shoulder. "I do not want you to become an enemy."

"I don't want that either." Morgen looked up at his face, touched by what was, for the first time, gentleness in his eyes. It made him seem far more approachable than usual, even appealing. Not that he hadn't been that before. It was hard not to notice the inherent sex appeal of all those chiseled muscles. "I should go back to the house," she said, halting her mind before it could wander down a dangerous road.

"Very well." He lowered his hand.

A part of her wished he hadn't. It had felt nice to have someone close. She wasn't cold and aloof, damn it. She liked having people around and occasionally being touched and appreciated.

"I will accept your offer of lodgings until such time that I'm able to rebuild the barn," Amar said.

"Okay. Good." Morgen smiled and meant it, though as she walked back to the house, she remembered his talk of hunting and hoped she didn't wake to deer organs or rabbit steaks being fried up in the kitchen.

17

DESPITE PHOEBE'S PROMISE THAT ONE COULDN'T LEARN WITCHCRAFT from books, Morgen was absorbing a lot as she inventoried Grandma's root cellar and created entries in a database she'd made for everything from civet paste to dogbane fiber to dried mugwort to sea urchin spines to coffin nails. What she couldn't find was much on bones. The internet promised her they played a role in some types of witchcraft, but in all of Grandma's odd collections, bones didn't make an appearance, and few of her books mentioned them.

"*Teeth* are where it's at," Morgen muttered, closing a grimoire that touted their natural affinity for magic.

Fossilized teeth, in particular, supposedly had inherent power, with great value being placed on those from the repeated glaciations of the Pleistocene epoch. According to the text, magic had been more concentrated among the fewer species that had lived in those difficult times. Some of the tusks and teeth from animals such as mammoths and cave bears were supposed to lend themselves well to curses, luck charms, and even tokens that could increase one's charisma or sex appeal.

It sounded like a bunch of mumbo jumbo. Nonetheless, unlike with the bones she'd hunted for and not found, Morgen discovered a couple of boxes of yellowed teeth on Grandma's shelves. The origins of most were unidentifiable, the choppers simply dumped together like bottle caps in a kid's shoebox collection, and it set Morgen's organization-loving jaws to clenching. But there was one neatly segmented plastic crafting container of twelve large teeth, each labeled in faded pencil. Perhaps those were more valuable—more magical?—than the others?

If the labels could be believed, the box contained a dire-wolf fang, parts of several mammoth tusks and woolly-rhinoceros horns, and two giant ground-sloth teeth.

"Funny how giant ground sloths never came up in the *Bewitched* reruns I saw as a girl," Morgen muttered as she pulled out her phone and read an online article on the extinct creatures. "Though there was a lot of nose crinkling in that show. Maybe it was inspired by the prehensile lips of the ground sloth."

Rustling and scraping came from the back of the root cellar. If Lucky hadn't been down there with her, Morgen would have expected rats. Instead, she suspected Lucky *smelled* a rat.

"Don't knock anything over back there," she said. "I haven't gotten to those boxes yet."

She set down the container of teeth and looked around. There were a *lot* of boxes she hadn't gotten to yet. Inventorying the contents of the cellar could take months, especially since she wanted to record what everything was and what it did, not simply stack things neatly on shelves. Maybe she should have remained focused on bones, but she kept getting distracted by all the things she *could* find down there. Even though she never would have considered witchery and all of its paraphernalia a passion, or even a vague interest, she had to admit that all the quirky old stuff was kind of cool. Who else's grandmother had dire-wolf fangs in the basement?

"Wait," Morgen breathed as Lucky's tail thwacked against something. "What if that magical clip from the motorcycle isn't made from bone? What if it's part of a tooth?"

She pulled it from the drawer where she'd tucked it for safe-keeping. Even though the root-cellar doors only opened for her if she had the amulet, she wouldn't put it past other witches to know how to get in, and since they'd been skulking around the property and setting things on fire, robbery might be right up their alley.

With the amulet on, the magical clip didn't buzz her, so she examined it from all sides, holding it up to the light from the single bulb hanging from the ceiling. If it had been in its original state, she trusted she would have been able to tell if it was a tooth or a bone, but it had been carved from a larger piece and polished, so she had no idea. An archaeologist might be able to tell, but what were the odds of finding one in town, wandering around with an *RV Life* T-shirt on?

"Maybe a werewolf would know." Morgen thought of the tooth that Amar wore on a thong around his neck.

That didn't necessarily make him an aficionado, but who knew. Maybe ancient teeth smelled different from ancient bones.

The rumble of a car sounded as Morgen climbed the steps to the yard, and a sedan with *Soto Real Estate Photography* on the side rolled into view.

Morgen swore and checked the time on her phone. She'd only meant to spend a couple of hours that morning organizing and then tidy up the house before the photographer arrived.

Admittedly, she didn't *want* to sell the property—and she suspected whoever put in an offer would care a lot more about the woods than the presence or absence of tidiness—but she always kept things back home neat and clutter-free, so it felt like a failing not to have properly prepared the house.

Sawing noises came from the top of the barn, along with the sounds of nails being ripped free. Amar sat astraddle a truss, pulling off burned wood and tossing it into a growing pile in the grass below.

The photographer, a middle-aged woman in a dress and heels, stepped out of the car and frowned at the charred barn.

"You can leave that out of the pictures," Morgen said, waving to her.

Realizing she didn't want anyone taking photos of the root cellar, she whistled for Lucky so she could close and lock the doors.

He bounded up the stairs with something that looked like a wig clenched between his teeth. Morgen *hoped* that was what it was, not that he'd found a dead gopher or raccoon in the root cellar. Surely, she would have smelled something like that, right? Unfortunately, his bounding took him straight toward the photographer.

She shrieked when he dropped his find at her feet. He wagged his tail and sat, as he'd been taught, for petting.

"What is that?" The woman pointed at the furry thing, horror contorting her face.

"Something I haven't inventoried yet," Morgen muttered and firmly closed the root-cellar doors.

The good news was that Lucky hadn't found a dead animal. The bad news was that it was some kind of fur hide from what had previously been an animal. Later, Morgen would have to look up hair and fur as it related to witchcraft, though she was far more interested in teeth at the moment.

"Hi, I'm Morgen. That's Lucky. He's friendly."

"And what is *that*?" The woman was still pointing at the fur.

"Something he found in the root cellar. This was my grand-mother's house. You know how it is when you clean out a relative's home. I'm finding all sorts of quirky stuff." Like giant ground-sloth teeth.

"Yes. Ah." The photographer made a point of taking several

steps from the lump of fur. She didn't pat Lucky, which confused him, since he adored all people and assumed they would adore and pet him. "I'm Joyce Soto. This should take about a half hour."

"Great." Morgen petted Lucky so he wouldn't feel bereft and waved for the photographer to head to the house. "I'd suggest taking more pictures of the woods and the property than the house, but you do whatever you think is best."

"What happened to the barn?" Joyce gazed up at Amar.

"We're remodeling."

"Do you want... pictures of it?"

"Maybe one from a distance that doesn't show the burned side. *Sides.* There's some cool artwork on the door that you could take a picture of." Morgen hadn't yet asked Amar how he'd done that. With the blowtorch? It looked burned into the wood rather than carved.

"Perhaps *just* the door."

Morgen let Joyce into the house, then trotted to the barn. "Amar? Can you come down for a minute? I have a question about the clip."

If it turned out to be made from tooth and she could figure out what kind of animal it had come from, she might have more of a lead than she'd had earlier that morning. She wondered if Phoebe sold teeth in her store and if she knew anything about them. Or maybe someone else in town sold them. And remembered who'd wandered in a couple of months earlier to buy one?

Amar ripped off a few more burned pieces of wood before sliding across a creaking beam toward the edge of the roof. Morgen held her breath as he swung over the side and jumped down without a ladder, landing in a deep crouch. If she tried that, she would break both legs.

"You didn't bring me more food, did you?" Amar stopped in front of her and eyed her warily.

"No, I've been working in the cellar. And you said you liked the cantaloupe."

"It was edible. The faux meat products were disgusting. If you're a vegetarian, why don't you just eat vegetables?"

"Vegetables don't have protein."

"I thought the watermelon seeds did."

"Those do, but it's nice to eat something warm and kind of similar to things I used to enjoy."

"You used to enjoy meat?"

"I used to enjoy bacon cheeseburgers from Wendy's."

His lip curled, as if he put that in the same category as her quasi-sausage patties. "I will bring you delicious elk steaks one day. *That* is meat."

"Thanks, but I'm trying to cut back on elk too. Here's my question." Morgen held up the clip. "I should have asked before. Can you tell if this is made from bone, which I assumed, or was it a tooth?"

"It's a tusk," Amar said, barely glancing at it. "Ivory."

"You're sure? It's been carved and polished so much. How can you tell?" She held it up to the wan sunlight filtering through the clouds.

"Bones have tiny pores where blood vessels ran through them when the animal was alive. Ivory is dead matter that grows on the outside of the animal, like fingernails. Bones taste better."

Morgen blinked at that addendum. "Got a nice crunch, do they? Like popcorn?"

He grinned at her, showing off his teeth. "The marrow is the best. You crack open the bone and lick it out."

"Are you purposely trying to disgust me?"

"You brought up fast-food cheeseburgers. I assumed that was to disgust me. No real predator would eat such mutilated, unappealing dreck."

"Lucky likes them."

Amar gazed toward the lawn where Lucky was rolling on his back in the grass—no, he was rolling on that awful hide. "That is not a real predator. That is a *pet*."

"I guess I can't argue with that. Is there any chance you can tell what kind of animal this tusk came from? The teeth from different animals apparently have different inherent magic. Also, maybe I could figure out if someone in town sells them." Not that she'd seen any signs on Main Street that said *mastodon tusks, inquire within*.

"The crystal witch sells many things." Amar took the clip from her and sniffed it but shook his head. "It is very old. Any scent that would have come from the animal has long faded and been covered by the polishing process. Perhaps, with a microscope, it would be possible to tell. Or you could cut it open and get a sample to examine."

Considering the thing had zapped her when she'd touched it, she couldn't imagine what it might do if she tried to drill a hole in it.

"I'll show Phoebe and see if she knows."

Morgen kept herself from saying that she was heading back to her shop this afternoon. Amar had made it clear that he didn't think she should associate herself with the witch. But Phoebe had answers, and Morgen wanted them.

"She may be the one who sold it to the murderer." His eyes narrowed. "Or she may have done it herself. If so, she will not answer you truthfully."

"Maybe I won't bring it up until I inventory everything in her store and see if I find any tusks for sale. I'll have to do that anyway to get her online store set up."

"Most people would find such a task onerous, but you sound excited."

Yes, because the idea of solving crimes through examining

evidence was a hell of a lot more appealing than asking strangers questions and risking getting into confrontations.

"One of my passions is wrangling data into easily searchable databases, and nothing gets me excited like figuring out how to provide a tidy way to access sequestered silos of information." Morgen realized from his forehead crinkle that her explanation may have sounded a tad... nerdy. "I like helping people keep track of their stuff," she clarified. "You can't run an efficient business if you don't know what you have."

Lucky trotted over to them with his prize clutched in his teeth again. Morgen grimaced and wondered how offended he would be if she tossed that in the trash.

He always approached warily when she was with Amar, and he did so now, dropping low to his belly to slink closer and deposit it at his feet.

"He's willing to give you gifts, even though you insulted his culinary tastes," Morgen said.

"He recognizes a superior predator and is acting with proper submissive behavior."

"By giving you an old hide?"

"It's a beaver pelt."

"Hm. Do you think it has magical properties? My grandmother must have kept it for a reason, right?" Morgen jogged to the truck. She'd taken most of the groceries into the house, but there was one item she'd left outside, because she'd known she would use it in the root cellar. "Here we are."

She tore it free of its packaging—frustration-free, yeah, right— and returned to Amar. Lucky was now lying on his back with his legs in the air. Amar deigned to pat his belly, though Morgen didn't think that was a wolf thing. Maybe it was an I'm-a-bit-of-a-softy-under-my-grumpy-predator-mien thing.

Using the label maker, she typed out *beaver pelt* and stuck it to the clump of fur. While Lucky was distracted, she returned it to the root cellar.

"I'm all done," the photographer was reporting to Amar when Morgen returned. "I'll send the pictures over to Mr. Christian as soon as I have some wifi. I know he's eager to get this property on the market."

Even though Morgen had explained her ruse to Amar, he glared at the poor woman.

"Thank you," Morgen said, hurrying to step between them. She doubted Amar would do anything more threatening than glaring, but there was no need to tempt fate. "I appreciate you coming all the way out here."

Joyce grimaced at the mud spattered on the sides of her sedan. "Mr. Christian paid me a bonus." She eyed the charred barn and glanced back toward where the beaver pelt had been before Morgen put it away. "I should have asked for more."

"Tell him he'll have to pay double if he wants the really good pictures."

"Really good pictures?" Joyce glanced skeptically back at the house.

"Or for you to withhold the really bad pictures?" Morgen suggested.

Joyce snorted. "That's closer to the truth."

"I'm going to run into town," Morgen told Amar once the photographer left. "Do you need anything to help with the rebuild?"

She waved at the barn, though she had no idea what she could have picked up if he asked. As far as she'd seen, there wasn't a hardware store in Bellrock, and she was only going as far as the Crystal Parlor.

"Such as geodes, crystals, and polished carvings?" Apparently, Amar knew exactly where Morgen was going.

"Yes. I saw a pretty amethyst heart that would go great over the door."

"I was thinking of putting the beaver pelt up there." He pantomimed nailing something to a wall. "Since it was a gift from your dog."

"Your decorating tastes are as questionable as your food tastes."

"Do you want me to go with you to town?"

"That's all right. I'll probably be there a while, and I'm sure you would rather be working on something than loitering against the wall outside."

"Stay away from the Timber Wolf."

"Oh, trust me. The meat trolley isn't calling me back."

"And take a weapon," he said.

A weapon? Like what? "Are you offering your blowtorch?"

"Since you aren't interested in crossbows, perhaps a witch weapon." His lips twisted, but he didn't take back the suggestion. "Aren't there wands in that cellar?"

"Yes, but I wouldn't know what to do with one." Morgen thought of the witches who had forced Amar to his knees with wands and wasn't sure she *wanted* to know how to use one. Such power would be handy if one were attacked by enemies, but she didn't want to hurt people.

"My experience is that you say supercilious things about how much better than a werewolf you are, point it, mutter something arcane, and zap your target."

"I would guess that first part is optional."

"Not that I've noticed," he said glumly.

She had the urge to hug him, but just because he'd deigned to touch her the night before didn't mean he wanted frequent physical contact from her. "I suppose I could take one and ask Phoebe how to work it."

She expected him to object, since he objected to everything about her.

"Yes," was what he said. "It's good to be able to defend yourself."

"Right." Once more, she returned to the root cellar. She eyed the three wands she'd found so far, two made from wood and one from silver, but opted for a much larger weapon. The staff with the antler horns attached to the top. If she couldn't learn how to summon its magic, she could prong enemies with the points.

Amar watched blandly as she marched past with it and tried several different angles before managing to fit it in the car around the dog crate.

Lucky, refusing to be left in the house this time, hopped into the back with it. Since Morgen worried the property might be in further danger, and that something could happen to her dog if she left him alone, she didn't mind. But she gave him the squinty eye when he sniffed the antlers with interest.

"Those aren't chew toys," she said. "No noshing."

That earned her a whine of protest. It only lasted until she turned the car on and rolled down the window so he could stick his head out.

"Good luck." Amar grabbed his hammer and returned to the barn roof.

As Morgen drove off, she wondered if she should have asked him to come along after all. She'd been thinking about defending herself in town, but if those three witches returned to the property, *he* might need protection.

But as long as the barn wasn't burning, and he wasn't distracted by trying to put it out, she doubted they would be able to sneak up on him again. She hoped.

18

"You don't mind if I take a core sample?" Phoebe asked.

Two hours into setting up the new computer and organizing the store, Morgen had casually brought out the bone—tusk—clip and asked her opinion on it.

"Not at all," Morgen said. "I'd like to know what animal it came from, and why it's oozing menacing magic."

"*Menacing* magic? Magic isn't good or evil. This has innate magic, but hm, there *is* something else."

"Yeah, menace."

Morgen expected a frown, but Phoebe only cocked her head as she rubbed the clip between her fingers and examined it.

"It's... almost familiar."

"Do you sell any ivory?" Morgen had searched every square foot of the store as part of her inventory, and she hadn't seen any, but maybe the Crystal Parlor had secret niches.

"Oh, not anymore. We used to sell a few pieces here and there, but the tourists were always asking us if we'd imported it illegally and how many elephants had been poached to finance our operation. They were *fossilized* tusks, mind you, and from mammoths and other prehistoric animals. Poaching was presumably at a minimum back then. But the tourists didn't get it, and it was annoying to deal with their accusations. The fossils weren't *for* them anyway. I'll happily sell crystals to all, but certain items are only intended as ingredients and only for our kind."

Even though Phoebe didn't give Morgen a significant look, she seemed to include her in that *our kind* category. It felt odd, since Morgen had spent all of her life not fitting into any categories, at least not those created by normal people. She and her sister—both awkward, bookish introverts, who got along better with animals than humans—had always struggled to gain friends and feel wanted.

If Morgen learned more about her blood, would she get along with—be accepted by—witches? Did she even want that?

Witches hated werewolves, three of them had half-burned down her grandmother's barn, and Phoebe was only helping her because she had been able to come up with a way to help her first.

"What happened to the ones you didn't sell?" Morgen asked.

"Oh, I'm not even sure. My sister was the one who set up and took down the display case." Phoebe shook her head sadly. "She was always more of a crafter of talismans, idols, and tools than I. Potions and tinctures are more my specialty." She held up a finger. "I'll be right back."

Phoebe stepped over Lucky, who had grown bored with the inventory process, and was snoozing in the doorway between the front room and the back room, but only frowned briefly down at him. Morgen was glad Phoebe had let her bring him in. She hadn't wanted to leave him in the car where he might be too warm—or where werewolves might target him to get at her. The thought made her shiver with dread.

Phoebe returned to the front room with something that looked like a microscope, though the blue and purple crystals embedded all over the casing were atypical for scientific equipment. She also carried an electric jewelry drill, something that looked out of place in the shop full of rocks and powders.

"Are you sure it won't zap you?" Morgen asked as Phoebe bent over the clip to take a sample.

"I'm protected from magic by numerous amulets and talismans."

"But are you sure it won't zap you?"

"Mostly."

"Reassuring."

Phoebe thumbed on the drill and applied it to one of the fatter parts of the tusk clip. Morgen held her breath, certain the thing would zap one or both of them. Or cause the ceiling to fall, the street to flood, and an earthquake to swallow the town.

Nothing happened. Phoebe took the sample and put it on a slide to examine.

"I was reading about those prehistoric tusks and teeth," Morgen said, "and how some of them are ideal for certain types of magic, such as luck charms, and others have a propensity toward other types. Such as curses."

Curses that caused brakes on a motorcycle to fail?

"That is what many of the grimoires suggest," Phoebe said. "As I said, I'm not a crafter myself, so I couldn't tell you much, but I do know that saber-toothed tiger and dire-wolf fangs are very desirable in the crafter community."

"The, uh, *witch* crafter community?"

"Yes. Mammoth tusks are popular too. I believe you can make charisma charms out of those. Who doesn't like being more charismatic?"

"My sister."

"Pardon?"

"She's kind of aloof. Except with orangutans."

Phoebe peered at her.

"Never mind. My family is just a bit eccentric. Let me know if you find anything, please. And thanks."

As Phoebe focused again on the sample she'd taken, Morgen returned to the computer and entering inventory into the new system, using a few of her favorite programs to make the process quicker. More quirky information on gems, crystals, and rocks than she would have guessed existed popped up.

Her phone buzzed while she was photographing and labeling chunks of amber.

"Hi, Zoe," she answered. "What's up?"

"You listed the *house*?"

"Ah, you saw that? From Seattle?"

"I've been monitoring Whatcom County listings to get comps. Just in case. *Morgen*. You said you weren't going to list it and that if you did, you'd use me. I already did research for you."

"I know." Morgen lowered her voice so Phoebe wouldn't overhear. "I'm not going to sell it. I'm just hoping to get offers and that one of them will be..." She remembered that she hadn't shared with her cousin that Grandma might have been murdered. "There's been some hinky stuff going on here. Someone lit the barn on fire last night. I want to know who's behind trying to get Grandma's property and why."

"So... you hired an agent, got him to do a bunch of work and pay for photos, and you're not planning to sell? You know he only makes money if a deal closes, right?"

"Yeah, but he's a dick. He deserves getting shafted."

"That's evil, Morgen."

"He was trying to talk Grandma into going into an old-folks home and listing the property for months before her crash."

"Really? Okay, he's a dick. Now I'm glad you didn't have me do the listing."

"I thought you might be."

"Hey, do you think..." Zoe also lowered her voice. "Do you

think Grandma's crash maybe wasn't an accident? Or have I been watching too many crime shows?"

"Well, the barn being lit on fire wasn't an accident, so who knows? I'll let you know what I find."

"You're not in danger, are you?"

Morgen snorted. She was in *so* much danger that she was not only worrying about herself but about the brawny killer werewolf she'd left working on the barn. Somewhere along the way, it had stopped seeming strange.

"I'm serious," Zoe said. "Maybe you should talk to the police."

Morgen had spent an hour talking to the authorities the night before, describing the three women she'd told them she'd seen running into the woods. She'd been reluctant to share that they'd been witches—not wanting to be dragged off to a mental institution by people who hadn't heard the news that witches and werewolves were lurking all over Bellrock—and that they'd threatened her werewolf friend. But she had described them in detail. A female deputy had written everything down, but Morgen doubted anything would come of it.

"I've already talked with the sheriff, three deputies, the fire marshal, and a first responder who insisted on taking my blood pressure and checking my oxygen levels because I looked stressed. I was more frazzled than stressed by that point." She'd also been worried about Amar being singed since he'd been firefighting naked after his failed attempt to shift forms.

"I wish Jun were there with you."

"Why, because he's such a big and intimidating man? I used to beat him at arm wrestling."

"Strange that it didn't work out."

"Ha ha. Do you want anything else?"

"Just be careful. Did you really say the barn burned down? Do you want *me* to come up this weekend?"

"No, thanks."

A part of Morgen wouldn't have minded if some of her family came up, but as far as she knew, none of them knew anything about grandmother's secret retirement career, nor how weird this town was. She didn't want to get them in trouble.

Another call came in, a familiar local number. Magnus Christian.

"I've got to go. Bye."

Zoe made a disgruntled noise as she hung up.

"Hello, Mr. Christian," Morgen said after she switched over.

"Please, call me Magnus. I've already received an offer on the property."

"Oh? That was fast."

Way too fast. She'd assumed prospective buyers would come out to see the house and that she, Lucky, and Amar could scope them out, those two with their superior canine senses, and her with the intelligent and probing questions she would casually ask while standing back and acting like a wallflower.

"Yes. It's wonderful when it works out that way. Mind if I come up to the house in person to present it to you? I'll be in the neighborhood later."

"Uh, I'm in town. Maybe we could meet at that coffee shop that you spoke so highly of."

The one he'd called froufrou and flavor-free.

"The coffee shop closes at four. I'm down in Sedro-Woolley, so it would be closer for me to meet you at the house. I've got a bottle of celebratory wine and some cinnamon rolls from the bakery here that I'd love to share with you. Not that you have to take this first offer, mind you. You might want to wait and see what else comes in, but it's all cash, which is amazing on an estate that size. The seller is giving you twenty-four hours to respond."

"Isn't it unusual for the potential buyer not to come out to see the house before making an offer?"

Unless this person had already *been* to the house and knew all about the property. Just how long had those three witches been snooping around inside and locking Lucky in the library before lighting the barn on fire? They'd said they didn't want the land sold, but it wasn't as if Morgen could trust arsonists.

"It's not that rare in a hot market and when they're more interested in developing the land than in the house. I'm sure they're just planning to tear it down. They didn't even care that the barn had recently caught fire."

How handy.

"Can you give me their name?" Morgen's fingers twitched. She was ready to do research.

"I'll get everything together for you and bring it over for you to look at. Meet you at your place at five? The seller did have one contingency, and I'd like to verify it for myself in case you decide to accept the offer."

"What contingency?"

"Something about a pond."

"A pond?" Morgen thought of the little spring that Amar had shown her—and the blue magical mushrooms growing beside it.

"Yes. I did think it odd, but I've learned to accept the eccentricities of buyers and sellers without judging them. You don't even need to worry about it. I'll take a look if I get there before you."

"All right. I'll meet you up there, but wait before wandering around, please. My... handyman is there, and he's protective of the place." She wondered if Christian had crossed paths with Amar before. Amar had been around during that first conversation between her and Christian, but she didn't think they'd interacted. "You might want to stay in your truck until I get there. Just to be safe."

"Because of your... handyman?"

"Yes. He was living in the barn, and he's a little grumpy that it was almost burned down."

"Ah. Understandable."

Never mind that Amar had been a little grumpy *before* it was burned too.

"I'm finishing up here, and I'll be on my way. Thanks." Morgen hung up and debated if she should head straight up to the house, but she wanted to hear the results of Phoebe's investigation.

She was about to check on her when two women in their mid-twenties walked into the shop. They wore black dresses, studded black-leather collars, dark lipstick and eye shadow, and had pierced noses and eyebrows.

"Trying a little hard, aren't we?" Morgen muttered.

They frowned at her and glanced around, no doubt looking for Phoebe.

"Who are you?" one asked, sniffing dismissively at Morgen's jeans and hoodie.

Clearly not appropriate attire for a witch.

"Tech support," Morgen said.

"There's *tech* here?"

Lucky bounded down the aisle, thwacking display racks with his tail, to greet the newcomers. One pulled back in horror, as if he were a rabid wolf. The other cooed and bent down to pet him. He accommodated by rearing up on his hind legs and planting his paws on her shoulders.

Morgen snapped her fingers and pointed at the ground. "Sit for petting," she whispered to him.

He dropped down into a sit, his tail swishing back and forth across the floor.

"There's tech *and* a new shop dog," Morgen told them. "I'm bringing the Crystal Parlor into the modern computer- and canine-loving age. Can I help you find something?"

They glanced at each other, the one who thought Lucky was a leper shifting to stand behind her friend.

"I'm sure you can't help," she said. "We need certain special *powders* from the back room."

"Uh huh. In stock, we've got banishing powder, pestilence powder, hexing powder, numerous dried herbs, witch salt, and cascarilla eggshell powder—only one ounce left of that." Since Morgen had just entered those items, it was easy to remember the list. "I believe Phoebe can do custom blends too."

"We'll take a bag of the hexing powder. Oh, and do you have anything to drive away annoying men who won't leave you alone?"

"You'll want to try the hot-foot powder for that," Morgen said. "The instructions are included in the jar."

"Two, please."

When Morgen headed toward the back to get the jars, she found Phoebe watching from the doorway as she tapped the tusk clip to her chin. Morgen hoped that meant she'd learned something about it.

"Are you *sure* you don't want a job working here?" Phoebe asked with amusement after Morgen bagged up the powders and took the women's payment. The Goth look was somewhat diminished by the perky pink Hello Kitty case that one carried her credit cards in.

"Though I'm sure it would be an excellent use of my database-management degree, I've got enough on my plate."

"Are you positive? You seem to be a quick study. You might not be too old to learn after all. I could teach you quite a bit if you stuck around for the summer."

Morgen thought of Amar's warning that she had better watch out for Phoebe and that he would prefer she *not* become a witch. "Let me think about it. Did you, by chance, learn anything about the tusk?"

"I did. It's a saber-tooth tiger tusk. And there's curse magic embedded in it."

"The kind of curse that could cause someone's motorcycle brakes to fail at an inopportune time?"

Phoebe frowned. "I can't tell, but witches are supposed to use their magic only to protect themselves and others, not to kill. We're a peaceful people unless we're driven to violence by those persecuting us. Even then, we prefer to use guile and wit over violence."

"Uh huh. Three witches came out of the woods and lit my barn on fire last night. Without guile."

Phoebe spread a hand. "I can't defend the actions of the younger generation. Know only that I don't teach such methods myself."

"Do you have any idea who made the tusk clip? And put a curse on it?"

Phoebe hesitated, then shook her head. "No."

Morgen, certain she was lying, was tempted to question her further, to try to wheedle the information out, but her face had grown tight, her eyes hard with disapproval. Morgen doubted she would get answers, not if Phoebe was protecting someone she knew. And she probably knew all of the witches in the area.

But would a witch have done it? Cursed Grandma's bike so she would die? If the three witches who'd shown up the night before could be believed, they wanted Wolf Wood preserved, not sold, so they should have wanted Grandma to continue living there.

"Would anyone besides a witch be able to put a curse on a tusk?" Morgen asked.

"Perhaps. There are others who practice magic in the world." Phoebe seemed happy to deflect the onus onto someone else.

Which made Morgen more and more sure it had been a witch. But why?

"Perhaps a werewolf was responsible," Phoebe said.

"I thought they were shaped by magic but couldn't perform it themselves."

"A strong werewolf might *force* a witch to do something for him. If we are prepared, we can handle their kind, but if we are unprepared when they come upon us, we are as mortal as the next woman."

"Maybe I'll ask Amar about it," Morgen said, though she knew he hadn't had anything to do with the clip.

"Yes, but be careful when confronting their kind." Phoebe held up a finger, then retrieved a pen and a piece of paper. "This is a more advanced incantation and usually takes a trained witch to succeed, but perhaps if you practice..."

"Practice what?"

"Make sure to wear your grandmother's amulet. You have the right blood, but that amplifies and enhances abilities that it would otherwise take years to learn to draw out." Phoebe wrote a sentence on a piece of paper. An *incantation*.

Under the moon's magic, turn the snarling hound from angry foe to witch bound.

"Hound?" Morgen asked.

"Our ancient brethren probably struggled to find a rhyme for wolf." Phoebe offered her the paper. "With this incantation, you may be able to control a werewolf, but be very careful. If your magic isn't greater than their innate power, you won't be able to take control. And they tend to get furious and kill you when you try."

Morgen lifted a hand, not wanting it. "That sounds like a good reason not to use it."

She couldn't imagine what Amar would think if she sauntered out with the paper in hand, mumbling as she memorized the words.

"Take it." Phoebe kept her hand out. "Memorize it. You may need it for self-defense, if a werewolf comes after you. Or, if someone else is threatening you, you can force a nearby werewolf to defend you."

"Amar would defend me without a spell."

Phoebe rolled her eyes. "He's not the only werewolf in town, and even if that were true, he can't be around you all the time. Besides, it's entirely possible that *he* was the one to force a witch to craft that clip. Who besides he would have had an easier time getting close to your grandmother—and her motorcycle—to place it?"

Morgen shook her head. "He didn't do it."

"Don't be naive. You've only known him for a few days. There's a reason his pack kicked him out."

She hesitated. "What reason?"

"He's an outcast. I'm sure there's a reason."

Meaning she didn't know. Morgen set her jaw, unwilling to believe Amar was the troublemaker. He'd helped her too many times.

"Take it," Phoebe said softly, shaking the paper. "Just in case. You don't want your life in some furry man's hands."

Morgen stared at the paper, again thinking how furious Amar would be if he learned she'd accepted it. But the phrase was short. She could easily memorize it and get rid of the paper. Then he'd never know. Unless she one day had to use it around him.

Or *on* him? Was it possible he'd lied to her and truly was a danger?

Reluctantly, she took it and stuck it in her pocket. "In case I have a run-in with the Loups again."

"Good." Phoebe nodded curtly. "And here's your clip. It won't work as well now that I've drilled a hole in it, but it should still have some power."

"The power to curse people?"

"Yes."

Morgen was as reluctant to take that as she had been the paper, but it would be better to get rid of it or at least hide it away than to leave it where it might be used for evil again.

"I better go. I have to meet—" Morgen caught herself before saying Christian's name. Since nobody wanted her to sell that property, she had better not let the word get out any more than it already had. "Someone."

"Just be wary of the werewolves," Phoebe said, as if she was sure that was who Morgen was on the way to meet. "They resent us because we can control them, but many of them are brutes, bullies, and savages. They need controlling."

"Not all of them are like that." Morgen realized that her experience with werewolves was very recent and very limited, but she wanted to believe that Amar was a good person. She wished Grandma were still alive so she could consult her. And... just because.

"Don't be too certain."

19

IT WAS GRAY AND DRIZZLY BY THE TIME MORGEN TURNED UP THE long driveway toward the house. Her nerves tangled in her stomach, some strange certainty telling her that this meeting wouldn't go well. Christian hadn't called again, but she couldn't help but feel that it was odd that he'd insisted on coming here. And checking on her pond? What was *that* about?

Lucky whined in his crate.

"You're the one who wanted to come along on errands today." Morgen had taken him for a quick walk at a park in town before heading out, but she hadn't wanted to delay. She didn't like the idea of Christian skulking around the property by himself if she was late. No, not by himself. Amar would have been there, keeping an eye on him. Maybe *threatening* him.

Lucky's tail *thwapped* against the side of the crate. Snuffling noises followed, and Morgen cracked a window. The smell of rain was thick in the air, and water dripped from moss dangling from the tree branches.

When she pulled into the clearing, Christian's Land Rover was there, and there was no sign of Amar. Morgen sighed in relief.

Maybe Amar had been gone the whole time and hadn't been here, threatening the agent.

She parked next to the big SUV and was about to let Lucky out when she spotted clothing on the ground beside Christian's driver-side door. Surprised, and wondering if Amar had stripped out of his jeans and vest again, she peeked around the front of the vehicle. Then reeled back in shock.

It wasn't just clothing but an entire person.

Magnus Christian lay sprawled on his back on the ground, his arms splayed wide. His eyes were open, staring up at the rainy sky, water spattering his face, but he didn't move. His throat was bloody—completely torn out.

Shaking with horror, Morgen stumbled backward. She clipped the bumper of the SUV and pitched to the ground. For a moment, all she could do was stare at the body, her mind refusing to parse that Christian was dead. Dead in her driveway.

Dead... by a werewolf's jaws?

It wasn't dark yet. Maybe it hadn't been a werewolf.

But as she glanced at the gray clouds, she remembered Amar's admission that he could change during the day if the cloud cover was heavy enough.

"Why?" Morgen whispered, digging in her pocket for her phone. "Why would he have killed him?"

She'd told Amar it was all a ruse, that she had no intention of selling the property.

And even if Christian was smarmy, she didn't think he could have been behind Grandma's death. He hadn't wanted the land, just his cut of the money from selling it.

Or so she assumed. What if he'd been in on it? And Amar had found out?

Morgen stared at her phone for a long moment as rain droplets struck the screen. She had to call the sheriff's office, didn't she? But what if they came out here, determined it had been Amar, and hunted him down?

If he'd killed someone, he deserved to be hunted down and imprisoned. Didn't he? Unless he'd been protecting her... or the property.

But even then, it wasn't okay to *kill* people.

Damn it. She rubbed a shaking hand down her face and dialed 9-1-1 for the second time in less than twenty-four hours. If Amar had murdered someone, she couldn't protect him from that, no matter what.

Lucky whined from the car.

"Sorry, buddy," she said. "I can't let you out yet. This is... a murder scene."

The dispatcher answered, and Morgen reported the death, her voice surprisingly calm. Or maybe it was numb. A man was dead in her driveway, and it was her fault. If she hadn't come up with the scheme to list the property, Christian never would have been here.

"Damn it," she said once she hung up. Why did everything keep going wrong?

An intense longing for her old life came to her, her life before the divorce and before she'd lost her job. Back when everything had been normal. Back before everything had fallen apart.

Not wanting to disturb the scene, Morgen started to get back into her car, intending to wait until the sheriff arrived. But she remembered that Christian had been bringing physical information on whoever had made the offer on the property.

Careful not to touch his door with her bare hand, out of some vague notion of the deputies coming and looking for fingerprints, she peered through the window into his passenger seat. Her heartbeat sped up. There was a folder lying in it.

She pulled down her sleeve and tried the door handle. It was damp from the rain, so her fear of leaving fingerprints was probably unfounded, but she didn't want to touch anything or risk somehow incriminating herself. She was a stranger in this town. Who would stand up for her if she ended up a suspect in this murder?

The door wasn't locked. She opened it and lifted the flap of the folder. Inside lay a printout of a real-estate contract. The offer the prospective buyer had put in?

Mason Arbuckle, the name read. There was a phone number.

In the dim light, with rain striking the windshield, Morgen took a picture of the page with the name and number. She turned to the next page, finding an offer for millions of dollars. It was surreal but not as surreal as the fact that she could see Christian's mutilated body through the other window. She tried not to look, but it was hard.

The rumble of a car coming up the driveway floated to her.

Morgen closed the folder, shut the door, and flung herself into the front seat of her car. She hadn't committed this crime, but she felt guilty anyway. Christian had been killed on her property, and she had a strong suspicion who had done it.

"Why, Amar?" she whispered, gripping the wheel, as if she could drive away from this whole mess and wouldn't have to talk to anyone else that day.

She ran a search for Mason Arbuckle and Bellrock, expecting the name to come up in conjunction with land development, but the only instance of it was in an archived online news article from a couple of years earlier. *Internet Entrepreneur Buys Rainwater Estate and Settles into Town.*

The article itself wasn't accessible without a subscription. She tried wider searches, hoping to find what the internet entrepreneur sold, but very little was linked to his name, other than fifteen-year-old track-and-field records from one of the state universities.

"A town named Arbuckle in Mason County, West Virginia. Probably not helpful."

Lucky *thwapped* his tail again.

"I'm afraid dinner is delayed," she muttered, then turned to open his crate, so he could at least have the freedom of the car.

He licked her cheek.

"I'll feed you after this." Morgen glanced in the rearview mirror as not one but two sheriff 's department SUVs parked behind her. "If I don't end up arrested."

Deputy Franklin was one of the drivers. Morgen didn't know whether to be relieved or not that someone familiar had been sent. He headed toward her car as the other man went over to look at the body.

Morgen made herself get out and face Franklin.

"Ma'am," he greeted her gravely. "Do you want to tell me what happened?"

Yeah, it was like with the deer in the driveway. But worse.

She took a breath and explained how she knew the agent and that he'd been like this when she arrived. Franklin gave her a long, assessing look. These people had to be growing suspicious of all the strange things happening at her property. Now including murder.

She wanted to blurt, *It's not my fault!*

But Franklin didn't make any accusations. He joined his fellow deputy, and they pointed at the body and marks on the ground. One called for a coroner.

Morgen waited, wondering if she should invite them into the house or keep sitting in her car. What was the protocol when dead people were found in one's driveway?

She glanced toward the barn, then started. Amar was walking out of the woods, off the trail he'd taken the other day to show her that spring, and he paused. He met her eyes across the lawn and frowned at the deputies and the body. She hesitated, not sure whether she should point him out to them or make shooing motions so he would know to leave.

If he'd done this, why had he come back?

She shook her head. He hesitated, then backed into the woods.

"Ma'am?" Franklin waved her over.

They hadn't seen Amar.

"Uh, I'm fine here." She'd already seen Christian once and knew the image of his throat torn out would remain with her forever.

Franklin opened his mouth, as if to object, but he seemed to understand that she was shaken. "There are prints. I think they're too big to belong to your dog."

"My *dog* didn't do this," she said, panic flaring in her chest. If they believed that, they would put him down. "He was in the car with me. I haven't let him out, and he doesn't tear people's throats out. He licks them and leans against their legs." She took a deep breath, realizing she was speaking too rapidly.

"Oh, I didn't think he'd done it, ma'am. We were just debating these prints and how fresh they are. They look like they belong to a giant dog. Or a wolf." He gazed at her, as if she should grasp the significance.

Unfortunately, she did. But did *he*? Did he know about Amar? And the werewolves in town?

"I saw similar tracks around that deer that had been dragged into the road the other day," Franklin said.

"Yeah," Morgen said. "This place has been... a lot creepier than I was expecting."

A lot more of *everything* than she'd been expecting.

"I understand. Did you ever see the wolf?"

She hesitated, tempted to lie, to cover for Amar, but so many people here knew about the werewolves that it was hard to imagine everyone in the sheriff's office being oblivious. Especially if the various packs had caused as much trouble over the years for the townsfolk as Phoebe had implied.

"Yes," Morgen said. "I've since learned that one lived—or was living—on the property here. He's a werewolf."

Franklin gazed grimly at her, neither acknowledging nor disputing the existence of werewolves.

"He claimed to know my grandmother," she continued. "He was living in the barn, but he's moved out now."

She nodded to the burned structure and neglected to mention that he'd moved into the main house the night before and slept in one of the guest rooms before rising to eat cantaloupe and granola and sneer at faux sausage.

Franklin exchanged a long look with the other deputy. "Maybe you should stay somewhere else for a while, ma'am. We'll do a search of the woods and try to find this... wolf, but it could be dangerous here for you."

"I don't have anywhere else to stay."

Morgen didn't bring up the Wild Trout. She wanted to look up the Rainwater Estate and learn everything she could about this Mason Arbuckle. She also wanted to talk to Amar, whether that was wise or not. If he'd done this, she had to know. If he'd been framed—she *hoped* he'd been framed—she had to know that too.

"We'll have someone stay the night and keep an eye on the house," the other deputy said.

"Oh." Morgen didn't want a babysitter, even if that could be wise, but she made herself say, "Thank you. I appreciate it."

"Why don't you take your dog inside while we handle this?" Franklin waved to the body as another car arrived. The coroner.

"Thanks," she said again.

More SUVs arrived, and uniformed men with rifles and armored vests hopped out. They barked orders about searching the woods and headed off in several directions.

Morgen watched numbly, hoping Amar could avoid them. And wishing she knew his phone number. Did he even *have* a phone?

After she retrieved Lucky, she walked him across the yard on his leash so he wouldn't disturb anything. As she took him in the house, she wondered how she was going to talk to Amar and find out what had happened. She also wondered what would happen if they caught him wandering around out there in wolf form.

20

AFTER FEEDING LUCKY, MORGEN SAT AT THE KITCHEN TABLE, examining Rainwater Estate via satellite imagery and trying not to think about Christian's death. She'd brought mushroom-quinoa risotto home from the grocery store, but it sat by her elbow, untouched. It was hard to contemplate eating with the memory of the garish murder so fresh in her mind.

She was also worried about Amar. Outside, night had fallen, but shouts from the forest wafted through the open window, and she strained her ears listening for gunfire. The entire sheriff's department had shown up to look for the fanged murderer. The fanged murderer that she still didn't want to believe was Amar.

"Focus on this," Morgen ordered herself, locking her gaze on the laptop.

Learning about Mason Arbuckle wouldn't bring back Christian, but it might lead her to Grandma's murderer.

According to her internet searches, Rainwater Estate was located on Fern Drive, a meandering road that started on the other side of town and headed out into the woods. The houses were on large lots, separated from each other by thick stands of trees. If that news article had been correct and Mason Arbuckle lived at the estate, could she pay him a visit? What would she do? Drive up, knock on the door, and ask if he'd bought a saber-toothed tiger tusk from a crafting witch and used it to kill her grandmother? That conversation was sure to go well.

She didn't even know if he truly lived there. That article was two years old.

Morgen called Zoe. "How do I find out who owns a property?" she asked without preamble.

"Go into the county GIS site and type in the address." Zoe's tone turned suspicious. "Why?"

"Someone made an offer on Grandma's property already, and I want to check him out. I haven't gotten the details, because someone killed the real-estate agent before he could share them, but I might know where the would-be buyer lives."

Given that Zoe was one of the chattier people in the family, the length of the stunned silence that followed was impressive.

"You need to get out of there," she finally said.

"I'm fine. There's a deputy sheriff who's going to spend the night."

"In your house?"

"Uh, I assume in his car in the driveway, but I didn't ask for details on how it works when they're keeping an eye on you. Do you think he'll expect a room?" She imagined having to explain that one of the guest rooms was unavailable because the possible murderer was staying in it.

"I think they stay in their car, but come on, Morgen. This has gotten serious. Just get out of there. You can sell the property and sign everything remotely."

"Grandma didn't want it sold."

"*Grandma* isn't here anymore."

"Yeah. That's one of the problems."

She said goodbye, glowered at the roof of Rainwater Estate on the satellite map, then found the county GIS site and typed in the address. There he was. Mason Arbuckle listed as the landowner. Rainwater Estate consisted of fifty acres outside of town and a sprawling house—she would call it a mansion—of more than ten thousand square feet.

So, what did Arbuckle need with Wolf Wood? And the pond. The *magical* spring, if Amar could be believed. Since she'd touched those blue mushrooms and been zapped, there had to be something to the place, but was fancy mineral water worth millions of dollars? How would anyone have even found out about it?

Admittedly, witches had been all over the property lately, and the forest was called Wolf Wood, so that probably meant wolves—and werewolves?—hunted out there often. Perhaps the whole town knew about the pool and had for decades.

A soft tapping at the window almost made her fall out of her chair. A dark shadow loomed, and the window creaked further open.

Morgen swore and lunged for the only weapon nearby, the fork she'd stuck in the vegetarian risotto. Little bits were wedged between the tines.

Since Franklin was out front in his SUV, she almost shouted, but she recognized the shaggy black-haired head that thrust itself through the window first. The rest of Amar followed, and he landed in a crouch, sniffing as he peered around the kitchen and through the doorways.

"Are you alone inside?" he whispered.

"Yes," Morgen whispered back. "Except for Lucky."

"Are you going to prong me with that fork?"

"I'm undecided. Did you kill Christian?"

His expression was grim as he met her eyes. "Against my will."

"What does *that* mean?"

Damn it, she'd wanted him to say that it had been someone

else. That one of those asshole Loups had done it. Or a real wolf. Or a mountain lion. Anyone but him.

Lucky had been sleeping on the couch in the living room, but he rushed in, as if he would bark to alert the world to this intruder.

"Ssh, sh," Morgen whispered to him, patting her leg so he would come over.

If the deputies heard him barking, they would be sure to knock on the door and ask what was going on.

But Lucky recognized Amar, despite his unorthodox entrance. All he did was go over and sniff his muddy boots before checking under the table to see if Morgen had dropped anything from her plate.

"The witches returned while I was working on the barn," Amar said softly, holding her gaze. He'd barely seemed to notice Lucky's arrival. "Christian had driven up a little earlier and gone into the woods. I didn't stop him. He said you were coming back to meet him."

Morgen nodded.

"I was working inside when the witches arrived. I didn't think they knew I was there and was debating if I should hide in the woods or attempt to drive them away. I assumed you hadn't invited *them* and had no plans to meet with them. I *hate* that they have the power to stop a werewolf, but since I know from experience that they do..." He rubbed the back of his neck and grimaced. "I sneaked out the back of the barn and headed into the woods. But as I was leaving, the call came over me. Far more intensely than it should have, especially given that it was still daytime."

"The call... to change into a wolf?"

"Yes. Last night, one of the witches with an amulet did something to me. I was in pain and didn't realize at the time that it was *permanent*." He rubbed the back of his neck again, glanced toward the window, then stepped closer to the table.

Morgen made herself stay put, though the urge to skitter back came over her. He'd just admitted to killing Christian. But if he had been under someone's control...

She thought of the incantation on the paper in her pocket. If a witch recited that, could it truly force a werewolf to do things against his will? To *kill* people?

Amar knelt on the floor and pushed his hair aside to show her the back of his neck. "Her mark is there, isn't it?"

Morgen stared at a raised red welt, a pentagram in a circle. He'd been branded like a steer.

"Yeah," she whispered.

"I was afraid of that." Amar lifted his head, and his shaggy hair fell back over the spot. "With her magical mark burned into my flesh—into my *soul*—it makes it easier for her to control me. I think she may be able to track me, know exactly where I am, but all I know for sure is that I couldn't deny her summons or her command to turn into a wolf. Her command to kill." He clenched his jaw, anger replacing the haunted look in his eyes. "This isn't the first time they've ordered one of our kind to do their dirty work. Why commit crimes themselves when they can command others to do it for them? Others who won't be believed if the authorities come to their door, because they're not native to this country, and they're not... fully human anymore."

"Do you know why she would have done it? Ordered you to kill Christian?" One day, Morgen would ask Amar how he'd ended up so far from his homeland, but it wasn't the most important thing now.

"Your agent had a buyer for this land. Somehow, the witches knew. I did not smell their scents when I was working on the barn, so they couldn't have been hiding nearby, but they knew."

"You didn't see any ravens, did you?" Morgen shifted on the kitchen chair, thinking of Phoebe's feathered familiar.

"Not a raven." Amar gazed thoughtfully at the dark window.

A car door slammed outside, making Morgen flinch. She was glad Amar was staying low. If one of the deputies saw him inside, she didn't know how she would explain his presence—and why she hadn't screamed for help when he'd climbed through the window.

"There was a fox in the garden earlier," Amar said. "I remember thinking it odd, because what in a garden would draw a carnivore, but then I thought he might be hunting the rabbits I see from time to time... Perhaps he was a witch's familiar." Amar pushed his hand through his hair in agitation. "I don't know what to do now, Morgen."

It was the first time she remembered him using her name.

"The deputies are after me. They know it was me. They know I protect Wolf Wood from trespassers. They know the tracks left here are mine, and they're not wrong. But I've never killed anyone who trespassed. It was always a bluff. I've... killed before, in defense or to protect the pack or someone I cared about, but that was far away, in another land with different rules. And they were enemies of the pack, not simple humans. They understood the law of the pack, the rules of the wild, and that when they challenged us, we would do what we had to do." He was looking out the window instead of at her, lost in memories. For the first time, he looked older than she, someone who'd seen a lot of life rather than the young man his wild hair and muscles had made him seem. She noticed flecks of gray at his temples.

"If a witch was controlling you and left a mark on you, maybe the sheriff will understand," she said.

"The law never does," he said softly. "The witches are from here. Born in this country. Citizens of this place. The legal system defends them. The sheriff would assume I'm the criminal, whether I was a werewolf or not." His mouth twisted bitterly. "I thought we'd found a place—that the pack had. Where our work spoke for itself and nobody cared where we'd come from, but now... Now I must leave. Go off into the wild and live alone."

"Neither men nor wolves are meant to live alone," Morgen said.

"What is the alternative? Staying here and being shot?"

"No. Staying here and..." Morgen glanced at her laptop, nudging it so the screensaver would drop. "Finding my grandmother's killer and keeping him from getting this land."

Amar's eyes sharpened, and he focused on her. "You know who it is?"

"I can't know for sure, but it might be this person who put a three-million-dollar offer on Grandma's property the instant it came on the market." Since she hadn't found anything online about Mason Arbuckle or his business, the only thing she could show Amar was the name, the address, and the property lines of Rainwater Estate.

Still on his knees, Amar leaned his arm on the table and scrutinized the map.

Having him so close made her uneasy. Even if he'd been under someone else's control, he'd still killed Christian. Ripped the agent's throat out like the wolf he was. What if that same witch commanded him to kill Morgen?

"I never would have sold it to him," she said. "If these witches would have simply come and talked to me..."

Morgen understood how it might have looked to an outsider—Hell, even Zoe had thought she'd genuinely wanted to sell the house—but a man was dead now because of a misunderstanding. For whatever reason, the witches cared about Wolf Wood and that it remain intact. Her grandmother had cared. All the werewolves seemed to care. They should have all been working on the same side, not fighting each other.

"What's the deal with that spring?" Morgen asked when Amar leaned back from the table.

"I don't know any more than what I told you, that Gwen said it had rejuvenating properties."

"My grandmother who was ninety and still living on her own and riding her motorcycle around town," Morgen mused. "Who outlived her own daughters, both of whom died of cancer." The usual chill went through her bones when she thought of that and the question of whether that ticking time bomb also resided in her blood.

"It is unlikely it's some fountain of youth," Amar said. "Those with magical blood often live longer than typical. But I do believe it has *some* special properties. The moss, mushrooms, and lichens around the spring would not glow in the dark if it didn't."

She blinked. "You didn't say the mushrooms glowed in the dark."

They *had* been vibrant. She remembered noticing how bright everything growing around the water had appeared, even though the trees and spring had been in the shade.

"And the moss growing on the sides of the trees, yes. Were there not deputies hunting all over the woods, I would offer to show it to you." Amar smiled sadly at her. "It is lovely out there in the evenings. Quiet, peaceful. I will miss Wolf Wood."

"You're not giving up and leaving yet."

She'd meant her words to be firm and commanding, but something niggled at her mind from her inventory of Grandma's root cellar. A couple of jars of green powder down there glowed green in the shadows. Given how much kooky stuff was in the cellar, she hadn't thought much of it. The jars hadn't had labels that explained what they were or what the substance was used for. But maybe it was something important. Something worth paying a lot for.

Something worth killing for?

"No," Amar agreed. "Before I leave, I will kill the man who killed Gwen."

Morgen held up a finger and tapped a search into her laptop.

"Huh. Bioluminescent moss is a thing." She refined her search to add witches and potions to the keywords, though surfing through Grandma's grimoires might have been more helpful. "Hm. Supposedly, there are several potions that rely upon something called daylight bioluminescent moss, a very rare variety that's usually outcompeted by other mosses. The more typical species of luminous moss, which is called goblin gold or dragon's gold, is found in caves and isn't as rare. Here's a site warning that unscrupulous sellers try to pass that stuff off as daylight bioluminescent moss and that you have to be careful with purchases from strangers. You should never, it warns, order it online. Actual daylight bioluminescent moss is *very* rare and very expensive."

"It dangles all over the trees around the spring. Gwen used to harvest it occasionally."

"We may have found the reason everyone wants Wolf Wood to be preserved. Specifically, that spring and the glowy things growing around it."

Morgen typed in another search, seeking hints of what the rare moss might be used for, but she didn't find anything. If Grandma had harvested it, she had to have known. A book downstairs might even have recipes for potions. Morgen had seen a couple of potion books during her inventory.

"This Arbuckle may sneak onto the property to harvest and sell it," Amar said.

Yes, what kind of *internet business* did the man have that had bought him a fifty-acre estate on the edge of town? And allowed him to offer millions for Wolf Wood?

Morgen wished she'd found a site that happened to be registered to Arbuckle and was selling the fancy moss. That would have been convenient.

"Does that happen a lot?" she asked. "People sneaking onto the property?"

"Occasionally. Usually, witches come into the woods. Women, not men. When I catch them, I scare them away and warn them not to trespass. Werewolves occasionally pass through on the hunt as well, but they have no interest in moss." Amar tapped his chin thoughtfully. "There is one person's scent that I've occasionally caught around the spring but haven't been able to track."

"A man?"

"No. A woman."

"Maybe Arbuckle has a colleague. Or a witch servant locked in his basement. The scent doesn't belong to any of our arsonists, does it?" Morgen assumed Amar had a nose as good as a hound's when he was in his wolf form.

"No. And it has been some time since I detected the scent. Since before Gwen died." Amar's eyes closed to slits. "This Arbuckle will tell me what he knows before I kill him."

The urge to take a closer look at Grandma's grimoires—and find out what the glowing moss powder did—came over Morgen.

Too bad she would have to walk outside to get to the root cellar. Would Franklin think it odd if she abruptly needed something? For all he knew, the canned tomatoes were kept down there, right?

She stood up. "I'll be right back."

Amar was back to gazing out the window, his face more determined than lost now.

"Don't go anywhere without me, all right?" Morgen closed her laptop, lest he be speculating on visiting Arbuckle by himself.

"It would be better if you didn't come with me," he said, practically confirming it. His fingers twitched to the back of his neck. "If the one who did this is out there, she could make me turn on you."

"Why would she be at Arbuckle's house?"

"To keep him from obtaining your property."

"She shouldn't have any way to know who made the offer." Morgen glanced toward the garden, though it was too dark out to see if any foxes were lurking among the carrot tops. Even if there was, a fox couldn't have read the folder in Christian's car. "She can't know. And we don't know anything yet either. We need proof before we confront anyone—especially if you're planning to confront him with fangs." She pointed at him. "Give me another day to figure this out, okay? I'm close. I know I am."

Someone knocked on the front door.

Morgen swore. "Stay here," she whispered.

Amar's expression grew mulish, but he didn't immediately spring for the open window.

On the way to the front door, Morgen grabbed the camp lantern she'd used the other night. Now was as good a time as any to visit the root cellar.

"Hello, Deputy Franklin," she said, deliberately stepping out onto the porch with him, even though he looked like he wanted to go inside.

"Ma'am?" He pointed toward the entryway. "One of my men was checking around the house and said he heard you talking to someone."

"My dog. Lucky is a good conversationalist."

Franklin frowned, his other hand on his pistol as he peered warily inside.

Lucky either heard his name or smelled a chance to go outside. He bounced into view, nails clacking on the wood floors, and ran out between them. Fortunately, the body was gone. Unfortunately, six vehicles were still parked in the driveway.

"Thanks for checking in." Morgen made herself smile at Franklin. "I need something out of the root cellar, but I was afraid to go down there alone in the dark."

"The root cellar?"

"Yes." Morgen pointed around the side of the house. "I'm making dinner and need..." Realizing he would expect her to

bring out whatever she named, she threw away the canned tomatoes idea. "My grandmother's cookbook."

"It's in the root cellar?"

"Yes. Thanks for escorting me. I'm distraught. Cooking will
help calm my nerves." Or looking up bioluminescent moss...

Franklin accompanied her around the house, and she debated
how to keep him from following her into the cellar. He stuck close,
as if he meant to be her permanent bodyguard for the night.

Morgen removed Grandma's amulet and used her body to hide
that she needed it to open the doors. She held up a hand to keep
Franklin from following her down. Fortunately, someone called
him on his radio, and he stopped at the top of the stairs to answer.

She darted down, grabbed one of several jars of the glowing
green powder, and skimmed through the grimoires on the shelves.
Since she'd organized them the day before, it didn't take her long
to find the two potion books. She skimmed the table of contents of
the first, but it didn't mention moss or ingredients at all. Neither of
the old tomes had indexes, but when she opened the second, a
folded piece of modern, college-ruled paper fell out. She opened it
to reveal a list of names, dates, and ounces sold.

"Ounces of what?" The paper didn't say.

Morgen eyed the jar of glowing green powder. Amar had said
Grandma had harvested the moss. Harvested it to sell? Or was this
something unrelated?

She didn't recognize most of the names on the list, but the
third one down was Phoebe. Two years ago, she'd been sold two
ounces. There was no mention of prices.

Morgen's breath caught as her gaze landed on another name
on the list, one that repeated three more times. Arbuckle. He'd
first received—first purchased?—moss two years ago. The last
purchase had been a year ago. That had been the last purchase
anyone had made. Had something about him or their interaction
caused Grandma to stop selling the moss?

"Ms. Keller?" Franklin called from the top of the stairs.

"Found it." Morgen stuffed the sheet in the book and closed it. "Coming."

Once she was back inside, she would do a thorough search of the contents. A recipe for that moss had to be in there. She was sure of it.

And then what? Visit Arbuckle's house to ask him how sales of his moss potions were going?

She would rather snoop around his home for clues—for more definitive evidence—before encountering him. Or *instead* of encountering him. But she'd never broken into someone's house in her life, and the idea filled her with even more anxiety than confronting strangers.

If she had Amar at her side, she would be less afraid of going snooping, but he wanted to *kill* Arbuckle, not look in his underwear drawers. And he was already in a lot of trouble. If he murdered someone else, he would never be able to find exoneration.

No, she had better not take him. They couldn't kill anyone, and they couldn't break into Arbuckle's house either. She would have to ring the doorbell and talk to the man.

Why did that sound more terrifying than dealing with witches and werewolves?

Halfway up the steps out of the cellar, she ran back and grabbed another grimoire she'd spotted earlier. *Incantations of Protection.* Maybe something in there would help if she had to defend herself.

Outside, Franklin waited with his arms folded across his chest. He cocked an eyebrow at the weathered leather-bound tomes.

"They're old cookbooks," Morgen said, closing the doors. "Full of ancient family recipes."

Fortunately, it was dark enough that Franklin wouldn't be able to read the titles. She hustled toward the front door before he could ask for details on what dish she planned to cook.

Lucky greeted her when she returned to the kitchen, but Amar wasn't there. She jogged around the house, looking for him, hoping he'd simply decided to hide out somewhere, but she knew in her gut that he hadn't. He'd gone to confront Arbuckle—if not kill him outright.

She shook her head bleakly. If he did that, the sheriffs would hunt him for the rest of his life, and he would never be able to return to Wolf Wood.

21

"DEPUTY FRANKLIN?" MORGEN APPROACHED HIS SUV, WHERE HE leaned against the door, watching the house while the hunt continued in the woods.

She would have preferred to walk to her car and leave without being questioned, but she doubted Franklin would allow that. She would have to convince him to let her go.

Even better would be if she could convince him to go with her. She didn't want to confront Arbuckle alone, and she also feared she wouldn't be able to stop Amar by herself. Even if it turned out Arbuckle had killed Grandma, Morgen couldn't let Amar kill him. He was *already* in trouble with the law. But with Christian's death, he'd been manipulated against his will. Maybe there would be a way to clear his name. But not if he murdered Arbuckle in cold blood.

"Yes, ma'am?" Franklin was peering into the woods and barely glanced at her.

Since Morgen hadn't heard any shots, she assumed that Amar had slipped out past the men and was on his way to Arbuckle's estate by now. It was on the other side of town, and he hadn't tried to leave in his truck—the deputies would have seen him if he had —so he had to be on foot. But that didn't mean she had a lot of time. If he traveled in his wolf form, he would be able to cross the miles quickly.

"I need a favor," she said.

"Yes, ma'am?" Franklin repeated, now eyeing her warily, as if certain her favor would be onerous—or put him at odds with his duty.

This could *help* him with his duty. If he went along with her.

"Could you give me a ride across town? I think I have a lead on..." Morgen gestured to where the body had been.

"A *lead*? You're not on the case, ma'am. You don't pursue leads." He squinted at her. "Unless that werewolf has been in contact with you. Has he? He didn't ask you to meet him somewhere, did he?"

That was the first time Franklin had admitted to what she'd suspected all along. That he—and likely the whole sheriff's department—knew about the werewolves.

"He didn't, no." No need to mention the chat she'd had with Amar at the kitchen table. "But before we were going to meet in person, Mr. Christian gave me the name of the person who put an offer in on this property. He'd just listed it for sale, you see. I thought it might be worth talking to that man about the murder." The murder of her grandmother, not the murder of the agent, but she kept that part to herself.

"If he wanted to buy the property, why would he have anything to do with the murder of the real-estate agent?"

"He might not have, but don't you think we should talk to him? Maybe warn him about this? I've learned from the local wit— er, locals that there are some people in Bellrock who don't want to see this property sold. If whoever killed Christian did it to stop the sale, the buyer might be in danger too." There. That seemed plausible, didn't it? Maybe it was even true.

Franklin's eyes had narrowed further at her slip-up—did he

know all about the witches as well as the werewolves?—and he regarded her thoughtfully for a long moment.

"Who's the buyer?" he finally asked.

"Mason Arbuckle."

"That guy?" Franklin looked like he meant to spit, but he refrained.

"Do the locals not like him?"

"He's got a lot of money and likes to show it off."

One of the other men came over, mud spattering his boots and uniform pants.

"Any luck?" Franklin asked him, holding up a finger to Morgen.

"We followed some big wolf prints, but there are a lot of them out there, and then a lot of recent prints from people too." The man looked down at Morgen's shoes. "They looked like women's prints. Not that big."

"I haven't been roaming in the woods, but there was an arson yesterday—" Morgen waved toward the barn, "—and I saw some women run into the woods as I drove up."

"This place is trouble," Franklin said. "I'm going to take Ms. Keller to a hotel in town."

Morgen tamped down her frown as she imagined walking to Arbuckle's estate alone all the way from the Wild Trout. From what she'd seen thus far, the little town of Bellrock wasn't serviced by taxis or ride-sharing services.

"That's a good idea," the other man said.

"Get your things, ma'am." Franklin pointed to the passenger side of his SUV.

She withdrew the antler staff from her car and joined him. "I've got everything I need."

He eyed the staff as well as the tomes she had tucked under her arm and was being careful not to let him see closely. "Such as your recipe books?"

"People get hungry in hotels."

"Is that for stirring?" Franklin pointed at the staff.

"It could be. Dough can be feisty."

Franklin looked toward the house, and Morgen expected him to remember her dog, so she groped for an excuse to explain why she would leave Lucky there instead of taking him with her. Because she had no intention of being gone all night or staying at a hotel...

"Right." Franklin pointed toward the passenger side again and climbed into the driver's seat.

She would have preferred to take her car, especially if he wouldn't come with her to Arbuckle's, but she didn't know if she had a choice.

After she buckled herself in, and they started down the long driveway, Franklin said, "We'll stop by Arbuckle's and warn him about this."

She glanced at him in surprise. "Oh, good. Thanks."

"Maybe one of our men should watch him tonight too. I don't like the guy, but we don't need another murder."

Morgen thought Arbuckle was more likely to be behind the murders than be a victim, but if the witches were after anyone trying to develop the property, maybe that wasn't true. She wondered if they would think of getting rid of *her* since she'd been the one to list it. Maybe they would hope that if she died, the next of kin would leave the place vacant and not do anything with it. If her sister inherited it, that might be exactly what would happen, since she hadn't been in the country for more than a year.

The night had grown chilly, and Franklin flipped on seat warmers for both of them. Morgen opened the potion book to resume her search for recipes calling for moss ingredients. As soon as she'd seen that Amar was gone, she hadn't dared linger for a leisurely perusal at the kitchen table. Now, she was stuck reading by the glow of her phone.

"Going to make a meatloaf at the Wild Trout?" Franklin asked dryly, glancing over.

"I'm a vegetarian. I don't make meatloaf."

"Soy loaf?"

"Even though food becomes *much* more appealing when pulverized and shaped into rectangular cuboids, loaves aren't really my thing."

"Odd."

"So my family tells me."

"Because you dislike loaves or because you use words like *cuboid*?"

"Those are two of the data points in the array, yes."

Franklin turned before reaching Main Street, taking a road that looped around the outside of town. Morgen paused in flipping pages. There it was. A recipe with four ingredients, including *daylight bioluminescent moss*. It called for two grams of the stuff.

"Performance-Enhancing Elixir," she murmured, reading the title at the top.

That was *it*?

Commercials for erectile dysfunction pharmaceuticals popped into her mind. Who would pay a fortune for a potion—an *elixir*—that helped with that?

But as she flipped through more pages in the book and didn't see any other recipes calling for the moss, it occurred to her that the elixir might help with other kinds of performance. What if it improved athletic ability? Or cognitive function? If it worked better than other stuff out there, she could imagine people paying handsomely.

She remembered the college track-and-field records she'd found with Arbuckle's name on them. The next commercial that came to mind was the old one that went: *I'm not only the Hair Club president, but I'm also a client.*

Morgen closed the book and gazed thoughtfully at the dashboard.

"I know about the witches." Franklin glanced at the books in her lap. He must have seen the titles, despite her efforts to hide them. "Everyone in the department does."

She didn't know whether to be relieved or chagrined at the news. Did that mean they believed in magic too?

"Do you know that they can control the werewolves?" she asked.

He grunted. "Is that what he told you?"

"It's what another werewolf said." And it was what the incantation in her pocket was supposed to do. She'd memorized it, just in case she needed it and didn't have time to pull out the paper.

"Don't believe anything they say," Franklin said. "They're dangerous. The witches are just kooky ladies who pretend they can put hexes on you. They're harmless."

Ah, maybe he didn't believe in magic after all, at least not witch magic.

"The werewolves are a different story," he continued. "There have been a lot more tourists disappearing since *they* showed up, not to mention the occasional murder. Like tonight. They're trouble. Both packs. But it's not easy to drive them out. Our department is small—the men you saw tonight are basically all we've got. Even then, a couple of those men were on loan from up north. Besides, the Loups have bought a bunch of real estate in town, and they're in with the mayor and some of the wealthy landowners. It's complicated." He grimaced.

"Sorry," Morgen said and opened the second book. Maybe she could find something useful in it.

But only a couple of minutes later, Franklin turned onto a dark, winding road without center lines. "We're almost to the property."

"So soon?"

That quashed her hopes of finding and memorizing a helpful incantation. Ideally one that erected a huge shield made from diamonds all around her and made her impervious to bullets, magic, and fangs. Sadly, she hadn't found anything like that. Most of the spells listed were for such mundane things as keeping slugs out of the garden, repelling termites from the house, and putting hexes on newspaper-delivery people who left the Sunday edition in a puddle instead of on the porch. She had a feeling the fantasy novels full of magic users flinging fireballs and lightning bolts at each other might not be indicative of the common witching experience.

"Bellrock is a small town," Franklin said.

Morgen's phone vibrated. She would have ignored it, but it was her sister.

The urge to speak with her before going into a possibly dangerous situation washed over her with startling intensity. Maybe her gut knew something that her brain didn't, that her desire to speak with Arbuckle would turn into more.

"Hey, Sian," Morgen said. "I don't have long to talk, but I'm glad you called."

"I am certain you are. As I was witnessing previously captive orangutans being released into the wild and discussing the threat of Sunda clouded leopards with a colleague, it occurred to me that you may wish some tips on dealing with your local predators, the wolves you mentioned. Assuming you truly are having encounters with such near Grandma's property and your previous call about werewolves wasn't a hoax."

"I'm dealing with such, yes."

"Wolves are wary animals and generally not dangerous to humans—most historical attacks involved rabid wolves—but it is possible that they will bite if they're provoked or have, through nearby habitation, lost their natural fear of humans. There have also been incidents when humans have greatly altered the wolves' environment."

"They can also be aggressive when you're innocently dining in an establishment that they partially own and consider their territory."

Judging by the long pause, Sian hadn't yet accepted that werewolves existed and Morgen truly was walking among them. Well, siblings weren't perfect.

"Perhaps I shouldn't have called," Sian said.

"No, I'm glad you did." Morgen glanced over at Franklin, but the dark road either demanded all of his attention, or werewolves owning restaurants was nothing new to him. She lowered her voice. "If anything happens to me... Grandma didn't want the property sold, all right? She left a letter. It's on the kitchen table and explains... Well, there's a lot she never explained to her children or grandchildren. But don't sell it, all right?"

"What is going to happen to you? Morgen, if you're in danger, you should call the police."

"Bellrock doesn't have police, but I'm riding in a deputy sheriff's car right now."

"That doesn't sound sufficient."

Franklin glanced over. Sian hadn't lowered *her* voice.

"It is," Morgen said. "There are seat warmers and everything. Just promise me that if the house ends up in your hands—the house and the land—that you won't sell it, all right?"

"*Morgen.* What is going on? Do you need me to call Jun?"

"He's the last person who could help with this, even if we weren't divorced."

"Oh, I forgot about that."

"I'll wager you don't forget which of your orangutans are together and which are split up."

"All of them are *split up*. Males are solitary and generally only remain with a female long enough to ensure a successful mating."

"Never mind."

"Don't do anything dangerous, Morgen. It would be inconvenient if I had to ask one of our brothers to send my bamboo underwear."

"You'd get something goofy instead. Didn't Rhett give you a *Goonies* T-shirt for your fortieth birthday?"

"Yes. Because I watched the movie as a child."

"You did watch it eighty-three times."

"It's a superior movie that was chosen for preservation in the United States National Film Registry by the Library of Congress."

"You wear that T-shirt, don't you?"

"Almost there," Franklin said, drowning out Sian's response.

"I need to go," Morgen told her sister.

"Don't do anything even an orangutan would know is foolish."

"Aren't they pretty smart?"

"Yes, but I hope for your sake that you're smarter." Sian hung up.

"Don't you love siblings?" Morgen asked Franklin.

He only grunted and turned up a paved driveway. It wound through dark trees, but landscaping lights on either side brightened the way.

Up ahead, more lights came into view. They were atop a tall stone wall that stretched into the trees on either side of the driveway and looked to wrap around the house on all sides. The entry was barred by a wrought-iron gate with two ornamental lion heads incorporated into the design. Through the bars, a four-story stone mansion was visible—it looked more like a castle than traditional Pacific Northwest architecture. Cameras perched atop the rock wall as well as on a porte-cochère that led to wooden double doors at the front of the mansion. Numerous signs proclaimed that the premises were protected by a home-security company.

"I bet *he* has towel warmers," Morgen muttered, glancing into the woods to either side, wondering if Amar might be skulking around out there in wolf form.

Franklin stopped at an intercom next to the gate and buzzed it.

"Yes?" a woman answered after a minute.

That wasn't likely Mason Arbuckle. Maybe his mom was visiting. Or he had servants to answer his intercom for him.

"This is Deputy Franklin from the sheriff's office. There's been an incident with someone Mr. Arbuckle might have been working with, and I have a warning for him."

"Show your badge to the camera, please."

Franklin turned and did so.

"Very well," the woman said.

The iron gate clanked open, and Franklin drove in.

That had been easier than Morgen expected, but when the front doors opened, and an older woman in a butler's uniform stepped out to the porte-cochère, she had a feeling they might not get to talk to Arbuckle. Not that she wanted to have a long, in-depth conversation with him. What would she even ask? *Did you kill my grandmother?*

No, she would pretend she was there to do just what she'd told Franklin, warn Arbuckle that he might be a target. If he didn't invite her in, she would say she wanted to discuss his offer. That ought to force a longer conversation and maybe give her an opportunity to snoop.

As long as the butler cooperated by inviting them in so they could speak with Arbuckle. She had to find out if he'd been responsible for the cursed tusk clip. One way or another. Too bad she hadn't stumbled across an invisibility spell in the grimoires.

Franklin parked before reaching the porte-cochère. "Stay here."

Stay there? Morgen was the one who'd wanted to come here. And she needed to go with him and somehow finagle an invitation to get them invited inside.

"Uhm."

"*Stay here*," Franklin repeated firmly.

"Sure. I'll just look for interesting loaves in my recipe books."

He shot her a dirty look, then hopped out.

Morgen waited to see if the butler would invite him in. If they both disappeared into the mansion, maybe she could slip out and admire the copious shrubbery, flower beds, and tidily pruned trees in the front and side yards. And find a back door that the butler had left ajar after taking out the trash.

"Yeah, right." More likely, she would set off the security alarm.

The butler listened to Franklin without inviting him in. She waved toward the front gate, either to indicate the deputy should go or that Arbuckle wasn't home.

Morgen willed Franklin to try harder to get them invited inside, but he'd already turned back toward the SUV, as if they were wrapping up the conversation.

The butler propped her hands on her hips, watching to make sure he left. A gray braid of hair hung over one of her shoulders, and Morgen sucked in a breath. She recognized that braid—and the black ponytail holder with something like a fabric spider decorating it. The butler was the cloaked woman who'd spied on her from across the street of the Wild Trout.

Abruptly certain that she needed to search the premises, Morgen tucked her books under her arm, grabbed the staff, and wrapped her fingers around the door handle. Thanks to the bushes near the driveway, and the fact that Franklin had parked so that the passenger door faced away from the mansion, she might be able to slip out without being seen.

But what then? With all that security, she was certain to be spotted on a camera somewhere.

The butler turned for the front door as Franklin neared the SUV. Morgen didn't have time to come up with a better plan.

She opened the door, ducked low, and eased out, not closing it for fear of making noise. The antlers on the staff clacked on the pavement. She winced and darted between two bushes, imagining Franklin chasing her down and tackling her. There was no way he would miss seeing her—*not* seeing her.

Still, she hoped vainly that he would believe she had a plan and that he should leave her behind to snoop. As she ran from tree to rose bush to flowerbed, staying low and trying to avoid the cameras and the windows with lights on, she angled around to the side of the mansion.

Up ahead, she spotted a door. Not surprisingly, it wasn't open. Neither were any of the windows. She tried to remember if any of the incantations in the grimoires had been for opening locks and thwarting security systems.

As she hurried toward the back of the house, a hand reached out of a bush and grabbed her.

It locked around her biceps like a vise and tugged her into the shrubs. She almost screamed before remembering that she was a trespasser and dared not make any noise. There was no help for her.

22

EVEN THOUGH MORGEN HAD DECIDED NOT TO SCREAM, THE MAN'S strong hand plastered over her mouth ensured that she couldn't. She whipped her staff around, hoping to bash her assailant, but the antlers snagged in the branches. She lost her grip on it as he twisted her to pull her back against his chest.

His hand against her mouth smelled strongly of damp dirt and made her think of gravediggers. She tried to pull away, but he dragged her farther back between two towering rhododendrons. She threw an elbow behind her, hoping to get him to release her, but she only clipped the man, and it didn't seem to hurt him at all.

"Don't make any noise," he whispered. "He's right behind you."

That voice had a familiar accent.

"Amar?" she tried to whisper but couldn't get anything out around his hand.

Even though she knew who it was, she didn't appreciate being restrained, and she had the urge to bite him. But rustling sounded in the yard, from the direction she'd come.

"Ms. Keller?" Franklin whispered loudly. "Come on. Where'd

you go? We don't have a search warrant. I can't roam around the property. And neither can *you*."

Her staff had fallen so that it stuck out from the bushes she and Amar were wedged between. There was enough exterior lighting around the mansion that Franklin was bound to see it. She pointed, hoping Amar would let her bend down and grab it.

"Ssh," was all he said, whispering in her ear.

In the back of the mansion, a door opened. Barks and snarls erupted, along with the sound of claws clacking rapidly on a patio.

Franklin swore.

From her spot in the bushes, Morgen couldn't see the dogs coming, but she had no trouble hearing them.

"Ms. Keller, come *on*. I can't shoot someone's dogs on *their* property."

Morgen leaned further back into the bushes, inasmuch as she could. Amar's hard chest was like a stone wall behind her.

He murmured another, "Ssh," and didn't move.

Foliage rattled as Franklin turned around and ran back toward his SUV. The dogs—two black-furred rottweilers—charged past the bushes. They were after Franklin, but what would happen once he left? They were sure to smell Amar and Morgen and return to check on them—or gnaw their favorite limbs off.

A car door slammed. More growling and barking came from the front yard. The engine roared, and Franklin drove off.

Morgen couldn't decide if she was affronted or relieved that he was leaving her here.

The gate clanked shut after Franklin drove out, shutting Morgen and Amar in. Shutting them in with two angry rottweilers.

Amar lowered his hand, but he didn't release her. What, was he afraid she would lunge out and fling herself into the dogs' path? If anything, she was tempted to burrow behind him and push him out to deal with them.

The dogs trotted back from the gate and stopped in front of

their hiding spot, two dark heads turning, two pairs of eyes focusing on them. The rottweilers growled low in their throats. Amar growled back, and the hair on the back of Morgen's neck rose. Even though he stood behind her as a man, that growl sounded canine—*lupine*—and very dangerous.

Amar eased past her, putting himself in front of her, and growled again.

The dogs whined and slunk off toward the back door.

"Any chance you can do the same thing with security cameras?" Morgen whispered.

"Growl at them?"

"And cause them to slink off, yes. Or at least *turn* off."

"That sounds more like witch magic than a werewolf ability."

"I've been perusing Grandma's grimoires. Security cameras aren't mentioned. But if you need slugs driven from the garden or an ice dam melted out of the gutters, we're covered."

With the dogs gone, Amar eased back between the shrubs with her. Being mashed against a muscular man might have been titillating if not for the likelihood that the butler would run out at any moment with a shotgun—or a wand.

"You smell like dirt," she whispered, the aroma wafting up again.

"I dug under the wall to get into the yard."

"As a man or..."

"As a wolf. There's magic about this place, including some kind of energy field above the wall. I spotted a few dead birds along the outside. It was enough to convince me not to try jumping over."

"Does that mean we're trapped inside?" Morgen was positive she'd heard the gate closing.

"Only if you're too worried about getting dirty to squeeze out through my hole."

"Is it large enough for a human?"

"I have the same body mass as a wolf that I do as a man, so likely so."

She imagined him stepping onto a scale on his hind wolf legs to test that hypothesis. "You don't have boobs and hips as either."

"They can fit."

"Okay, then I'm game. *Dirt* isn't my primary concern tonight. Did you have a plan when you came here?"

"Kill Arbuckle."

"Ah."

"Did *you* have a plan when you fled the deputy?"

That had been a touch impulsive, but she'd had a plan at one point. "Find Arbuckle, pretend I want to discuss his offer, and snoop around while doing so."

"Killing him would be simpler. You believe he arranged Gwen's death, don't you?"

"I can't be positive without more evidence. If you kill him when you're already in trouble for Christian, you'll end up with a life sentence."

Or a *death* sentence. Morgen grimaced as she thought of the deputies tramping around in Wolf Wood with guns.

Amar sighed. "That is likely already in effect. I'd hoped... I'd hoped to take care of this before you showed up. Right now, you're not guilty of anything, as far as I know. Nobody believes you've had anything to do with any of this. Better things stay that way. I'm already in trouble. It hardly matters."

"So you're going to kill more people?"

"Just one," he said grimly, no remorse in his tone.

If this Arbuckle had arranged Grandma's death, could *she* feel remorse over him being killed? Maybe not, but until they knew for sure...

"He's not here," Amar added. "I can smell others in the house, that butler and perhaps another female employee or lover, but Arbuckle is not here."

"You know what he smells like?"

"I can smell the difference between men and women when I'm in wolf form. His scent is so faint I almost missed it."

What did that mean? That he was out of town? That he hadn't been here for a while? Morgen frowned in confusion. Arbuckle was the one who'd put in the offer on Grandma's property. Of course, he could have done that remotely. Everything was handled online now.

"Interestingly," Amar added, "I've caught one of the women's scents before. Near the spring in Wolf Wood. She's the one who always managed to make her trail disappear somehow, so I was never able to follow her and find out who had trespassed."

"I want answers, Amar."

"I want revenge."

She shook her head, unwilling to agree to that.

"Let's go into his house and find..." Evidence, she almost said, but it wasn't as if they were here legally and whatever they found could be used to construct a court case against Arbuckle. If anything, *they* would end up in court for trespassing.

"Where the dogs bed down for the night?" Amar asked.

"I guess what I'd like to find is a room full of tusks and the blueprint for the clip that sabotaged Grandma's motorcycle." Morgen didn't mention the moss, though she was sure that was tied in to all of this.

"Yes," Amar growled. He lifted his nose in the air and sniffed.

"Is he coming back?" Morgen had no trouble imagining Amar able to smell someone turning off the main road a mile away. After all, Lucky could do that, assuming that someone was a favorite person or carrying a pound of brisket.

"No. Not yet."

"Is someone else coming?"

Amar hesitated. "Another werewolf. One of the Loups. It's possible he's just passing through the forest on a hunt." He waved toward the wall around the house and the yard, reminding her of the woods beyond it—and the fact that there weren't any neighbors nearby. Nobody to hear her scream if she ended up locked in some castle dungeon. "Either way, we can't linger. It's possible the butler believes the deputy was the only one out here, and that the dogs scared him off, but it's also possible she's watching us right now on one of the cameras."

Since they were wedged into the bushes and couldn't see the side of the house from there, Morgen doubted that, but she allowed that it was likely someone knew she was there. Her escape from Franklin hadn't been smooth.

"I suppose you want to snoop," he grumbled.

"Does that mean you approve of that?" Morgen peeked out to check the yard. Was it wrong that she was secretly delighted that Arbuckle wasn't home? She might not have to confront him or talk to him at all. What a relief.

"No, but you didn't spring from the deputy's SUV for a night stroll. You'll snoop whether I approve or not."

"True." By now, she felt committed to that line of action. As long as she was trespassing on his lawn, why not stroll through his mansion? "Are you going to join me or keep leaning against that rhododendron like a misplaced rake?"

"I just protected you from rottweilers, and you're comparing me to garden tools?"

"Sorry, that was rude. If you help me get into the house for my snooping, I'll make you breakfast in the morning."

"Plant-based sausage patties aren't going to inspire me to risk my life."

"I don't need you to risk your life, just growl at the guard dogs. And I saw some boxes of pork-sausage links wedged into the freezer. I could make those for you." Assuming the entire sheriff's department wasn't still hunting around the house when they finished here.

"Gwen used to make those. And omelets. She got a lot of boxes of them and a lot of cartons of eggs because of me." He sighed. "I miss her."

"Yeah," Morgen said, though she mostly wished she'd spent more time with Grandma before she passed. "I'm sure she appreciated your company."

"Let's go in now if we're going to do it. I'll watch your back the best I can. If there's magical security... it may be beyond me to thwart it. Or protect you from it."

"Don't worry. I've got a staff with antlers on it and a witch's grimoire. I'm a force to be reckoned with."

"Do you know what either of them does?"

"I told you about the slugs-be-gone incantation." Morgen hefted her books. "And one of the antlers gouged a hole in the upholstery of my car, so it's clearly a formidable weapon."

"Just stay behind me."

"Wait." Morgen gripped his shoulder before he stepped out of the bushes, moved to say something in case... in case this didn't go well. "Thanks, Amar. Thanks for helping me tonight and for being there for my grandmother."

"You are welcome."

He led the way to the back of the house, staying behind bushes and trees in an attempt to avoid the security cameras. He crouched near what Morgen could only think of as a tower—a round stone tower that rose up five stories. It had a pointed metal roof instead of crenellations, but it still put her in mind of castles. A window on the third floor was open.

"Are you suggesting we climb up there?" she whispered. "When the dogs used a lovely back door around the corner?"

"It'll be locked, monitored by a camera, and likely the dogs. They won't back down as easily if I try to enter their house."

Before Morgen could think of more objections, such as the fact that the smooth stone wall had neither trellises nor conveniently

placed ivy anchored into the mortar, Amar jogged toward the
tower and sprang onto it. Even though she watched him scramble
up the side, she couldn't tell what he used for hand and footholds.
The windows were set into the stone, so they didn't even have
frames or ledges to grab.

Amar reached the third-story window without trouble, eased
the pane farther open, and squeezed his big frame inside. Morgen
stood in the bushes below with her books and staff and wondered
if there was some witch incantation that assisted with climbing.
Even if a handy rope ladder had dangled down, she would have
struggled to get up there with her unwieldy items in hand. As
much as she hated the idea, she might have to leave them behind.

"Note to self: take a backpack on future enemy-compound
infiltrations."

Amar leaned out and lowered the end of what looked like a
dusty blue velvet rope down to her. A handmade rope. It was little
more than strips of fabric tied together. From sheets? A comforter?
Maybe velvet duvets were popular in castle mansions.

Reluctantly, Morgen hid the staff and the books under some
bushes before approaching the end of the makeshift rope. Amar
glanced backward, making her think someone might be
wandering around on the third floor, so she dared not hesitate.

Awkwardly, she started up the velvet rope, doing her best to
laboriously pull herself up while having flashbacks of gym class in
elementary school and her PE teacher assuring her that climbing
up to ring the bell at the top was far more satisfying than playing
Oregon Trail in the computer lab.

Partway up, the rope started moving, and she nearly squawked
aloud. Amar must have lost patience with her meager climbing
skills. He was pulling her up.

"Would you be offended if I told you your grandmother was a
better climber than you?" he asked softly as he pulled her through
the window.

"No," she whispered, worried about the dogs hearing them. "I know where my talents lie, and I'm self-assured and confident in my abilities." That had been truer before she'd been let go. Funny how that rankled more than her husband leaving her.

"What did you say you do for a living? Something with computers?"

"Program databases."

"Does that mean you can hack the security system if we come across the control panel?"

"No. It means I can maintain, program, organize, and manipulate the crap out of any databases we find in this castle." She eyed shreds of velvet on the floor and realized he'd used curtains for his rope.

"I've not seen any of those things done by the thieves in heist movies." Amar pulled up his rope, tossed it in a corner, and closed the window. They were fully committed now.

"That's because Hollywood lacks imagination. As for the rest, since the window was open, it probably means the security system isn't armed." Something she wished she'd realized *before* she'd started up the castle wall.

Oh, well. Morgen glanced around but didn't see any interior cameras. They were in a bedroom, the lush velvet duvet matching the now-shredded curtains. Bottles of perfume and possibly potions rose from the top of every flat surface like stalagmites in a cave. The carpet smelled like it had been marinated in patchouli.

Morgen's phone buzzed in her pocket, startling her. She was glad she'd set it to vibrate instead of ring, but in the quiet room, it still sounded noisy. As she tugged it out to silence it, Amar sniffed at the air.

She didn't recognize the number, but it was a local area code, and it wasn't the caller's first attempt to make contact. She must not have noticed the first vibration when she'd been climbing. An alert for two voice messages popped up. She had a feeling they were from Deputy Franklin, wanting to know what the hell she was doing.

As she stuffed her phone back into her pocket, certain she couldn't come up with a satisfactory response if she answered, Amar touched her shoulder and pointed at the door.

She almost swore aloud. A cloud of green vapor was wafting in under the crack.

Images of being knocked unconscious—or killed—by a toxic substance flashed through her mind, and she tried to think of something she'd read in the grimoire that might help, but she'd only memorized two incantations thus far, the one that revealed secret weaknesses and the one that Phoebe had given her to control werewolves. She had no idea yet if that one worked.

Amar strode around, opening the windows to air the room out. But the currents didn't seem to affect the green vapor. The cloud thickened in front of the door, then swirled about. So far, it didn't smell like anything that Morgen could detect, but that didn't mean it couldn't kill them.

It thickened even further, and letters formed within the cloud. *HELP ME.*

23

"IS THAT MESSAGE FOR YOU OR ME?" MORGEN WHISPERED, POINTING at the words in the thick green cloud of vapor. She used her phone to take a picture of it.

Already, the help-me message was dissipating.

"Nobody asks a werewolf for help." Amar cocked his head. "I can hear the dogs on the first floor, and the butler is walking around down there too.'"

"Do you think *she's* the one who needs help?" Morgen couldn't imagine it, since the butler had been able to amble out the front door and had controlled the gate. "Wait, you mentioned another woman too, right?"

"Yes."

"Do you hear, or smell, anyone else here?"

"Not yet. Her scent is all over, including in this room, but I am not sure where in the mansion she is now."

"Not on this floor, I hope."

"I don't think so."

"Let's look up here for an office full of evidence of wrongdoing." Morgen would prefer to check for—and find—that evidence on a floor without any dogs or people on it.

"I think most people keep things like that in a basement or garage."

"Or root cellar." Since Morgen couldn't smell whatever accounted for the green cloud, and didn't feel any ill effects from its presence, she crept toward the door.

"Your grandmother's doing wasn't wrong. Just eccentric."

"The owners of the eyeballs floating in jars might disagree," she said, though she doubted Grandma had killed anyone for those. She'd probably picked them up at the witch version of a flea market.

"I don't think their owners needed them anymore."

The door wasn't locked, and Morgen opened it carefully, peering into an empty hall dotted with rugs over the floorboards. She expected the area to be full of the green smoke, but only a faint haze filled the space. It didn't seem to have come from the hall—or anywhere. It was as if it had poofed into existence.

She was about to step out, but Amar brushed past her and took the lead.

"Do you know where you're going?" she whispered, trailing him down the hall.

"No. I'm going first in case we're attacked. I must protect you."

"I knew you didn't want to miss me cooking you breakfast."

Amar shot her an unamused look over his shoulder and raised a finger to his lips. He opened doors, looking for an office, but they only passed more guest rooms, a cinema room, and an area full of arcade games and a pool table. The necessities.

Morgen closed her mouth on another snarky comment and continued around a corner after Amar and past a wider section of the hall that had plush chairs facing each other over a low table. A railing let them see down to a marble foyer on the ground floor.

A floorboard creaked, and Morgen winced and hurried past the open area.

Dog barks drifted up from below, and she braced herself for the rottweilers to charge up to their floor. The clacks of claws on marble floors came from below.

Amar lifted his chin—no, his nose. He strode past several closed doors, turned another corner, a stairway coming into view, and stopped in front of a door no different from the others lining the hall. He opened it.

"Office? Huh." He stepped inside.

"Isn't that what we were looking for?"

"I thought it would be a storage room. I smell... powders. Musty, mildewy, and pungent. The air is similar to that in the Crystal Parlor."

Morgen stepped into the office after him, and he shut the door. That would keep the dogs out, but the butler was sure to come up to see what they were barking at. And then what? Morgen couldn't let Amar attack the help, even if the butler had been the one spying on her days earlier. The woman probably just did what Arbuckle paid her to do.

Inside the office, Amar prowled around, sniffing. On the far wall, two large windows overlooked the front gate. The furniture in the room was sparse, with only a desk and a laptop on it. There weren't any bookshelves, cases, or filing cabinets full of the evidence Morgen had hoped for. She didn't see any powders, musty or otherwise.

"Now, the scent almost reminds me of the forest," Amar said softly. "Wolf Wood."

Morgen tried sniffing, but all she smelled was whatever disinfectant the cleaning service used. She trusted Arbuckle didn't mop his own floors.

The sparseness of the office made her doubt this was his primary work area. It seemed more like a guest room.

Hoping she was wrong, Morgen hurried over and opened the laptop. Not surprisingly, it required a password for logging in. Alas, hacking wasn't among her specialties.

She peeked into the desk drawers while Amar returned to the door, though he continued sniffing and now scrutinizing the room from that spot. Looking for the powders he smelled?

The drawers held such innocuous objects as packing tape, staplers, and already-created shipping labels. That made her pause. If Arbuckle shipped things, where were all the boxes? And where was the inventory he mailed?

She plucked out a packing slip addressed to someone who lived on Cauldron Cove Court in Canada. Her breath caught. Two four-ounce vials of daylight luminescent moss powder were listed on the invoice above a total charge of over twelve thousand dollars.

Her mouth sagged open. If it wasn't a mistake, the stuff sold for almost as much as pure gold.

But where was the powder?

"Could there be a secret storage room accessible from here?" she wondered, folding the invoice and sticking it in her pocket. It wasn't exactly condemning evidence, but it was something.

"Try there." Amar pointed at wainscoting and a beige-painted wall no different from the other three walls of the room.

Barks alternating with sniffing came from the other side of the door. Amar growled softly through the wood.

The barks paused, and the sniffs grew less certain. Morgen spotted a wadded-up piece of tape on the floor near the wall Amar had indicated. She walked over and ran her hands along the wainscoting. Castles often had secret doors, didn't they? Why not this one?

Never mind that it was a pretentious wannabe castle in Bellrock, Washington, not a legitimate medieval dwelling surrounded by a moat overflowing with cranky alligators.

"The butler is coming," Amar murmured.

Morgen spotted a crack and tried to tug open what was possibly only in her imagination a secret door. "Remind me to find an incantation that thwarts locks."

"Gwen did that with a wand."

"Great, I didn't grab one of those."

"You should have. They're easier than a staff to climb with and less likely to maim car upholstery." Amar jogged over and peered at the crack, acting like a drug-sniffing dog at the airport as he ran his nose along it.

The claws clacking in the hallway outside the door set Morgen on edge. What would she say when the butler barged in? That she'd gotten lost on the way down the driveway?

Amar prodded a spot on the wall. It didn't look like a button or anything at all, but a soft click sounded, and a door swung inward.

For the first time, Morgen smelled what Amar must have been smelling for several minutes. A musty, decomposing leaf scent wafted out, as if they'd found the passageway into a dying forest. In was dark in the new room, so she couldn't see much, but light glinted off glass on the far wall. A glass jar of moss powder?

In the hallway, the dogs resumed their loud barking.

"Someone up here, Hans?" a muffled female voice came from the hallway.

Morgen crept into the dark room while wondering if the butler would call the sheriff's department and if Deputy Franklin would be sent in to retrieve her.

After stepping in after her, Amar closed the door. Darkness engulfed them.

Morgen patted along the wall, looking for a light switch, but she didn't find anything.

"Witch light glow," Amar whispered.

The amulet hanging around Morgen's neck brightened, shedding enough greenish light to illuminate bags of packing peanuts and stacks of flat cardboard that hadn't yet been folded into boxes. It also showed shelves and shelves of small glass jars of various powders on the far wall. A faint glow came from behind them.

"Should I feel distressed that you know more about being a witch and activating magical items than I do?" Morgen crossed the room, pushed jars aside, and revealed a smaller stash of vials of glowing green powder.

"I visited your grandmother more often than you did."

"That's because she invited *you* to live in the barn. She didn't even ask me up for the holidays."

"You lack my charisma."

"More like your sexy muscles." Morgen wondered if her ninety-year-old grandmother had appreciated such things.

The sound of the dogs charging into the office came through the wall. Amar stayed by the hidden door, bracing it with his hand. If the butler knew about this room, she was sure to check it.

"Trapdoor," Amar whispered, pointing down and toward a corner.

Morgen turned her chest—and her light source—in that direction. The square he'd spotted in the floor was less hidden than the door in the wall. A little ring was set into it. If they'd been on the bottom floor of the mansion, Morgen would have assumed it led to a crawl space, but who had a crawl space under the third floor?

"To... the room underneath this one?" She grabbed one of the glowing jars of moss powder and headed for the trapdoor.

The sniffing sounded right at the hidden door in the wall. The dogs knew exactly where they were. Amar growled softly again, so low only the dogs would hear it. A whine penetrated the wall.

"Wait there, boys," the butler said. "The wolf is coming."

"The wolf?" Morgen mouthed. The werewolf Amar had scented outside?

"Go down." He pointed at the trapdoor.

Morgen lifted the metal ring, turned it, and pulled. Her weak light shone into a vertical shaft with stone walls descending into darkness. Iron ladder rungs ran down one side.

A loud howl came from somewhere in the castle. Morgen jumped, almost dropping her jar.

"That wasn't a dog," she whispered, tucking the jar in her pocket.

The dogs in the next room whined again in fear. She'd thought it was because of Amar, but maybe it was because another werewolf was coming.

"It was not," Amar agreed, then repeated, "Go down. *Now.*"

Morgen stepped onto the ladder. She had no idea where it would take her—hopefully, not a dungeon where she would be trapped—but it was a foregone conclusion that they couldn't go back the way they'd come. Amar might have fought and won against the butler and two dogs, but what if that werewolf was his equal? Or *more than* his equal?

"Amar?" Morgen paused several feet down. "Are you coming?"

The howl sounded again, much closer. Whatever had made it was on this floor now.

"I'll delay him. Get out of here with your evidence."

"Him who? Do you know him? Is it the Loup?"

"Yes."

"Is he dangerous?"

"Yes."

"Sounds like you should avoid him. Come with me." She waved for him to follow her down the rungs, but wood snapped, as if whoever was out there had broken down a door—or through a wall—and Amar didn't look back at her. He took a few steps away from the hidden door and crouched, facing it. Ready for someone to charge in. Ready for a fight.

"Amar..." If he wouldn't flee and leave an enemy at his back, maybe she could help him. "Phoebe taught me an incantation for controlling werewolves," she admitted.

"She *what*?" Amar gaped over his shoulder at her, fury—or was that betrayal?—in his eyes.

"In case I need to defend myself."

"By controlling us?" He smacked a hand to his chest. It was as if he meant *by controlling me.*

"Just the bad guys. Let me stay and help."

"No," he snarled. "I'm not bringing conniving *witch* magic to an honorable fight."

"This isn't about honor. It's about us getting out of here alive."

His nostrils flared, and his eyes widened. That was definitely fury this time. "It's *always* about honor."

"Amar...."

"Go." He thrust his finger at the ladder.

"You may need help."

"*Go*," he repeated, his voice a snarl again. "Get out of the house as soon as you can. Call the deputy to come get you."

Morgen swore, but if he was determined to stay and fight an enemy werewolf, she couldn't stop him. She descended further, pulling the trapdoor back into place. Just before it settled, the hidden door creaked open. An ear-splitting howl preceded something large and heavy charging into the room.

Afraid for Amar and afraid for herself, Morgen kept climbing down into the darkness.

24

THE GLOW FROM THE AMULET GAVE OUT HALFWAY DOWN THE SHAFT.

Morgen was about to repeat the illumination command that Amar had used, but clatters, snarls, growls, and yips of pain echoed down from above with such noise and ferocity that she felt safer in the dark. She wanted to believe that Amar would be victorious, but if the other werewolf won... she didn't want light seeping up through the cracks, letting him know where she'd gone.

Though she was tempted to go back up and stand by Amar's side. He didn't want her assistance, didn't want her "conniving" witch magic, but she'd helped him in the restaurant parking lot. Surely, she could do something.

Morgen was about to turn around and go back up when her feet clunked down onto cement. A *snap-thud* sounded above her as a breeze whispered across her cheeks. Frowning, she tried to climb back up only to find that something barred the way. Some kind of door or hatch had dropped down, leaving the sounds of the fight distant and muffled.

When she pushed against it, nothing happened. Had she climbed down into some pit where nosy intruders were locked up?

"Hell." Morgen groped around, hoping for a door.

Stone wall, stone wall, stone wall, and... stone wall. She shoved against them. The third one moved, grinding loudly as she pushed it outward. She winced at the noise and also the light that slashed into her shaft.

Afraid of attack dogs, and wishing she still had the staff, she held up her arm and squinted at the brightness. Had she descended to the first floor? Or deeper into the castle-mansion?

As her eyes adjusted, a cement floor and walls came into focus. They were nothing like the marble foyer she'd seen, so this had to be a basement or garage. Or dungeon.

No, as soon as she crept out, she spotted a strange contraption that looked like a miniature helicopter with a single seat. The term gyrocopter came to mind, but she'd never seen one and wasn't sure if this qualified. This had to be an underground garage, though she didn't see a door large enough to let the contraption out. She didn't see a door at all, save for a dark corridor on the far side.

As she walked warily around the quirky vehicle toward what she hoped was the exit, Morgen eyed workbenches, cabinets, and counters along two of the walls in the windowless room. She wanted to hurry and find a way out, in case she had to go back up to help Amar, but one of the workbenches made her pause. It was full of carvings and tools for cutting ivory. Tusks.

She held her breath as she crept closer. Several short pieces of tusk lay on the bench, carvings in progress. One was shaping up into a clip similar to the one from Grandma's motorcycle. A saber-toothed tiger tusk ready to curse another vehicle?

A rack on a wall above the workbench held straight sticks about eighteen inches long. Wands?

Jars of powders rested in shelves above another workbench.

The surface was scattered with dried bits of moss. Vibrant moss that Morgen wagered glowed in the dark when the lights went out. And had been stolen from Wolf Wood.

Maybe even using that gyrocopter. That could explain why Amar had never been able to track the owner's scent.

With shaking hands, Morgen pulled out her phone and took pictures of the gyrocopter and the ivory carvings. She'd found all the evidence she could ever want.

But was this Arbuckle's lair? Or someone else's? Amar had mentioned smelling another woman's scent in the mansion. And he'd said the person he'd struggled to track from the spring in Wolf Wood had been a woman.

"Does Arbuckle have a witch lover?" Morgen whispered, slipping her phone back into her pocket.

It was time to get out of there.

"He *had* a witch lover," a woman spoke from the mouth of the corridor.

Morgen spun toward the speaker.

A brunette in her forties or fifties stood with a wand in one hand and the other propped on her hip. She wore an ankle-length black dress with mesh sleeves and had black polish on her artificial nails, though she had no piercings or black lipstick to match the Goth girls from the Crystal Parlor. She radiated confidence and power, and Morgen doubted this was a *pretend* witch in the market for hexing powder.

"I admit," the woman said, strolling forward to lean against the nose of the gyrocopter, her wand pointing loosely in Morgen's direction, "when I sent that imploring message for help, I was worried the strapping werewolf would barge down here to find me, not Gwen's daughter, but my faithful lover already caught him, so you're my only guest. Perfect."

"I'm her granddaughter," Morgen said, though her mind

almost stuck on the words *caught him*. Did that mean Amar had lost the battle?

"Really? I hadn't realized she was that old." The woman sniffed —why did her face seem familiar? "Though she did always swear by that water. The tests on it, however, were inconclusive. The real gem is the moss."

"Which you've been flying over and stealing for Arbuckle since my grandmother stopped selling it to him, right? Who are you?" Morgen glanced ceiling-ward, worried for Amar and wondering if she could get past the woman to run back up to find him. What exactly could that wand do?

"An entrepreneur." She smiled cryptically.

"I thought that was Arbuckle." Why did Morgen get the feeling that this woman—this *witch*—was trying to stall her?

A distant thump came from somewhere above them. Maybe the woman had lied and the battle was still going on upstairs.

"My name is Calista, and Mason was nothing until he met me. A pity he was so poor at acknowledging that."

"You know how men are." Morgen took a few steps sideways, toward the corridor she hoped led to a way out.

"You're not going anywhere." Calista—if that truly was her name—lifted her arm, pointing the wand at Morgen's chest. "Not until you sign the documents."

"Documents?"

"The agreement to sell your grandmother's property."

"What's the matter? You're afraid you won't be able to sneak in anymore to steal moss from the trees if there's a new owner? I saw how much you charge for the powder, but it's not *really* worth millions of dollars, is it?"

"You fool." Calista lost her smug smile, and her fingers tight-ened around the wand. "You'll kill the golden goose if you sell that land to someone else. The developers will cut *down* those trees.

They'll cut down everything, destroy the spring, and destroy the magic of that place."

"I wasn't planning on selling it. I just wanted to draw out the very eager buyer." Morgen squinted at her. "Are *you* the one who killed my grandmother? Or was it Arbuckle? Or were you working together?"

"Oh, you *will* sell the property. To *me*."

"I don't think so." Morgen wanted to run, to rush into the corridor and find Amar, but if that wand was like a gun and could shoot her in the back, she dared not.

She took a couple more steps to the side, as if she meant to flee, but when Calista shifted the wand to track her, Morgen changed direction. She rushed the woman, hoping to surprise her and knock the tool out of her hand.

Calista muttered a few words under her breath. Terrified she wouldn't reach her in time, Morgen crouched to duck an attack and dive at her legs, to tackle her to the ground.

"...and be my loyal servant!" Calista finished with a flourish, stabbing her wand in the air like a fencer's foil.

Nothing so deadly as a blast of power or a fireball slammed into Morgen, but between one step and the next, she forgot what she was doing and stumbled, barely keeping from falling.

She peered around the basement blearily. Where was she? What was she doing here?

"Are you ready to obey me?" The woman smirked at her.

"I..." Morgen struggled to wave away the dense fog that had descended on her mind. "That sounds reasonable," some power compelled her to say.

Wait. No, it *didn't* sound reasonable. That wasn't her speaking. This was... a control spell. Yes, that was it. This woman—who was she?—was using magic to control her. Magic that took over her mind. Control spells seemed familiar, but Morgen didn't know how to fight them.

"Good," the woman said. "I've got something for you to sign."

She reached into the cockpit of the gyrocopter and pulled out a tablet, tapping the screen to bring it to life. A form glowed on it, an online documents service showing a real-estate agreement with Morgen's name and personal details already entered.

Had Christian typed that up before he'd met his end? An agreement to everything without a counter of any kind? He shouldn't have done that before Morgen had even seen the offer. Before she'd signed anything. Maybe someone else in his office was on Arbuckle's payroll. Or had been willing to take a one-time bribe.

If the witch—Calista, she remembered—had managed all that, Morgen was surprised she hadn't been able to forge the electronic signatures. Ah, but it required her to click an email verification link to sign in. One that was, she wagered, sitting in her phone's inbox. She hadn't looked at her email all day.

"Log in and sign it," Calista ordered.

Sign away Grandma's house? And Wolf Wood? No, that wasn't right.

"It's more than a fair payment. More money than you've ever seen."

"Arbuckle's name is on it," Morgen murmured. "Not yours."

Calista smiled. "I'm taking care of things for him. Open your email, click the link, and start signing."

Morgen's hand twitched toward her phone. Her amulet lay against her chest, its weight noticeable.

"Under the moon's magic," she blurted, "allow me to sleuth and reveal thy silvery truth."

Calista didn't stop her from uttering the incantation, but she didn't look worried either. Morgen stared at Calista, hoping an illusion would form, revealing a secret weakness that she could exploit. But for the first time since Morgen had tried the spell, nothing happened.

"That won't work on a good witch," Calista said dryly. "Now quit screwing around and sign the documents."

Damn it. Why didn't Morgen know an incantation that would allow her to take back her mind?

This time, Morgen couldn't keep her hand from delving into her pocket, from pulling out her phone. The prompt for the passcode came up. She willed her thumb to enter the wrong numbers or not do anything at all, but it wouldn't obey her. She gained access, tapped open her inbox, and found an email from the documents service with Christian's address listed. It had been sent after his death.

Morgen's thumb twitched toward the email to open it, but once she clicked on the link and started signing, Calista would have won. If only Morgen could trick her mind into ignoring the woman's orders. Or forgetting what to do.

She tried uttering the incantation that would supposedly allow her to control werewolves, even though she doubted it would work on witches. Though Calista again didn't look worried, Morgen noticed that her thumb stopped moving when she was focused on reciting the words. Maybe if her mind was busy working on something else, it kept her body from following the commands.

An urge built in her to open the email. Her thumb trembled as she tried to resist.

She muttered the incantation again.

"Knock it off." Calista rapped her wand against Morgen's knuckles, eliciting a sharp stab of pain. "That's for werewolves. It won't work on me either. Even if you knew something useful, it wouldn't work on someone with my power."

Morgen shook her head. Saying the incantation over and over wasn't enough, especially since it didn't do anything. Who was she fooling? She wasn't a real witch. She was a database programmer from Seattle. When other kids had been playing fairies and magic at recess, she'd been in the school's computer lab, learning to code silly programs in BASIC.

She thought of one of those early programs, of using recursive loops to make a ball bounce down a set of steps over and over again.

That was what she needed now. To get her mind stuck in a loop so she never got to the mental line of code that involved opening her email and signing the digital papers.

"Check for spam before opening important email," she muttered, managing to get her thumb to delete another message instead of opening the one from the documents service. But that was the only junk message in her inbox.

She hit the refresh button. There was *always* more spam on the way, right?

"If there's no spam, then check for new spam," she said.

"What are you doing? That's not an incantation."

"If there's no spam, then check for new spam," Morgen repeated, hitting the refresh button. Nothing like a good old IF-THEN statement to set up a loop...

Calista smacked her knuckles again.

Morgen grimaced but hit the refresh button on her inbox. "If there's no spam, then check for new spam."

"*Stop* that." Calista's wand shifted away from Morgen as the woman grabbed her arm and tried to open the email herself.

Morgen reacted without thought, lashing out with her other hand. Her palm connected with Calista's chin, sending her reeling away.

"You're under my control," the witch snapped before Morgen could lunge after her and press the attack.

The will to strike her again faded, but Morgen went back to repeating her mantra to herself, and that tricked her mind into believing she couldn't open the important email until she'd completed that task. She couldn't obey, even if the witch controlled her.

Calista snarled and brought her wand to bear again. "If you won't sign these documents, then I'll get rid of you, and whoever inherits the property after you can sign them."

Her sister. Would Sian care enough to honor Grandma's wishes? Or would she simply sign away Wolf Wood from halfway across the world, not wanting to deal with the hassle of coming up here and getting involved in the Bellrock craziness? She might never meet Amar or learn that witches were picking on werewolves.

"Get in," the witch said, then pointed at the gyrocopter.

"Uh." Morgen didn't want to, but her legs moved her toward the one-man vehicle.

Calista pulled something out of a fold in her dress. A garage-door opener? But there wasn't a garage door. Was there?

Calista clicked it. One of the cement walls—what Morgen had *thought* was only a wall—tilted outward, rising like an old one-piece garage door.

Cool misty night air wafted in as an opening wide enough and tall enough for the gyrocopter to fly through appeared. Outside, it had started raining, and heavy droplets splashed down on a cement driveway. The poor weather would make it dangerous for flying, but somehow, Morgen suspected that was what Calista wanted.

"You're going to take it for a flight, having stolen it while illegally trespassing on the Arbuckle estate." Calista drew another compact device. A remote for the gyrocopter? "Alas, you're going to crash in a canyon and won't live to see morning."

"The way my grandmother crashed? Why did you kill her?" Morgen watched Calista's face, wanting to hear the confession, wanting to know for certain that this woman had been the murderer. Did Arbuckle even exist? "She wasn't planning to sell the property. You could have kept stealing the moss from her for years."

Calista sneered. "That damn werewolf was there every time. Even flying in to take samples was dangerous, and the moss wouldn't grow anywhere else. Trust me, I tried to get it to."

"Why did you have to kill Grandma?"

"She was even nosier than you. She figured it all out and was threatening to put a halt to my operation. Get into the gyrocopter." Calista recited the incantation again, reestablishing control.

The urge to obey compelled Morgen to lift a foot to climb in, but she made another loop in her mind. *If the weather is too dangerous for flying, then wait for the sky to clear.*

She lowered her foot. For whatever reason, the simple commands, the simple logic loops, let her resist the compulsion.

"You don't have to be conscious for your flight," Calista growled, stepping over to a workbench and opening a drawer.

Morgen turned, but her body was too slow to obey. She couldn't keep Calista from drawing a gun.

A bang sounded in the corridor before she could point it at Morgen, and a door slammed open.

A great furry gray wolf charged into the garage.

It wasn't Amar.

25

THE WOLF CHARGING IN MUST HAVE BROKEN CALISTA'S SPELL, FOR Morgen found she could move without tricking her mind into loops. She turned toward the open garage door, but Calista blocked the way. Her eyes lit not with alarm but with triumph as the wolf raced across the garage.

It headed straight toward Morgen, saliva gleaming on its fangs.

Morgen wanted to punch the triumphant expression from Calista's face, but there wasn't time. She spun and dove under the gyrocopter, her knee cracking on one of the landing skids.

Maybe she should have dived *into* the vehicle, but it didn't have an enclosed cockpit. The wolf lunged for her legs. Morgen yanked them fully under the contraption as jaws snapped inches from her shoes.

"Drag her out," Calista ordered.

Morgen glanced out the other side as she debated whether to stay under the gyrocopter or try to crawl out and sprint away. But sprint where? The ways to the garage door and the corridor were blocked, so the only place she could run was back into that shaft, and the hatch that had dropped ensured she couldn't escape that way either.

Where was Amar? Did this wolf's presence mean he was dead?

The gray wolf lunged under the gyrocopter, snapping for her leg again. Morgen jerked it away and kicked at its face. It dodged, too fast for her meager human speed, and she knew it would succeed in grabbing her and dragging her out.

But before those fangs bit into her leg, a snarl came from the corridor.

Another wolf charged in, an even bigger one. Amar? All she could see were legs.

With her attacker distracted, Morgen pulled herself out on the far side of the gyrocopter. She gripped her amulet, wishing she knew more useful things to do with it and the witch blood that supposedly flowed through her veins.

The second wolf smashed into the first, knocking it to the ground as jaws snapped. The growls and snarls were so loud and fierce that it sounded like an entire pack had rushed into the garage.

Morgen scrambled to her feet, keeping the gyrocopter between her and the wolves—and the witch. Calista was waving her wand about, focusing on the wolves—no, on Amar. The patterns in his black and gray fur were distinctive.

He was larger than his foe, and it seemed he should have the advantage, but Calista drew what looked like sparkling silver sand from her pocket and flung it at them. Maybe she bought hexing powder after all.

The wolves rolled sideways, jaws sinking into each other's shoulders as they tried but didn't quite reach throats. As they thrashed about, they almost knocked Calista down. She stumbled as she skittered back, and the gun flew from her hand. It skidded across the cement and disappeared under a workbench.

A part of Morgen wanted to take the opportunity to flee, to get out of there, but she couldn't leave Amar. Not when Calista was targeting him.

Since her incantations had been useless, Morgen settled for a non-witchy method of dealing with problems. She ran around the gyrocopter, bypassing the snarling and biting wolves, and launched herself at Calista.

The woman saw her coming and jerked the wand toward her but not quickly enough. Morgen crashed into her, grabbing her around the waist and bearing her to the ground. She snatched the end of the wand and tried to tear it free. But even discombobulated, Calista wouldn't release it.

They each gripped one end, playing tug-of-war with the wand as Morgen tried to maneuver on top of Calista to keep her from rising. The woman's dress was bunched around her thighs, but that didn't keep her from kicking and thrashing like a trapped honey badger.

A canine cry of pain came from behind them. Morgen couldn't tell if it belonged to Amar or the other wolf, but out of the corner of her eye, she glimpsed blood spurting from a severed artery. It spattered on the gray cement floor as if flung by a macabre paintbrush.

Fear for Amar slammed into Morgen's heart, and she pulled on the wand as hard as she could. Finally, it slipped in Calista's grasp. Just as Morgen thought she would wrest it away, Calista shifted under her and jerked her knee up. It struck Morgen in the abdomen, and she almost lost her grip on the wand.

The witch started chanting the control incantation again.

Cursing, Morgen pinned her to the ground and clamped her hand over Calista's mouth. Afraid that wouldn't be enough to stop the spell, Morgen slammed her forehead down on the woman's nose.

Cartilage crunched, and Calista cried out, but she'd gotten out the last word of the now-familiar incantation.

Morgen braced herself, fearing that her body would once again betray her, that it would obey Calista instead of her own desires. But maybe she'd disrupted the incantation after all, for nothing happened to her.

A hand gripped her shoulder, yanking her backward so hard that she flew away from Calista, landed on her back, and skidded across the cement floor. She bumped something furry. Amar?

No, it was the other wolf. The big gray lay still, his life's blood pouring from the severed artery.

Amar had changed back into his human form, his clothing abandoned who knew where, and he strode toward Morgen. His muscles were bunched, his fingers ready to grab her. Grab her and tear her limb from limb. She realized in an instant who'd thrown her. Amar was under Calista's control.

Morgen rolled away from him and scrambled to her feet, though she knew she couldn't outrun him. She half-expected him to reach her and grab her throat before she could take a step, but he didn't lunge quickly after her. He walked after her, inexorable, powerful, and determined, but not fast.

She sprinted around the gyrocopter, glancing for something to use to deter him. If she ran out the garage door, would he break into a run?

"Faster," Calista urged. "Get her. *Kill* her."

Amar strode around the gyrocopter. For a second, it looked like he would switch to a sprint, but his eyes were full of conflict and emotion. He didn't *want* to do this, didn't want to be a witch's pawn again. He was fighting her.

His face contorted from the effort, the veins in his neck standing out. His stride faltered, and he almost managed to spring over the gyrocopter toward Calista, but she pointed her wand at him, and he jerked and turned back toward Morgen.

Morgen gripped her amulet as she backed farther away. Maybe her control incantation would override Calista's. Since Amar was fighting hers already, maybe it would be enough.

Unless he resented Morgen trying to do the same thing Calista was doing and fought her just as hard...

She had to try. She had no choice.

"Under the moon's magic, turn the snarling hound from angry foe to witch bound," Morgen whispered, staring intently into Amar's blue eyes, hoping he understood. She didn't want to control him, simply wrest him from Calista's control.

His face didn't twist with rage or indignation. He seemed to understand what she was trying to do, but she couldn't tell if her incantation had made a difference. Amar kept striding toward her, unable to break Calista's control.

But something disturbed Calista. She frowned intensely at them, pointed her wand at Amar, and repeated her control incantation.

Morgen repeated hers, saying it loudly this time, not whispering. She had no idea if *volume* mattered with spells, but she would try everything she could.

Amar's movements grew jerky. He kept coming, but it was as if he were walking through molasses. He mumbled under his breath as he lifted his hands to reach for Morgen.

"Fight it," she whispered after another recitation of the incantation. "Don't let another witch turn you into a criminal. Not again."

"Must protect... protect you," Amar said, his fingers shaking.

Morgen took another step back, but her heel clunked against the wall. She'd been so focused on the incantation that she'd let herself be backed into a corner. She crouched, ready to try to charge past him if she had to, but he halted three feet away.

Calista shouted another incantation. Amar froze.

"Get *her*, Amar," Morgen whispered. "She's the one who made the bone clip and sabotaged my grandmother's motorcycle. Because she didn't want anything to interrupt her being able to steal that damn moss from the property."

Amar snarled, like the wolf he'd been a minute earlier, and launched himself. Not at Morgen but at Calista.

She shrieked, the high-pitched noise echoing from the cement walls and flowing out into the night.

Amar leaped over the gyrocopter and barreled into her. She tumbled backward, her wand finally flying from her grip. It clattered across the cement floor.

Morgen lunged after it. What she would do with it, she didn't know, but she had to keep Calista from getting it back.

The woman shouted something incomprehensible. Morgen wrapped her fingers around the wand an instant before an explosive went off.

The ground shook, and a shockwave threw Morgen backward as smoke filled the garage. A thunderous wrenching crunch sounded as the gyrocopter tipped over. A male yelp of pain came from the other side of the garage as Amar slammed into a wall.

Morgen skidded across the floor for the second time that night. Somehow, she managed to retain a hold on the wand. She stared blearily into the smoke, ready to chant the control incantation again.

But the garage fell silent, neither Amar nor Calista making a sound. If the other wolf was still alive, he also wasn't making any noise.

Morgen pushed herself to her feet. A hint of damp misty air wafted in, stirring the smoke. It cleared slowly, revealing Amar standing naked in the doorway of the garage, peering out into the night.

Morgen glanced warily at the downed wolf, decided it was dead, and looked for Calista. She had a feeling the witch had gotten away. Amar wouldn't be looking off into the yard if she hadn't.

As Morgen walked over to join him, a distant siren wail reached her ears. Had Franklin already been on the way back with reinforcements? That explosion couldn't have been reported so quickly.

"She got away?" Morgen asked, though she already knew.

"Yes."

"Was that werewolf—I assume it's a werewolf?—controlled by her?"

"Yes. I believe they were also lovers, so it might not have taken much magic, but..." Amar shrugged. "We were too busy fighting for me to get the details."

"Oh." Morgen didn't know what else to say.

Amar glanced toward the front of the house. "We need to go. Our presence here will be difficult to explain." He gazed back at the dead wolf on the floor. "And I am a wanted man." His expression grew forlorn and wistful but only for a moment before he looked at Morgen. "But only for *one* murder."

"Yeah, I'm pleased it wasn't two."

It almost had been, and they both knew it.

"As am I," Amar said softly, holding her gaze.

If he resented her for having used that incantation on him, he didn't show it. His eyes were almost gentle. Or maybe just sad.

Morgen groped for something heartening to say, wanting to offer him hope that they could figure out a way to clear his name, or at least make the sheriff's department understand that a witch had been responsible for the agent's death, but Morgen didn't even know where she stood with the law after sneaking out of Franklin's SUV and running away from him.

The sirens grew louder along with the sound of multiple vehicles roaring toward the gated property.

"I can't let them catch me. This way." Amar jogged into the yard, still naked, and headed toward the back wall.

Morgen diverted long enough to grab her books and staff. A shame she'd dragged them all the way here and hadn't gotten to use them—pronging Calista with antlers would have been satisfying. But climbing down that shaft with the weapon would have been awkward if not impossible.

Morgen caught up to Amar at the hole he'd dug under the wall.

"You're coming back to the house with me, right?" she asked.

What if he disappeared forever? She'd barely gotten to know him, and she felt like she owed him for what had happened. Even if this wasn't her world, everything revolved around her grandmother's property, and since she'd shown up, he'd had his belongings burned, his work destroyed, and now, he was a wanted man and couldn't show his face in Bellrock again.

"I promised to make you breakfast, remember?" she added.

Amar was slithering on his belly through the dirt hole and didn't reply. Maybe he hadn't heard her.

She dropped to her knees to hurry after him, afraid he would take off as soon as he reached the other side. If the deputies started searching the woods around the property right away, he would have to.

The staff wouldn't fit, so she had to throw it over the wall. Yellow light flashed around it, and the air sizzled as if it had sailed into a bug zapper. She winced, remembering Amar's admonition about magical security and dead birds, but the staff continued on its trajectory. Maybe the magic couldn't harm inanimate objects.

She squeezed through the hole, scraping her hips and clunking her head on the stone wall above.

"I remember." Amar helped her out and handed her the staff. Fortunately, it wasn't noticeably charred or damaged in any way.

"And you agreed that it was scintillating and couldn't wait to eat it, right?" She gripped his arm as she stood, reluctant to release him, lest he take off.

"I'll return to the house with you tonight."

"And tomorrow?"

Car doors slammed and shouts echoed through the woods as the authorities jumped out.

"We'll see," Amar said quietly.

26

Morgen found bacon as well as sausage in the freezer and fried up both for Amar while her vegetarian patties and hash browns sizzled in another pan. Sunlight streamed in the window, and she yawned loudly. If she hadn't promised Amar a breakfast, she might have slept until noon. It had been well after midnight by the time they'd gotten home.

"Home?" she mused.

Grandma's house was hardly that, not for her. It was just the kooky place that she needed to figure out how to take care of and what to do with, now that she'd decided not to sell it.

Lucky padded around the kitchen, sniffing and wagging. She'd already caught him with his front paws up on the counter as he contemplated how to steal sausage and bacon from a hot frying pan.

"I know you're excited that I'm cooking meat, but it's not for you."

That earned her a pitiful whine. There were times when she was positive he understood more than the handful of words she'd taught him.

"If you go tell Amar breakfast is ready, *maybe* I'll give you a piece of bacon."

Lucky woofed but didn't leave his frying-pan vigil. Well, he didn't understand everything.

Morgen turned off the burners, pushed the pans far enough back that he wouldn't be able to reach them, and went to knock on Amar's door.

When he'd returned with her the night before, they'd found the sheriff's vehicles gone and the search called off, so she'd been able to talk Amar into staying in the house, but he'd been noncommittal on whether he intended to remain on the property —or anywhere near Bellrock.

They'd survived their tangle with Calista and the Loup were-wolf, and they'd disappeared before the authorities barged in, but it wasn't as if they'd cleared Amar's name or solved a crime. The fact that Calista had escaped made Morgen uneasy. All she could hope was that people were done scheming against her to get Grandma's property. If she removed it from the market, told everyone that her family was keeping it, and went back to Seattle, would that be the end of it? Would the townsfolk be happy?

Except... what was she supposed to do with the house if she returned to Seattle? And for that matter, what was there for her back there? Not a job. Not a husband. Not an intriguing new part of herself that she'd been learning about these past few days.

Amar didn't answer the door. She knocked again, but her stomach gradually sank as she realized he might already have left.

The idea of him disappearing without leaving a note or saying goodbye distressed her. After all, she'd promised to make him breakfast—actual *meat* sausages. If he hadn't intended to stay, he should have let her know.

She opened the door to make sure he wasn't lying abed, afflicted by grievous injuries that he hadn't admitted to the night before, but it was empty. Empty, with little sign that he'd ever been in the room.

But then, he'd lost his belongings in the fire, so what would he have brought over? The thought of him having to walk away with nothing and start over in life saddened her.

A couple of soft bangs came from outside. Morgen hesitated, worried the deputies had come to question her—or search around the property again. After scant hours of sleep, she didn't want to deal with them.

She walked around the bed to look out the window. There weren't any cars out front besides hers. The bangs came from... the barn. Amar knelt on the roof-in-progress, attaching new ceiling joists.

"Hah. Not gone after all." Morgen trotted down the stairs to tell him breakfast was ready.

But as she opened the front door, a familiar SUV drove up. Deputy Franklin's.

Swearing, she lunged to the side of the porch to yell a warning up to Amar. But his hearing was better than hers, and he'd already disappeared into the barn or some other hiding spot.

Fortunately, Franklin looked more relieved than angry when he stepped out of his SUV and spotted her. Since she'd ignored all of his texts and calls the night before, eventually putting her phone in airplane mode, she had no idea what he thought of her disappearance—or if he'd been among the men who'd returned to the Arbuckle estate.

"I'm pleased to see you alive, ma'am," he said. "When you didn't return any of my messages last night, I feared the worst."

"Sorry. I was trying not to make noise."

"Because you were illegally trespassing?" He raised his eyebrows.

"Actually, I was invited in to sign some paperwork." Admittedly *after* she'd illegally trespassed... "Eventually."

"Did you? Sign it?"

"Despite a magical spell trying to compel me to do so... no. I've decided not to sell the property."

His eyebrows twitched at the words *magical spell*, but all he said was, "That's probably good since the potential buyer's remains were found under a cairn behind his house. I'm waiting to hear back from the coroner, but it looks like he's been there for weeks."

"Weeks? His signature was on the paperwork."

"It seems his former lover has been digitally masquerading as him, including running his business and collecting his payments, since her werewolf lover killed Arbuckle. This is according to the butler, who rushed out to greet us and was pleased that you and *your* werewolf lover—" his eyebrows went up again, "—had taken care of the odious one who supposedly didn't treat her well."

"We're not lovers."

"Ah."

"If she wasn't happy with the situation, why didn't she quit after Arbuckle, uhm, disappeared?" Morgen assumed the butler had originally worked for him, not Calista, but she supposed she couldn't know that.

"There aren't that many jobs for butlers in the area. Also, Calista Aetos has a reputation for being someone you don't want to cross."

And Morgen had crossed her. Wonderful.

Wait, that surname sounded familiar.

"Aetos?" Morgen asked. "Is she related to Phoebe?"

"Her sister, yes."

"I thought the sister was dead."

But Phoebe hadn't actually said that, had she?

"Just estranged, I gather. You'd have to ask Phoebe what happened. We'll be trying to find Calista and charge her for Arbuckle's murder. We'll also keep looking for the person responsible for Christian's murder."

Morgen blinked. "You don't think... ah."

If he'd changed his mind about a werewolf doing that, she didn't want to say anything to dissuade him.

"The butler mentioned that witches can sometimes control werewolves." He removed his hat and pushed a hand through his mussed hair. "I miss when this was a sleepy town that everybody zipped past on the interstate without noticing."

And before the werewolves moved in, she wagered. The witches had probably always been around—Grandma certainly had—but maybe they'd been less of a problem in the past.

"Is Amar Guerrero here?" Franklin asked. "I have questions for him."

He spoke casually, but Morgen didn't quite believe that the sheriff's department had absolved Amar of guilt or would treat him fairly.

"As far as I know, he left town last night." She was a horrible liar and gazed out toward the trees instead of meeting Franklin's eyes. "I don't think he's coming back."

Franklin paused. "I see."

"Why did Calista—and her werewolf—kill Arbuckle?" Morgen asked to change the subject.

"The butler was a little vague. I think she fears reprisal. I have some calls out and am gathering more information, but I've already learned that a couple of months ago, Arbuckle's lawyer advised him not to add Calista to his bank accounts or credit cards. She was apparently vying for that."

"She was helping him make the magical powders that I believe he was selling, so she probably thought they should be equal partners."

Franklin wiggled his fingers, as if he would neither agree nor disagree with that, or maybe with the idea of magical powders in general.

"Either way," he said, "per his lawyer's advice, he wouldn't add her to his accounts. Shortly after..."

"Cairn?"

"Cairn."

"So, she was with Arbuckle for his money and business while keeping a werewolf lover on the side?" Morgen asked.

"A werewolf something. He might have been a servant or employee or who knows what. Arbuckle actually had a relationship with the Loups that goes back a few years and paid them to do jobs here and there."

Morgen remembered how well-dressed the werewolves in the parking lot had been. A far cry from the laboring Lobos at the construction site.

"We may never know exactly what happened. It'll be best for our town if we can catch Calista, or, barring that, if she never comes back, but you'll want to watch out if you're going to stay in the area. Are you?" Franklin looked like he wanted her to say no.

Had she truly been that much trouble? Morgen didn't think any of it had been her fault...

"I haven't decided yet," she said.

"Ah. Do you want us to have someone stay here to keep an eye out for you for a while?"

She resisted the urge to glance toward the barn.

"You can imagine how much we enjoy protecting people who don't answer our calls, texts, or emails," Franklin added.

"There were emails?"

"You didn't notice?"

"Sorry. It was an eventful night."

"No kidding."

"I don't need anyone to stay. I think that if I spend more time looking through my grandmother's resources, I can figure out how to put some security in place around the house."

"I'll pretend you're referring to her Brink's manual and not anything that requires me to stretch my imagination overmuch."

"Isn't your imagination already stretched by the acknowledgment that witches and werewolves exist?"

"Stretched. Tied in knots. Something like that." Franklin tipped his hat toward her. "Good day, ma'am. And don't take this the wrong way, but I hope not to hear from you for a while."

"Given my disinclination toward replying to voice mail, texts, and emails, that seems like a reasonable hope."

"Good."

Franklin climbed into his SUV and headed down the driveway. Before the vehicle had fully disappeared from view, Morgen noticed someone standing near the porch, half-hidden by the bushes. Had Amar been listening to everything?

"I'm not on Deputy Franklin's favorite-persons list," Morgen said.

"No?" Amar vaulted over the railing to land on the porch beside her.

He'd found clothing since losing his last set the night before, but she couldn't help but wonder how many changes of jeans and vests he could have in his truck. Maybe she would offer to buy him a few new shirts. It would be unfortunate if he had to work on the barn naked.

"My opinion of you has improved since we met," he said.

"I'm touched, but the first day we met, you threatened to rip my throat out while glaring at me with loathing in your eyes. I'd be distressed if we'd gone downhill from there."

He only grunted. No apology for the threat—or the deer head and carcass.

Well, he'd risked his life helping her the night before. That counted for a lot.

"I was thinking of leaving right away," he said.

"I know. Why didn't you?"

"I told you I'd fix the barn. Also, Calista is still alive. And you've ruined a good thing for her."

"The good thing where she murdered her boyfriend and was masquerading as him while enjoying his castle, his riches, and her werewolf lover?"

"A *very* good thing. She may be angry with you and seek revenge."

Morgen sighed. "I know. I truly am going to try to figure out how to secure this place against vengeful witches, pyromaniacs, moss thieves, and anyone else who wanders too close."

"But not lone wolves?"

"No. I don't want them deterred from showing up when I make breakfast. I'm sure as hell not eating that sausage and bacon."

"No? It smells good. If you *have* to eat your meat cooked, fried in bacon grease is the way to go."

"Are you trying to disturb me?"

"Not at all. I wouldn't want you to revoke your offer of a room before I finish with the barn. The rainy season is approaching."

"I wouldn't do that. You're welcome to stay as long as you want." She hoped there wouldn't be a reason for the deputies to keep coming up here so it wouldn't be safe for him to do so. "Maybe we can figure out a way to officially clear your name."

From Franklin's words, Morgen hoped the sheriff's department would stop looking for Amar, but she wasn't positive that would be the case. That also wasn't the same as being absolved of the crime.

He sighed and rubbed the back of his neck, the spot where that witch's brand now was. Would it be possible to remove it? Or would that witch continue to be able to control him from afar? Morgen shuddered at the idea.

"The clearing of a name," Amar said, "is something done to those who are believed guilty but are in fact innocent. I killed the man."

"That doesn't mean you're not innocent. If we could force that witch into admitting that she controlled you..." Unfortunately, Morgen didn't know the names of any of those three witches, where they lived, or anything about them. She also didn't know what the difference was between the werewolf-control spell and the brand he'd received. Was the latter stronger? And longer lasting? *Permanent*?

"Do not try," Amar said. "Those witches are dangerous, and you're a neophyte."

"Only until I learn more." Which she intended to do. She wouldn't remain helpless in this strange place full of werewolves and witches.

"That takes a long time. If you want to be given the time to learn, you have to leave them alone. Don't make enemies—any *more* enemies."

It wasn't bad advice, but Morgen had no intention of letting Amar be blamed because of those witches. She would figure out how to help him get out of their clutches, one way or another.

"Does the determined set of your jaw mean you intend to defy me?" Amar asked.

"No." Yes. "It means I'm concerned about my kitchen smelling of bacon all day. I need you to go in and devour your breakfast and take care of that."

He gazed at her through slitted eyes. She decided it was unlikely that werewolves could read minds, but he might be good at guessing people's thoughts. Maybe she smelled different when she lied.

Amar stepped closer to her, making her aware of his height, his wild hair, and the muscular arms his vests always left on display...

"I'll even lick the pan," he said in a rumbly voice.

"Lucky does that. You two share gastronomic habits."

"Do tofu pans not move you to lick them?"

"Not usually. I am working on my saucier skills though, so that might change."

"You'll enjoy licking once you try it." He lifted a hand, touched her cheek, and walked into the house.

Morgen raised her eyebrows, not certain whether that had simply been an acknowledgment that he didn't loathe her anymore or... if he'd been flirting with her.

"My life has gotten very strange lately," she murmured and followed him inside.

THE END

Thank you for picking up the first Witch in Wolf Wood adventure. I hope you enjoyed visiting Bellrock.

If you have time to leave a review, I would appreciate it! If you want to read more about Morgen and Amar, the series continues with Book 2, *Spell Hound*.

Made in the USA
Monee, IL
11 February 2022

91099641R10152